# Lost in the Outcome

## Rowan McAllister

Dreamspinner Press

Published by
DREAMSPINNER PRESS

5032 Capital Circle SW, Suite 2, PMB# 279, Tallahassee, FL 32305-7886 USA
http://www.dreamspinnerpress.com/

This is a work of fiction. Names, characters, places, and incidents either are the product of author imagination or are used fictitiously, and any resemblance to actual persons, living or dead, business establishments, events, or locales is entirely coincidental.

**Lost in the Outcome**
© 2014 Rowan McAllister.

Cover Art
© 2014 AngstyG.
www.angstyg.com
Cover content is for illustrative purposes only and any person depicted on the cover is a model.

ISBN: 978-1-63216-200-7
Digital ISBN: 978-1-63216-201-4
Library of Congress Control Number: 2014943207
First Edition August 2014

Printed in the United States of America
(∞)
This paper meets the requirements of
ANSI/NISO Z39.48-1992 (Permanence of Paper).

# Readers love ROWAN MCALLISTER

## *Never a Road Without a Turning*

"The story was well told and I found the characters multidimensional and interesting."

—Prism Book Alliance

"Rowan McAllister is a good author who writes a wonderfully engaging story and fans of this genre will enjoy this sweet novel."

—The Novel Approach

## *Hot Mess*

"I like finding these gems every once in a while. Read it for the enjoyment of reading. Read it to fall in love with the bad boy, while secretly hoping that he has a HEA with the good boy."

—Gay List Book Reviews

"I really liked this story, yes I was aggravated with both men at times, but I was also invested and wanted to see them get it together and be happy."

—Hearts on Fire

"Really good read with much more depth than I expected."

—Live your Life, Buy the Book

"It is just downright amazing. I cannot get over how much I love this novel."

—MM Good Book Reviews

By ROWAN MCALLISTER

Cherries on Top
Cuddling (Dreamspinner Anthology)
A Devil's Own Luck
Feels Like Home
Grand Adventures (Dreamspinner Anthology)
Hot Mess
Lost in the Outcome
My Only Sunshine
Never a Road Without a Turning
A Promise of Tomorrow
Riding Double (Dreamspinner Anthology)
Uniform Appeal (Dreamspinner Anthology)

Published by DREAMSPINNER PRESS
http://www.dreamspinnerpress.com

To all the romantic souls out there who know, when you've met the right one, all the hard work is worth it.

# Chapter One

NATHAN JOLTED awake to the sound of a garbage truck outside. The way his head felt it might as well have been driving through the room. He groaned, clamped his eyes shut, and wrapped the pillow around his head until the squeal of bad brakes, the whine of hydraulics, and the bang of metal against metal subsided. When it finally moved on to torture someone else, Nathan let the pillow fall. The only sounds left in the room were the buzz of street traffic and the rattling of the vertical blinds above the air conditioner.

Hoping there would be no more skull-splitting noises in his immediate future, Nathan cautiously opened his eyes again. As he looked around in the intermittent flashes of daylight through the swaying blinds by the hotel room door, three things occurred to him at once. First, he was in a room way below the caliber of the places he usually chose when he traveled. Second, he had no idea how he got there. And third, he wasn't alone.

Nathan could just make out the outline of a body in the bed next to him, beneath the crumpled cheap polyester bedspread. A hint of a tanned shoulder peeked above the blanket, but the head and arms were buried beneath a pillow, giving Nathan no clue as to who shared the bed with him. He dragged his hands down his face and groaned.

*What the hell happened?*

He swung his legs over the side of the bed, but he had to wait a few seconds for the room to stop spinning before he could get up and relieve the urgent pressure in his bladder. Stumbling blearily, he headed away from the light, toward the back of the room, tripping over the clothes and shoes strewn all over the floor.

The bathroom had to be around here somewhere. Lord knew he'd been in enough hotels that he should be able to find it with his eyes closed, even if he was a bit more used to sprawling suites than cheap generic rooms.

He closed the door to the bathroom and flipped on the blinding fluorescent light; flinching away from it, he stumbled to the toilet. When the afterimages cleared from his eyes, he finished his business and then turned to the sink to splash a little water on his face. With his arms braced on the counter, he reluctantly lifted slitted eyes to the mirror.

He looked as bad as he felt. His normally well-groomed wavy brown hair was lank and plastered to his forehead. His dark blue eyes were bloodshot, puffy, and red-rimmed. He had a livid mark on his neck, obviously a hickey. And his complexion, underneath a day's growth of whiskers, had a greenish tinge to it instead of the normal pale but healthy ivory he'd cultivated from years of sitting in front of a computer from dawn 'til dusk. Granted, fluorescent lights were never very forgiving, but he usually looked better than *this*.

He splashed a little more water on his face and grabbed the skimpy, overbleached towel off the small rack above the toilet to rub a little life into his skin and give himself a cursory wash. The shower tempted him. But since he was utterly off-balance and drawing a complete blank about whom he'd shared the bed with, he decided to wait until he could get back to someplace familiar. As fastidious as he was, he didn't think he could take a shower with a complete stranger only a few feet away.

After a quick but intense scrubbing, he at least looked a little better, even if his memory still wasn't cooperating and his body felt like that trash truck had run over him. Leaving the bathroom door open, he used the light from it to search among the pile of discarded clothes on the floor for his pants and underwear, studiously ignoring the empty condom wrappers. His gray slacks and black boxer briefs were buried underneath a pair of faded jeans that seemed somehow wrong to him, but he didn't waste time examining them. He just tossed them aside and hurriedly tugged on his clothes. Thankfully, his phone and his wallet were still in his pockets, and none of his cards appeared to be missing.

Once he'd pulled on his undershirt and buttoned up his navy dress shirt, he felt a little more in control, a little less vulnerable. But now he was more awake, the fact that he still couldn't remember a single detail of how he got there was really starting to get to him. The last time he'd drunk until he blacked out had been in college. And even then, he'd only done it once, on a dare because his roommate thought he was way too much of a bookworm and wasting his college experience. He was too old for this kind of thing now.

A quick glance at his phone told him it was 9:13 a.m., Saturday, September 7, so he hadn't lost more than a night. The guestbook on the small desk by the door let him know he was at a HoJo's, and the tourist pamphlets were all for Houston attractions.

Houston.

Yes. That much he remembered.

He was in Houston on business, vying for the biggest contract of his career, one that could put his company—his baby—in the big leagues. Rubbing his temples with his fingertips, Nathan sat down at the desk and mentally ran through what he could remember of the past twenty-four hours.

He'd left the offices of his prospective client, Frontier Global Energy, after his introductory meeting with one of their VP's Friday afternoon. He'd gotten a cab back to his suite at the Sorella. He'd taken a shower and changed into the slacks and dress shirt he had now. He'd had a brief conversation with his business partner, Sean, to let him know how things went and then answered a few e-mails and reviewed his notes from the day.

He remembered being tired from his early flight from San Diego and the stressful day that followed. His competition for the contract was steep, and he was the underdog at the table, so the whole situation was straining his already questionable interpersonal skills. He was a programmer at heart, not a salesman, but he was the boss and knew the most about what his company could offer, so it was up to him to make the pitch. Last night, he'd wanted to go through the bid one more time so he would have the rest of the weekend to make any changes before his presentation on Monday, but Sean—ever the mother hen—had made him promise not to look at it again until he'd had some rest.

Nathan was self-aware enough to know he wouldn't be able to keep that promise if he stayed in his room, so he went down to the hotel restaurant to unwind and have dinner. But after that, everything was a complete blank. He might have had a couple of glasses of wine with his steak, but that was it—nothing that could account for blacking out the rest of the night and how truly miserable he felt now.

He lifted his head and glanced over at the bed, but his erstwhile companion hadn't moved. Nathan didn't want to be rude to the woman, especially if she felt as hungover as he did, but he needed some answers before he really started to freak out.

"Uh, excuse me. Hello?" he called out from where he sat, keeping his voice pitched low for both their sakes.

The lump on the bed groaned. It was a surprisingly deep sound and not at all what Nathan expected. Nathan's already queasy stomach did a little flip, and his palms began to sweat as he watched the pillow and awful slick-sheened bedspread fall away, revealing a head of spiky blond hair and a tanned and very well-muscled—very *masculine*—naked torso.

*What the—*

Nathan's brain seized up in shock for only a moment before his thoughts flew immediately to the numerous condom wrappers on the floor, his own nudity when he woke up, and the hickey on his neck.

*Holy shit!*

The man gave him a sleepy smile at first. But when Nathan continued to stare at him in shock, the smile fell quickly.

"Um, mornin'," the naked guy on the bed said.

Nathan couldn't seem to get his brain or his voice to work enough to respond.

"*Oh my God*" was all the help his muddled brain seemed capable of.

For a wild moment, he wondered if this was some sort of practical joke, if he was being *Punk'd*. He looked around the room for a camera or a place someone could be hiding, but there was nothing but cheap hotel art, bad wallpaper, and worse carpeting.

"Are you alright?" the guy asked into the uncomfortable silence that stretched between them.

"Yeah, I'm… yeah," he managed to croak out finally.

"Okay. If you say so."

The guy waited, studying Nathan's face in the dim light, but when Nathan didn't say anything more, he shifted on the mattress and looked away toward the window. A muscle in his jaw ticked as he said, "I guess I should be going now, huh?"

Without waiting for an answer, he got out of bed and started rooting around in the pile of clothes on the floor. Nathan turned his head away, embarrassed. When he looked up after a few moments, the guy had his back turned and was pulling on a tight green T-shirt over faded blue jeans.

"Okay, so, uh, thanks for the room. Maybe I'll see you around," the guy mumbled as he picked up his shoes and headed for the door. He had to pass Nathan on his way, but he made no effort at eye contact.

When the fact that his only link to the last twelve hours was leaving finally sunk in enough to overcome his shock, Nathan sprang to his feet. "Wait!"

The guy stopped with the door half-open and looked over his shoulder. In the light from outside, his vivid green eyes looked almost hopeful until Nathan spoke again.

"I, um… I'm sorry, but I have to ask. Who are you?"

The shy, hesitant smile that had been curving the man's lips died as Nathan's question hung in the air. "What?"

"I don't…," Nathan started, then sighed and ran his hands nervously through his hair. "I'm sorry, but I need a little help figuring out what happened last night and where I am."

The guy stared at him for a moment in disbelief before a scowl twisted his lips and he said, "Look, Nate. I don't know what you're playing at, but you don't have to be a dick. It's sooooo not necessary. I'm already out the door. If you don't want to see me again, you won't."

He turned to go, but Nathan crossed the few feet between them and pushed the door closed before he could disappear. "Stop, please," he said. "Look. I'm not playing any kind of game here. I'm serious. I can't remember anything after about six last night, and it's really starting to freak me out. Please. I need to know what the hell happened to me."

The guy's amazing green eyes narrowed in suspicion, but he made no move to push Nathan out of the way. After a few beats, the guy let go of the door and stepped back, putting some space between them again. The look on his face was far from friendly as he leaned against the wall and crossed his arms over his chest. "Okay. I'll play along for a minute or two, if you really want me to," he said with obvious reluctance.

Nathan sighed in relief and took his hand off the door. He hit the light switch so they could see each other a little better and walked back to the chair. He probably should have stayed by the door, just in case the guy tried to leave again, but he felt like shit, and he really needed to sit down.

After a moment's pause, the guy stepped away from the wall, walked to the bed, and sat on the edge of the mattress.

"What's your name?" Nathan asked as the guy started putting on his shoes.

"Tim," he answered shortly, without looking up from what he was doing.

"Okay, Tim. Thanks for helping me out here," Nathan said awkwardly, trying to figure out how to start this conversation.

Tim lifted his head and gave Nathan a look that clearly said "Seriously?" and Nathan realized how ridiculous that probably sounded. He wasn't interviewing a prospective employee. But he was so far out of his depth, putting on his business face was probably the only way he was going to be able to get through this without having a meltdown.

Nathan chewed on his lip and swallowed at the queasiness in his stomach. He opened his mouth to say something and then closed it again when he realized how equally ridiculous anything he was coming up with sounded. None of the books he owned on interpersonal communication covered this kind of scenario. He had some gaping holes in his personal self-help library that he would probably want to address when he got home. Of course that didn't exactly help him now.

Tim's eyebrows drew together as he watched Nathan struggle, and eventually Tim shook his head, the movement drawing Nathan's attention back from where it had wandered. "You aren't shitting me, are you? You really don't remember last night? At all?" he asked, watching Nathan intently.

Nathan let out a relieved breath at the fact that he wasn't going to have to run this conversation on his own. He even smiled a little. "No. I'm not shitting you. The last thing I remember from yesterday was eating dinner at the restaurant in my hotel. Everything else is a blank," he answered honestly.

"Shit," Tim swore. He dropped his head into his hands and after a few seconds snorted out a bitter laugh. "I knew I couldn't be that lucky.

I just knew it. But I never would have expected this one. Let me guess, you're straight and married with kids too, right?"

When Nathan grimaced but didn't respond right away, Tim groaned and flopped back on the mattress. "Fuck me. Can this get any better?"

Nathan cleared his throat uncomfortably. "I'm not married, and I don't have kids."

"Well, thank heaven for small favors" was the snarky reply from the bed.

At that moment, Nathan really wished he'd had a chance to have a cup of coffee before starting this conversation. He wasn't thinking clearly yet, and he really needed all of his mental faculties in a situation like this... not that he'd ever been in a situation like this before, but he certainly wasn't scoring any points thus far. He cleared his throat uncomfortably and tried to get back to basics. "Will you tell me how I got here?" he prompted.

Tim sat up and propped himself on his elbows. He looked at Nathan with a pained expression for a few moments before he shrugged. "Suuuuurrrre, no problem. We met at South Beach."

When Nathan only gave him a blank look, Tim rolled his eyes and said, "It's a gay club a couple of miles from here. I saw you dancing, and I thought you were pretty hot, so I made my way over. The guy you were with didn't seem too happy when you started dancing with me, but... you were kind of *insistent* that I stay with you once you got your arms around me, so eventually he gave up and left. Personally, I would've never let you go that easily, but...." Tim paused there, a blush creeping up his tan cheeks as he studied Nathan's face, clearly searching for something and not finding it.

Nathan felt a twinge of guilt for hurting the guy's feelings, but he was having a tough morning, and it didn't sound as if it was going to get any better. He couldn't have hidden the shock he felt at Tim's revelations even if he'd wanted to.

*I was at a club? Not just a club, but a gay club?*

"Anyway," Tim continued, after dropping his gaze to where his fingers picked restlessly at the ugly bedspread. "We left the club a little while later, and you offered to pay for a room for us, so... here we are. That's all I know. I swear. I mean, you were a little hyper, but I thought you'd just taken something to get you in the mood to party. You didn't act like you were completely trashed or out of it or anything."

It was Nathan's turn to put his head in his hands as he tried to absorb what he'd been told. Apparently some time last night, he'd made his way to a gay bar, danced the night away, picked up a guy, then took him to a hotel for a one-night stand.

Did he have some kind of psychotic break brought on by stress? Some sort of stroke? Kidnapped by aliens? Was he possessed?

"Um, Nate? You okay?"

Nathan lifted his head to find Tim watching him with concern. He forced a smile. "I'm sorry. This is a lot for me to take in. I'm trying to wrap my head around it. It's just going to take me a bit."

"Oh. Yeah sure, I understand. I guess I'd be pretty freaked out if something like that happened to me," he said. "I wish I could be more help, but…." He shrugged.

Now that Nathan could see Tim a little better, he had the crazy and completely unhelpful thought that the guy kind of reminded him of someone he went to high school with—Jeremy Dawes, star of their varsity basketball team. Like Jeremy, Tim wasn't that tall, but he was all tan, lean, well-defined muscle, and boy-next-door good looks. Nate felt his cock stir a little, as if it remembered what had happened the night before, even if Nathan didn't. But a moment later, Tim's resemblance to Jeremy made Nathan's stomach drop for an entirely different reason.

"Uh, Tim, how old are you?" he asked, not sure he really wanted to know the answer.

Tim's eyebrows shot up, and a somewhat evil smile twisted his lips. "How old do you think I am?"

When Nathan blanched, Tim rushed to say, "Sorry, sorry. That was mean. Dude, you didn't rob the cradle. Don't worry. I'm twenty-seven, more than legal. I promise."

"Oh, thank God," Nathan sighed as the urge to throw up receded.

Tim's smile turned sad as he studied Nathan for a few moments more before he seemed to come to some sort of decision. "Look, Nate, as tons of fun as this conversation is, I don't think I have the answers you're looking for, and I should probably get going." He climbed to his feet and took a few steps toward Nathan. He stopped a couple of feet away, put his hands in his pockets, then stood, rocking on the balls of his feet, looking uncertain. "Is there someone I should call for you? Do you want me to help you get a cab to the hospital or something?"

As Tim waited, his eyes filled with concern, Nathan felt a strange fluttering in his chest. Tim seemed like a really nice person, and there was no denying Nathan was attracted to him, even if Tim was probably the first guy Nathan had looked sideways at since college. It was a shame the whole situation was so incredibly screwed up. If he'd been at a different place in his life, or if this had been any other week, Nathan might have been willing to explore this attraction further, maybe....

Well, he didn't exactly know what he would've been willing to do. But the contract *was* far too important. The situation *was* unbelievably screwed up. And now was definitely not the time to explore his sexuality. He had dozens of employees counting on him to take the company to the next level. He so did not have time for personal complications.

"Thank you, Tim, but I'll be all right. I can take care of myself from here," he managed to say.

"Okay, good," Tim said, dropping his gaze to his feet. "I guess I'll be going, then, if you don't need anything else."

Nathan might not have been the sharpest tool in the shed when it came to dealing with people, but Tim wasn't exactly a difficult read either. He could see the hurt written plainly across Tim's face, and he felt a sudden surge of guilt for being so wrapped up in his own troubles. He probably had every right to be self-involved right now, but his mom hadn't raised him to be insensitive—maybe clueless sometimes, but not insensitive. "Tim, I'm sorry, I—"

"Don't sweat it, man," Tim interrupted him. He gave Nathan a half smile that didn't reach his eyes. "I have nothing to complain about, really. And I hope whatever made you black out isn't serious... but I should really get going."

With that, Tim grabbed a beat-up black leather jacket off the chair tucked into the corner by the window and walked out of the room before Nathan could gather enough of his wits to say anything else.

While Nathan sat there, the door clicked shut with heavy finality and Tim's footsteps faded away. A strange weight settled in Nathan's chest, but he had bigger things to worry about than a guy he'd probably never see again. He was still no closer to figuring out what really happened to him, and he only had the rest of today and Sunday to practice his presentation for FGE.

# Chapter Two

*FUCK*!

The word echoed in Tim's head for the hundredth time as he banged it against his steering wheel in the hotel parking lot. It wasn't very creative of him, but it pretty much summed up his feelings.

*The best night of my entire life, and my dream man can't remember a single minute of it... oh yeah, and he says he's straight too. Fuck!*

Despite the chill of late January in Texas—barely forty-five degrees, *brrrrr*—the interior of his car was already warm in the late-morning sun. And after banging his head a couple more times, Tim dropped back in his seat and let the heat soothe some of the tension from his body. A night of dancing and marathon fucking usually left him a little sore, but it was the morning after that really did a number on him this time.

In an effort to shake off some of the emotional pain as well as physical discomfort, Tim cracked his neck and stretched as far as the seat would allow before letting out a long, disappointed sigh. Sitting around crying about it wasn't going to change what happened. He'd learned that lesson a long time ago. Of course he should have also learned by now that the only luck he ever had was bad. But judging by how crushed he'd been when Nate didn't even remember his name, he apparently needed another kick in the teeth before it really sunk in.

He still wasn't absolutely sure he bought Nate's amnesia story, although he couldn't fathom any reason why the guy would bother with such a crazy lie. But the end result was the same either way. He wouldn't be seeing Nate again. Ever.

He'd had one amazing night with someone he thought was incredible, and now it was back to the same crappy life he'd had before. But even with that thought ringing in his head and the hurt still squeezing his chest, Tim couldn't bring himself to drive away yet. Telling himself he was a complete idiot the whole time, he sat in that parking lot and waited until a cab pulled up and Nate climbed in. Tim wasn't going to follow the guy or anything, but, just in case Nate wasn't lying, Tim would feel better knowing he wasn't still alone in that room.

As the cab drove away, Tim sighed in resignation and sent up a prayer that his car would start without any problems before turning the key in the ignition. His twelve-year-old beige Civic was cranky about starting on the best of mornings, and he didn't think he could handle fighting with it today. After a few grinding wheezes, the engine turned over, and his old heap was ready to take to the road… even if he wasn't.

He pulled out of the parking lot and headed straight for the nearest YMCA. He needed a shower pretty bad. His dreams for the morning had originally involved a lengthy shower with Nate, taking up where they'd left off the night before. When that was blown to hell, he hadn't been able to bear the thought of hanging around long enough to shower by himself. And Drew was in town, so Tim couldn't go back to Matt's apartment until Sunday night. Therefore the Y was the only option he had left.

He usually avoided the place on the weekends. The building would be packed with kids, and he'd have to wait for a spot on pretty much any of the exercise equipment, but maybe he'd luck out for once and miss the worst of the morning crowd by the time he got there. He needed a good hard workout to release some of his frustration, almost as much as he needed a shower.

Unfortunately, his luck was about the same as always. The parking lot was packed when he pulled in, and he had to wait forever to use his favorite machines. The locker room was packed too, so he couldn't take the long shower he really wanted. And the cherry on top of the shit cake that was his morning happened when he dug through the bag he packed every weekend when Drew was in town and realized his uniform shirt wasn't there. He'd forgotten it in his rush to get out of Matt's apartment, and he couldn't go to work without it.

*Fuck me.*

Angry with himself and the world in general, Tim stuffed everything back into his bag, pulled on the tight T-shirt he'd packed for clubbing that night, grabbed his jacket, and hurried out to his car. If he was quick, he'd have just enough time to run back to the apartment for it before work. Matt would be pissed, but Tim didn't have any choice. He couldn't afford to miss even one shift at either of his two part-time jobs.

As he pulled into the parking lot of the apartment complex, all the tension he'd managed to work out of his neck and shoulders came rushing back. He wasn't looking forward to the confrontation ahead. Not that there would be much of one, not really. Matt was a great guy and generous to a fault. He'd let Tim couch surf at his place for almost a year now. Friends didn't get much better than that. But the deal was, Tim had to make himself scarce on the weekends when Matt's boyfriend, Drew, drove up from school to see him. And Drew was probably going to pitch a fit when Tim showed up knocking on the door. Feeling like he did now, Tim wasn't sure he could handle that, and he didn't want to do that to Matt either, but he really had no choice. No work, no eat, and no money to pay Matt even the piddling amount he could afford to contribute to the rent.

Once inside and standing in front of Matt's door, Tim drew in a deep breath and knocked, hoping against hope that maybe the two men had decided to go out for lunch and he'd be able to sneak in without anyone knowing.

No such luck.

After a few seconds of silence, Tim heard footsteps and someone at the door. A moment later, the deadbolt slid back, then Matt was peering at him through the crack, frowning.

"Dude, what are you doing here?" he hissed, glancing worriedly back over his shoulder toward the open door to the apartment's single bedroom.

"Sorry, man. I forgot my uniform shirt," Tim whispered back. "If you could just snag it for me, I'll be out of your hair."

"Matt?" Drew called from the other room.

Matt cringed and groaned. "Hold on," he said before closing the door again.

Tim shuffled anxiously from foot to foot as he waited in the hall. He could hear voices in the apartment, and he felt a twinge of guilt for making trouble for Matt. Drew didn't like Tim at all. He hated that Matt let Tim stay there in the first place, let alone the fact that he was still there after almost a year. But Tim still couldn't afford a place of his own.

He'd come close a couple of times. At one point he'd saved up enough he thought he could find a place with two bedrooms to share—with a real roommate instead of bumming Matt's couch. But then his car had broken down, he'd needed new tires and a root canal… and on and on and on. With his student loan to pay back and everything going on with his dad, most of the time, Tim felt like he'd never get out from under the black cloud. He was barely making it day to day as it was, and his prospects didn't seem too bright for that to change for the better anytime soon.

The sound of the chain sliding back and the door opening woke him out of his pity party, and he smiled his gratitude to Matt as the man handed over his black polo shirt. "Thanks, man."

Matt didn't return the smile, and when he stepped out into the hall with Tim and closed the door behind him, Tim felt the muscles in his neck tighten up even further in apprehension.

"I need to tell you something, and I know you're not going to like it," Matt said, looking over Tim's shoulder at the elevator instead of meeting his eyes.

"Look, Matt. I know I shouldn't be here. Tell Drew I'm really sorry, and I promise it won't happen again, okay?"

Matt shook his head, and with obvious reluctance met Tim's gaze. "That's, uh, what I wanted to talk to you about, actually." He paused there and blew out a long breath before he said, "I'm sorry, man, but I don't know how else to break it to you. Drew's decided to transfer up here for spring semester. He just got word this week that he can get into at least a few of the classes he wanted, so he's moving up here next weekend. He says you gotta be out by then."

Tim's stomach dropped, and he had to prop up against the wall because his knees didn't want to work for a second. "Shit."

"I'm really sorry, man. I know this is crappy, springing this on you, but we hadn't really talked seriously about it until last night. I love him, and I want to see where this goes. And you know how he feels about you staying here. He—"

"Hates me, I know," Tim finished for him.

"He doesn't hate you. He's just a little on the jealous side, and he doesn't trust that I can resist a stud like you." Matt let out a chuckle that sounded a little forced and punched him lightly on the arm, but Tim couldn't bring himself to tease back.

*What the hell am I going to do now?*

Matt was looking at him so guiltily, Tim managed to dredge up a smile from somewhere. "Don't worry about it, man. You've been more than cool, letting me crash on your couch for as long as I have. I'll figure something out."

When Drew opened the door a moment later, dressed in nothing but a pair of boxer briefs and a sour expression, Matt withdrew the hand he'd placed on Tim's shoulder and took a step back. "Let me know if I can do anything to help. If you need to borrow a little money to get by until you find something...."

Drew made a little sound of protest in the back of his throat at that, his ordinarily pretty lips twisted in disapproval. But Matt didn't take back the offer, and the smile Tim gave him this time didn't need to be forced.

"Thanks, man. I'll get out of your hair now. I'll talk to you next week. Nice seeing you again, Drew. And congrats to both of you on the moving in together." Tim waved at them with a hell of a lot more enthusiasm than he felt, threw his work shirt over his shoulder, and headed for the elevator before the weight of his situation could really sink in.

On the way back to his car, Tim's brain was only able to focus on one thing regarding his future. After the disaster that morning with Nate, Tim hadn't been sure he wanted to go back to the club that night, even if it meant he had to sleep in his car. But now? Now he *definitely* was going to the club. He was going to get shit-faced. And he was going to hook up with someone, even if he had to drop his standards well below the norm to do it. The rest of the disaster of his life was just going to have to wait until Sunday night. At least he had most of next week before he was sleeping in his car full time.

# Chapter Three

AFTER A long and scorching shower, Nathan wrapped himself in a hotel robe and collapsed onto the king-sized bed for a long nap. When he woke for the second time that day, he was feeling a little more like himself, and he went to the couch and set to work sifting through e-mail while he waited for room service to bring him a pot of coffee and a late brunch. After he finished his first cup, he decided he'd procrastinated long enough, and he picked up the phone and called Sean.

"Hey, boss man. I knew you'd eventually find something wrong with the bid if you stared at it long enough. What changes do you have for me?" Sean said cheerily.

"No changes. And I'm not your boss, remember? That's what it meant when you agreed to be my partner." Sean blew a raspberry into the phone, and Nathan smiled his first real smile of the day. He sobered quickly, though, as he got to the point. "I'm not actually calling about the bid, anyway. I'm calling to talk to my friend, not my business partner."

There was a pause before Sean asked, "Is everything okay?"

"Not exactly."

"What's up?"

"This is going to sound weird, so I want you to hear me out before you freak. Okay?" After Sean made a noise of consent, Nathan plunged ahead. "I woke up this morning at another hotel, and I can't remember how I got there or anything else past about six last night when I went to the restaurant in the hotel for dinner."

"*What?*" Sean shouted loud enough Nathan had to pull the phone away from his ear.

"Shhhhhhh. Jesus, Sean. I told you not to freak. Dial it back a little, man. My head is still killing me."

"Sorry. But God, Nate, what do you mean you can't remember? Like you blacked out? Were you drunk?"

Nathan rubbed at his temples a bit before heaving a deep sigh. "No. I don't think so. At least, I don't remember drinking more than one glass of wine. And yeah, I guess I blacked out. I don't know. I got nothing from last night until I woke up this morning."

"Did you go to the ER?"

When Nathan remained guiltily silent, Sean growled, "Are you kidding me? Goddammit, Nate, go now!"

"Stop yelling!" Nathan shouted back and then cringed at the sudden stab of pain in his skull. "I'm fine *now*, except maybe feeling a little hungover. What are they going to do for me at the hospital?"

"Oh, I don't know. Maybe check you out and make sure you didn't have a stroke or something, oh brilliant one…. You know what, I'm going to find someplace and get you in there. I'll have the hotel get a car for you as soon as I have the details. You just be ready when it gets there. You got me?"

"You don't have to—"

"Hell yeah, I do," Sean interrupted him. "If I don't, you won't go. I know you. You'll ignore it, even though you know it's the right thing to do. You'll sit there and pretend the reason you won't get help has nothing to do with your little hang-ups about crowded public places or unfamiliar social situations. You'll hide out in your hotel room and work on that damned presentation we've already gone over a million times. And the cleaning service will discover your dead body collapsed on top of your laptop. I'm finding you someplace *now*, and you're going."

"Yes, Mom," Nathan answered snarkily, too tired to argue with the man anymore.

"You better be grateful I'm not your mom. She'd be on the next flight down there if she knew about this," Sean shot back, the warning implicit in his tone.

Nathan cringed. He loved his mom to death, but the last thing he needed was her here demanding he get every scan known to man while he was trying to make the business deal of a lifetime. "Fine. *Okaaaaay*."

"Good. We'll talk after you've seen a doctor," Sean said primly before hanging up on him.

Nathan stretched out on the couch and pulled a pillow over his face. He really should take this time to go over their bid again before he had to waste his day sitting in a waiting room somewhere. But maybe another little nap wouldn't kill him.

Sometime later, the phone in the room startled him awake in the middle of a very erotic dream involving a certain tanned and toned body he hadn't been able to get out of the back of his mind since that morning. The car Sean called for had to wait an extra five minutes for Nathan to throw on some clothes before he hurried down to the lobby.

The driver took him to a rather elegant and expensive-looking urgent care clinic instead of a hospital. Of course Sean had to pick the priciest place he could find. The man was always the one telling Nathan's assistant, Tonya, to make reservations for the nicest hotel suites and most expensive restaurants, insisting they had an image to project, and if Nathan had to spend all his time drumming up business, the least his company could do was make sure he was comfortable while he did it.

Five years ago, Nathan had considered it a ridiculous expense. But now he'd kind of gotten used to the finer things in life. His business was a success. Why shouldn't he enjoy some of the perks of that? But did he really need a doctor with a five dollar-symbol rating too? He supposed it was better than sitting in a crowded waiting room at an ER, at least. Sean was right about that.

While ordinarily Nathan could handle public places like restaurants or mostly empty movie theaters—where everyone had their own designated personal space—just thinking about going to a busy hospital where the staff, the sick, and the injured were all rushing around and crowded into waiting areas made him feel queasy. How he'd managed to go to a gay bar and not collapse into a full-blown panic attack was a complete mystery.

After about an hour at the clinic, during which Nathan was poked, prodded, and had shiny lights burn out his retinas, the doctor had his bodily fluids and his insurance information, and Nathan had an appointment at the hospital for an MRI late Monday, *after* his presentation. Nathan's blood pressure and heart rate were normal, and nothing seemed out of whack, but the doctor was going to rush the blood and urine tests, and he recommended Nathan take it easy until he heard back.

Feeling a little grumpy, and like he'd just wasted his time, Nathan went back to the hotel and ordered tea before logging on to his laptop and skimming his e-mail. He'd checked it on his phone in the waiting room at the doctor's office, but it was part of his routine to always to check e-mail before getting down to work. That way he knew how best to prioritize his time, in case something urgent came up. Routine and normalcy were what he needed most right now.

There were six new e-mails in his box since the last time he'd checked, an hour or so ago, about average for a Saturday. A couple were from clients, and Nathan only skimmed them before forwarding them to Sean. Some, from salesmen, he'd probably never open. But the last one was from a strange address he didn't recognize. It looked like spam, the sender a weird combo of letters and numbers, but the address ended with @anonymizer.com. Nathan would have deleted it without opening it, except the subject line caught his attention. It said: "*SDS, FGE is not for you.*" Frowning, Nathan opened the e-mail.

> *To: Seward Development Solutions*
>
> *Mr. Seward,*
>
> *If you do not cancel your company's bid presentation and remove your company from the running before Monday morning, the attached images, along with others, will be forwarded to every e-mail address in FGE's directory as well as your own company.*

It was unsigned, and there were three JPEGs attached. The thumbnails were enough to give him the gist, but Nathan clicked on the first anyway. It was a picture of him, his shirt opened to his belly and barely clinging to his shoulders, surrounded by a sea of barely clothed men bumping and grinding on each other.

*How the hell...?*

Nathan slumped back on the couch and stared at his laptop screen with his mouth hanging open. It took him a few minutes to wrap his head around the fact that someone was actually trying to blackmail him.

*Who even did that?*

*And why would they bother?*

This contract was huge business for his little company, but most of the other corporations vying for it were already big names in their own right. Nathan was the underdog at the table. It didn't make any sense.

He so did not need this right now.

As he sat fretting on the couch, he felt a sudden prickle along his spine and then another on his shoulder. He scratched at the itches, but they kept coming back until he was forced to take his shirt off and scramble over to rub against a doorjamb, like a bear with a pine tree, until it stopped.

*Great*. The stress was going to give him hives. He just knew it. He didn't have an action plan for this sort of scenario, and he was definitely not good with surprises.

*Does Amazon even sell a "Blackmail for Dummies" book?*

After several calming breaths, Nathan went to get the free moisturizer from the bathroom. It smelled like lemons and something herby, but he didn't care. Once he was slathered up and his back felt a little better, he went back to the couch to stare at the e-mail again.

Nothing had changed. The words were the same as they'd been a couple of minutes ago. He dropped his head into his hands and forced himself to calm down enough to think.

*Focus, Nathan.*

Honestly, the pics weren't exactly *Enquirer* material. So he was at a gay bar. So what? Under most circumstances, he wouldn't have given a damn if the pictures went viral. He wasn't married. He didn't even have a girlfriend. And while his folks might be a little surprised— since Nathan had never really had reason to discuss the intermittent *flexibility* of his sexuality before now—he was pretty sure it wouldn't cause any big family rifts or anything. His whole family was pretty accepting as a general rule.

In fact, the only reason Nathan wasn't calling the cops right now or e-mailing the asshole back and telling him where to shove those pictures, was that Richard Hamlin, CEO and majority shareholder in FGE, was a notorious "conservative"—PC for bigoted and homophobic jerk. FGE was smart enough to keep that fact under wraps publicly and never institute any blatantly discriminatory policies or programs that would end in lawsuits or bad PR, but it was a well-known secret nonetheless. If Hamlin got even a hint of those pics, Nathan and SDS would be out of the running before they even started the race. Nathan couldn't have that. He'd worked far too hard for far too long on this bid. Sean, his employees, *everyone* who'd invested in his company was depending on him to take SDS to the next level, and this was their best shot to get their foot in the door of some pretty heavy hitters.

Nathan groaned and started scratching at his shoulder again. He had to call Sean.

"Hey, man. What did the doctor have to say?" Sean answered after the first ring.

"Nothing much. He took blood and had me pee in a cup. I have an MRI on Monday, just to cover all the bases, but I think he believes I just partied too hard and he was humoring me."

"Humoring you is the best any of us can do," Sean replied with a long-suffering sigh.

Nathan smiled, feeling some of the tension in his shoulders relax. "Ha, ha, ha. Very funny. Anyway, that's not why I called. We've got another problem, and I'm trying not to completely freak out about it, but I'm not sure what else to do."

"There's more?"

"Yup. I'm going to forward an e-mail to you, but you have to promise me two things first. One, you won't flip out, because that's what I'm trying not to do. And two, you won't share it with anyone, *ever*. Okay?"

"Uh, okay."

"All right. I just sent it."

There was a pause, and Nathan could hear Sean's kids yelling and stomping around in the background, until the sounds were cut off by a door being closed. Sean must have gone into his home office.

A few moments later…. "What the fuck? Is this for real?" Sean practically shouted into the phone.

Nathan grimaced and rubbed at his forehead again as he held the phone away from his ear. "Unless you know something I don't."

"Nate… I don't…. What am I looking at here?"

"If you mean the pictures, I think that's me dancing at a gay bar."

"Yeah. Thanks. I got that part, smartass. When were you at a gay bar, or *any* bar for that matter?"

"I'm guessing last night, since I don't recognize them," he answered wryly.

There was a long pause, and then, in a strained voice, Sean said, "So let me see if I'm getting this straight. You woke up this morning in a strange hotel. You have no memory of last night. And now there's pics of you at what looks like a gay bar, and someone's trying to blackmail you into giving up our bid on the FGE contract?"

"That about sums it up, yeah." Nathan held in the hysterical laugh by sheer force of will.

"What are we, on an episode of *Law and Order SVU*?" Sean said incredulously.

"They base a lot of their stories on actual events, you know." Nathan threw that unhelpful little tidbit out there, hoping to lighten the mood so they both didn't lose it.

"Nate? Are you sure you're okay? You're sounding a little weird... even for you."

Nathan snorted and flopped back against the couch cushions. "I love you too, man. If Isobel hadn't snatched you up, I would have made you my wife years ago."

"Uh-huh. Speaking of which. A gay bar? And you don't remember? You, uh, think anything, uh... you know... *weird* happened?"

Nathan's smile fell away, and he let out a long sigh. He might as well tell Sean everything. "If by weird you mean did I hook up with anyone, the answer is yes. I wasn't alone when I woke up in that hotel."

"Seriously? Jesus, man, was it a dude?"

"Well, I was at a gay bar so, uh, *yeah*."

"And you didn't tell me?"

"You were too busy mothering me."

"Shit. I forgot about that. Okay, let's put the whole man-love thing aside for now. We'll get back to that later. Do you think the guy was part of this blackmail thing?"

"I don't—" Nathan stopped. He was going to deny Tim's involvement outright, but did he really know that for sure? He'd barely shared two words with the guy before letting him walk out the door. God, he was an idiot.

Nathan sat up and grabbed his laptop. He clicked on the last of the three pictures, and there was Tim, draped all over him. An odd corner of Nate's mind noted how happy he looked with his arms full of Tim, but suspicion soon replaced any warm fuzzies.

"Nate?"

"Sorry. I was just thinking."

"About?"

Nathan opened his mouth to answer, but his phone beeped, indicating another call was coming in. It was the clinic.

"Hey, man, the doctor's calling. Let me call you back."

"You better," Sean said before hanging up.

Nathan switched over.

"Mr. Seward?"

"Yes."

"This is Dr. Holland. We got preliminary test results back on your urine sample, and I wanted to get back to you."

"Okay."

"Mr. Seward, we found traces of 7-aminoflunitrazepam in the sample. Do you know what that is?"

"No."

"Its more common name is Rohypnol."

"Are you serious? You mean like roofies? The date rape drug?"

"It's been called that, yes. Memory loss *is* one of the side effects, so without any other evidence of a stroke, seizure, or any other history of memory problems, I believe we may have found why you blacked out last night. I don't think the MRI will be necessary, although you're certainly welcome to keep your appointment, if you want to be sure."

"No. I—" Nathan had no idea what he wanted to say. His mind was a total blank.

Someone had actually slipped him a Mickey?

This day just kept getting weirder.

"Mr. Seward?"

"Yeah. I mean no." Nathan shook his head, even though the doctor couldn't see him. "I understand. I'll cancel the MRI. Thank you, Doctor."

"If you have any more problems or symptoms, don't hesitate to call or go to the hospital if it's after hours. But there shouldn't be any lasting effects, beyond the memory loss. I would recommend you drink plenty of fluids today and continue to take it easy, but beyond that, there isn't much to be done but wait until it's flushed from your system."

"Thanks. I appreciate you calling me back so quickly."

"Certainly, sir. Now, I believe you said you don't remember taking anything of your own volition, so I'd be happy to send you a copy of the lab results, if you intend to contact the police."

"I'd appreciate it. Thanks again, Dr. Holland."

Nathan ended the call and sat staring at the picture of him and Tim on his laptop screen.

*Son of a bitch*!

His phone beeped, telling him he had a text.

*What's happening? What's the Dr. saying? Don't leave me hanging here, man.*

Nathan sighed and dialed him back.

"So?" Sean said impatiently.

Nathan winced and braced for Sean's reaction. Pulling the speaker away from his ear, he said, "So… I was drugged."

"What?"

"The doctor said I was given roofies."

"Holy fuck, Nate! What the hell is going on?"

"You promised not to freak."

"That was earlier. I have every right to freak now."

Surprisingly enough, the fact that Sean was flipping out helped keep Nathan calmer. The whole situation was so surreal it was like it was happening to someone else. He cultivated that feeling. A little distance was what he needed so he could think. And really, he was actually more upset about the possibility of losing his chance at the contract than any of the rest of it at that moment.

"Did you call the cops?" Sean asked.

"I just got off the phone with the doctor, Sean. No. I did not call the cops."

"Oh, yeah. Well, I'll let you off so you can call them now. But you better call me back as soon as you're done."

Nathan was silent.

"Nate? You are going to call the cops, aren't you?"

When Nathan remained silent and deep in thought, Sean growled, "Fine. I'll call for you, then."

"No."

"Nate—"

"No, Sean. I'll take care of this."

"By doing what exactly?" Sean asked suspiciously.

"Don't worry about it."

"Don't worry about it? Are you kidding me? You were *drugged*, Nate. Someone's trying to blackmail you. You can't seriously be thinking you're not going to the police."

Nathan stood up and started pacing the room. "What are they going to do? If I go to the police, even if they take me seriously, what's going to happen? They'll start investigating, asking questions of our competition and people at FGE, because they're the only people who would have any motive for this. I don't know anyone else in Houston. It's going to get out, and we'll lose any chance we had anyway. FGE won't say it outright, and they'll still let me do my presentation. But you know as well as I do it'll be a complete waste of everyone's time, because they'll have already made up their minds. You've heard the same rumors about Hamlin that I have."

The growl on the other end of the line was one Nathan hadn't heard before. "The contract? You're seriously not going to the police because of that contract? Are you nuts? I don't give a damn about the contract, Nate. I *do* give a damn about you. There'll be other clients."

"No, Sean. This is the big one. We need this."

"That's bullshit. We're doing just fine. Besides, there's no guarantee we'll even get the contract anyway."

"Even if we don't, FGE could still open a lot of doors for us if we impress them. We might not get this contract, but they'll have others. Everyone's counting on me."

"This is *your* baby, Nate. You're the one who's been obsessing over it for months. The rest of us would be just—"

"I gotta go." Nathan cut him off. "I have to check some things out. I'll call you later."

"Oh no you don't—"

Nathan hung up on him and went to find his shirt and jacket. As he was pulling on his shirt, his phone starting ringing, but he ignored it. A moment later the hotel phone started ringing as well, but Nathan stepped out of the room and let the door close on the sound.

He put his cell on silent and made his way to the elevator. He knew what he had to do. He didn't have any illusions of being Sherlock Holmes or anything, but he couldn't sit in his room and stew all night either, or he really would get hives. There was no way he'd be able to concentrate on his presentation. Trying to piece together the night before was all he could think about, so he might as well get started.

The elevator doors opened, and he stepped in next to an attractive woman in a very short black dress and gold hooker heels. Nathan pressed himself against the wall farthest from her and tried to make a plan. Problem solving was what he did, and the best place to start with any problem was back at the beginning. Tim was his only tangible link to last night. But the only clue he had to finding him was the name of that club, South Beach, and chances were, even if Tim was going to be there tonight, he wouldn't arrive until late. Now that Nathan thought about it, a place like that probably wouldn't even be open for a few more hours. Mumbling to himself, Nate pulled out his phone and looked the club up, ignoring the missed calls, texts, and voice mail notifications. The club didn't open until nine. That left him a few hours to kill.

When the elevator doors opened, Nathan stepped out into the lobby and froze in indecision, not sure what his next move should be. The lady he rode down with gave him a look like she thought he might be insane as she tottered past him, and Nathan quickly shook himself out of his preoccupation. He was in public now. He needed to at least try to appear normal. He was tugging his jacket and smoothing his hair in the mirror on the wall outside the elevator when a young woman in a dark navy polyester pantsuit came up to him.

"Excuse me, sir. Are you Mr. Nathan Seward?"

She had a gold name tag emblazoned with the hotel's logo identifying her as Susan Black.

"Yes."

"Sir, there's a phone call for you at the front desk."

When Nathan hesitated, waffling between going with her and telling her to take a message, her bland smile turned a little pained. "Sir, the gentleman on the line told us to look out for you. He said to tell you, and I quote, 'If you don't get your ass on the phone right now,' he's going to call the police."

Nathan let his shoulders slump in defeat and reluctantly followed the woman to the front desk. They directed him to one of the house phones, and Nathan picked it up.

"Hello?"

"If you ever hang up on me like that again, I really will call your mom," Sean growled at him.

"Sorry," Nathan grumbled back.

"You should be." Sean drew in a long breath and let it out. "Look. I get that for some crazy reason—all your own—you don't want to call the cops, so I'm going to let that one go for the moment. But I need to know what's going on with you, and if you don't keep me in the loop, I'm flying down there to kick your ass in person. Got me?"

"Andy's birthday is in two days, Sean. You're not going anywhere."

"Don't make me, then."

"I'm not."

"Yes, you are."

"Fine."

"Fine."

They were both silent for a little while, and Nathan was the first to crack up.

"Did we just make up?"

Thank goodness Sean laughed too. "You aren't getting make-up sex out of this, so stop asking."

Nathan snorted, and his smile was wide and happy… and relieved. Even though he'd never admit it, he wished Sean were here with him right now. Sean was the practical one, while Nathan was the more creative side. That's why they worked so well together. Nathan had pushed his company as far as he could on his own—after investing in enough self-help and "be the entrepreneur you want to be" books to fill a public library—but Sean was the one who'd kept it going. So much of the "people" side of things, Nathan just didn't get. He could keep the mask in place only so long before people started to see the cracks in it. While Nathan had the technical know-how and vision to bring the clients in, Sean was the one who kept them happy in the long term. He also kept Nathan grounded and in touch with the here and now when his brain wanted to go far, far away. Nathan could use a little of that right now.

But he was a big boy. He couldn't go crying to Sean every time something in his life didn't go according to plan. And besides, if he did manage to track Tim down, that conversation would be a hundred times more awkward if Sean were there.

"Look, Sean. I know you're worried. And the situation is so damned weird I don't blame you. But just let me handle it in my own way, okay? If anything else happens, I promise I'll go to the cops."

Sean let out another long sigh before he said, "Okay. I think you're crazy… even for you, but I'll let you handle things as long as you continue to check in with me. And if you don't pick up or call me back within fifteen minutes when I call you, I *am* hopping on a flight down there, and I *am* calling the cops for you. You got it?"

"Got it."

"I hope you know what you're doing, boss man."

"So do I."

Nathan let the "boss man" slide this time and ended the call with a simple good-bye. His stomach growled as he set the receiver down, reminding him he hadn't eaten since before he went to the clinic. This, in turn, reminded him that he actually did have another avenue he could explore with the time he had left before the club opened.

He crossed the lobby, walked into the hotel's restaurant, and asked to be seated. The hostess wasn't the same as the night before, so Nathan decided to take a more direct approach and asked to see the restaurant manager after the hostess seated him. A few minutes later a young woman with short-cropped black hair in a smart little black skirt suit approached him with a cautiously inquisitive smile.

"Hello, sir. I'm Candace, the manager. Cherise said you wanted to speak to me?"

"Yes, uh—" Nathan cleared his throat uncomfortably. He took a moment to square his shoulders and put on his business face. "Were you here last night, Candace?"

"No, sir. I'm here the rest of the weekend, so I was off yesterday."

"Oh," he replied stupidly. Now that he'd started, he wasn't exactly sure how to proceed. Did he just come out and say "Someone on your staff may have drugged me, and I'm trying to figure out who"?

Thinking that probably would be a bad idea, he said, "Could you tell me who was working last night?"

Her brow crinkled a bit as she said, "We have a rather large staff of servers, chefs, and kitchen workers, sir. Perhaps if you could tell me what this is about, I might be of more help."

Nathan's wince was purely internal. On the outside, he continued to look calm and collected as he scrambled to think of a way to ask the question without really *asking the question*. The last thing he wanted was to stir up a shit storm by flinging accusations around, even if he was pretty damned sure he had to have been drugged at the hotel. He never would have left that night, otherwise.

"I, uh, may have met someone here and left with them last night, and I was hoping, if I knew who'd waited on me, that I could ask them about it. See if they remembered me," he said lamely.

The creases on the poor woman's forehead didn't ease at all, and she drew back just the tiniest bit, but the pleasant smile never left her face as she said, "You 'may have,' sir? You don't know?"

One of the wonderful things about expensive hotels was, no matter how crazy they thought you were, as long as you had the money to pay and tipped well, they humored you. Nathan reminded himself of this before his nerves got the better of him. "Things are a little foggy." Nathan deliberately glanced in the direction of the bar and let the woman draw her own conclusions.

"Oh, okay," she responded, with a little nervous chuckle. "Well, I can check the schedule for you, sir. A lot of the same people work both Friday and Saturday nights here. I'll ask if any of them had your table last night, if that helps."

"Thank you."

She left, and when his waiter came, Nathan ordered their pork chop special and an iced tea, not wanting to risk anything alcoholic at this point, no matter how sorely he was tempted. He felt a little twinge of concern and hesitated when the waiter brought his drink, but he couldn't spend the rest of his life worrying if someone was drugging his food every time he went out to eat. He'd starve or end up poisoning himself if he had to survive on his own cooking.

While he waited, Nathan spent the time looking up any web article he could on Rohypnol and its side effects. Even if the information didn't exactly make him feel much better about what might have happened to him Friday night, while he'd been under the influence, at least it didn't seem like he had much to worry about from now on.

Shortly after his salad arrived, Candace returned with another woman in the white shirt and apron and black vest and pants all the waitstaff wore.

"Sir, this is Felicia. She was working last night when you came in. She says she thinks your server was Ian, but he went home sick, and he's not on the schedule tonight. I'm sorry."

He had a name at least. "You wouldn't have a last name and number for Ian, would you?"

Candace shook her head regretfully. "I'm sorry, sir. I'm afraid I can't give that out without his permission. I would gladly pass on a message for you, if you'd like."

Nathan swallowed his irritation. The woman was only doing her job, and Nathan wasn't going to be one of those rich assholes people in the service industry always complained about. He really hadn't expected her to say yes anyway, but it was worth a shot. "Thank you. Yes, I would. My name's Nathan Seward. I would appreciate it if he would call the hotel so I might ask him a few questions about last night."

"Certainly, sir."

They turned to leave but stopped when Nathan called out to them. "I'm sorry, Felicia, is it? I know you weren't my server, but did you happen to see me with anyone last night? Here at the table or when I left?"

The young woman smiled shyly and shook her head. "I'm sorry, sir. I only saw you come in. We were pretty busy."

"Thank you."

He had a little more information but not much. Should he be suspicious that this Ian guy left early after waiting on him? Was that just a coincidence or some sinister plot? Hell if he knew. He could call Sean and ask him, but he knew he'd have to listen to Sean go on about how much more information the police would get if they were the ones asking the questions. And besides, Nathan had only just started at this amateur sleuth stuff. He wasn't going to get discouraged yet.

He finished his dinner mechanically. The food was excellent, but he didn't enjoy it much. His mind was on what would happen later that night. He was nervous about talking to Tim again, especially after the dreams he'd had that afternoon. But mostly he was dreading spending any time whatsoever in a crowded, noisy club. The thought twisted his stomach into knots and made his food turn to ash in his mouth.

*And if Tim doesn't show up?*

He was much too busy trying to psych himself up for confronting his social anxiety to worry about that now.

After Candace came back to tell him she'd left a voice mail for Ian, Nathan killed another hour at the restaurant drinking a couple of cups of coffee and picking over a crème brûlée he didn't actually want. By twenty after eight, his brain had talked him into—and his nerves had talked him out of—going to the club about a dozen times. His brain won. The final consensus was that he'd drive himself insane if he stayed at the hotel anyway, so the possibility of a quick and dirty anxiety attack at the club was preferable to hours of fretting in his room and maybe years of beating up himself over being too chickenshit to follow through with his plan. Sean was going to give him no end of shit about pretty much everything that happened on this trip anyway, so that didn't factor into the equation.

When his waiter came back again, Nathan decided it was time. He charged the meal to his room, stopped at the front desk to leave his cell number in case Ian did actually call, and headed out front so the doorman could get him a cab.

"South Beach club, please," Nathan said to the driver as he climbed in.

The guy gave him an odd look for a few beats in the rearview mirror before he said, "Sure thing."

Nathan slumped back into the seat and did his best not to think the whole ride there. There was already a line outside when they pulled up, and he had to force himself to get out of the cab. The scantily clad young men and women in line ahead of him gave him a few disapproving and measuring looks as they shivered and huddled together against the cold, talking way too loudly and animatedly for Nathan's comfort, but otherwise he was left alone to stew as he inched his way closer to his own personal hell. By the time he'd paid the cover and stepped inside, he was a nervous wreck, wondering what he thought he was doing.

It was still early, so the place wasn't packed yet, despite the length of the line he'd had to wait in, but there were still enough people around to make him tense and cranky. He found a quiet corner not far from the door and hunkered down to wait and watch. He would be fine as long as he didn't have to actually leave his corner and mingle. He'd staked out a space that was all his, far enough away from most of the action and the bars, so no one should bother him, and he had a good view of everyone coming in the doors.

Unfortunately, as the hours passed, the noise and the crush of bodies increased by leaps and bounds. With each passing minute, he felt the crowd getting closer and the air growing thicker, despite the cold breeze that came in with each new arrival. He'd watched the door for over two hours now, and there was still no sign of Tim. He wasn't sure how much longer he could take the place, and he was feeling more and more like an idiot the longer he stayed.

What had he been thinking? He wasn't a detective. He was a programmer, for God's sakes. He belonged behind a nice quiet desk with a computer screen between him and the rest of the world. He didn't do up close and personal unless it was for work, and only then because he had to.

Nate was just working up the courage to pack it in for the night and make a mad dash for the door when he caught sight of Tim making his way to the nearest bar. Nathan had no idea how he'd missed him coming in, maybe on one of the two tortuous trips to the bathroom he'd needed to make because of all the coffee he'd had at the hotel.

Despite all of his anxiety and his suspicions about Tim's involvement, Nathan felt a surge of relief the moment he spotted him, followed closely by a surge of something much more primal. Tim looked good. Nathan didn't know if it was echoes from his subconscious or simply whatever strong attraction had led him to pick Tim up when he was drugged out of his mind, but there was no denying the pull he felt. Tim's blond spikes were artfully mussed, and his thin blue T-shirt stretched tight across thick arms and sculpted pecs, reminding Nathan of how good Tim had looked without his clothes on. And with his dream from the afternoon still fresh in his mind, Nathan was finding it a little hard to remember why exactly he was there until a young man in a white tank top and torn jeans draped himself over Tim's shoulder and spoke into Tim's ear, leaning close to be heard over the music. The smile Tim gave the guy was inviting and flirtatious, and that's when Nathan's temper returned.

How dare Tim party and flirt like nothing had happened when Nathan's life was being turned upside down?

Nathan headed for the bar with blinders on. He let the anger drive him through the tight press of bodies, ignoring any protests or groping hands as he went. He pushed through to Tim's side just as Tim was picking up his drink and clamped a hand on Tim's wrist before he could take a swallow.

"I need to talk to you," Nathan yelled over the thumping bass of whatever club crap the speakers were pumping out.

Tim's eyes widened at first in what Nathan assumed was surprise, but his welcoming smile faded quickly as he searched Nathan's face. "Okay."

# *Chapter Four*

TIM ALLOWED Nate to drag him away from the bar and the little cutie in the tank top. He threw an apologetic smile over his shoulder, but the cutie was already moving back toward the dance floor, in search of another partner. Not that Tim minded. The cutie was hot, but Nate was definitely hotter.

At first, Tim was so happy to see him again—and buzzed—he nearly flung himself at Nate and kissed him, but then he remembered their morning after, and some of his enthusiasm waned. Plus, the look on Nate's face wasn't exactly encouraging. He actually looked pretty mad, and while Tim would have loved to believe it was jealousy, he had a feeling that wasn't it at all. The feeling was confirmed when Nate all but dragged him into a dark corner and shoved him up against the wall, spilling Tim's third rum and Coke of the night. He'd ordered the first two the minute he got into the club and pounded them back in less than five minutes, but that didn't mean he could afford to waste the third. He had a feeling he was going to need it by the end of the night, if the look on Nate's face was anything to go by.

Before Nate could make him spill any more of it, Tim chugged what was left in his glass and set the empty on a nearby table.

"What?" he yelled when Nate crowded him again.

"I want you to tell me what the hell happened last night, and I want the truth this time. No bullshit," Nate said through bared teeth.

All Tim could think was God, Nate looked good. His dark blue eyes were sparking, his nostrils flaring. He was acting so fucking take-charge and sexy, Tim was having trouble focusing on what the man was talking about. "What?" he repeated stupidly.

Nate's eyes narrowed at him, and it looked like he was grinding his teeth. He glanced around them, and only then did Tim notice they'd drawn the attention of several people nearby. When Tim turned back to Nate, the man growled something Tim couldn't hear and pushed him back against the wall again. A moment later, Tim felt rough hands groping him. He thought it was his lucky night until Nate stepped back abruptly and jingled a set of keys in Tim's face... *his* keys.

"Outside," Nathan shouted at him before turning and disappearing into the crowd.

*Oh shit!*

Panic soon chased whatever lust and alcohol remained in Tim's system. His car was pretty much all he had left. It was where he would be sleeping tonight if he didn't hook up with anyone who had a place of his own or was willing to pay for a hotel.

Tim chased after him as fast as he could, earning a great many insults shouted at him as he went. For one horrible second, once he got outside, he couldn't find Nate, but then he spotted him by the streetlight across the parking lot. As he jogged over, Tim started to get a little mad himself.

"What the fuck are you doing?"

"I want to know what the hell is going on," Nate shouted back.

"Well, so do I. I have no idea what you're talking about."

Nate got up in his face. "I'm talking about the fact that I was drugged! I'm talking about the goddamned e-mail I got this afternoon trying to blackmail me with pictures from this club... pictures with you in them. That's what I'm talking about."

Tim took a step back, some of his anger cooling into confusion. "You were what?"

"Drugged, asshole! Drugged! Do I need to call the cops to get you to tell me what's going on?"

"Wait. Wait. Hold on a second. Holy shit." Tim needed a moment to process. "You think I had something to do with that?"

Well, that hurt. There was a big difference between Nate not remembering him and Nate thinking he was the kind of guy who'd do something like that.

"Nate, I told you this morning. I don't know anything. I wasn't lying. I met you here, and we went back to the hotel. That's it. I swear."

Nate's angry mask wavered a little, and Tim decided to press further. "Look, I'm freezing my ass off out here. Can we go somewhere and talk? Please?"

Nate finally seemed to realize Tim was only in a T-shirt, and while Tim had enough rum in him to make him sweat in the club, now that he was outside, his nipples could cut glass, something he was sure Nate noticed because the man was staring at his chest.

"Where?" Nathan asked.

"Well, back inside the club would be warmer, but it'll be kinda hard to talk."

Nathan's face went stony. "I'm not going back in there."

Something in his tone clued Tim in that there was more going on there than just an aversion to dance clubs. It didn't really matter. Tim wanted Nate all to himself anyway. "Let's go to my car. I haven't been here that long. The engine should still be warm." There wasn't a lot of gas in it, but there'd be enough to idle for a little while. Tim just sent up a prayer that it would start and not completely embarrass him.

He held his hands out for the keys with as reassuring a smile as he could manage, but Nate shook his head. "Show me," Nate demanded.

Tim's car was near the back of the lot, and they passed a couple of vehicles with steamed-up windows on their way. Tim tried really hard not think about that. He wanted to be in a bed with Nate so bad he was afraid he'd bust the zipper in his jeans if he thought even the tiniest bit about what was going on in those cars.

He didn't really *need* a bed. The backseat would be okay, and there were already blankets there.

No.

Tim took a couple of deep breaths to clear that image from his mind and stared resolutely ahead of him. He had to use his big brain if there was going to be any possibility of not screwing up the only second chance with Nate he was likely to get. Nate was classy, a white-collar guy. Tim had to play it cool.

Nate climbed in the driver's side and started the engine while Tim got into the passenger's seat. It was a strange sensation, given that Tim didn't think he'd ever been in the passenger's side of his car before, but he definitely liked the way Nathan looked in the driver's seat.

He was not going to think about sex.

He was not going to blow—

He was not going to think about sex.

Once the heat was on full blast, the fan rattling embarrassingly loudly, Nate turned to face him again. "You swear you had nothing to do with this?"

Purposefully holding Nate's gaze and with as much sincerity as he could muster, Tim said, "I swear. I don't know what's going on. You were really drugged?"

Nate nodded and turned to stare out the windshield, his forehead creased. After only a few moments, he sighed deeply and let his head fall back against the headrest. "I guess that's it, then. If this guy, Ian, doesn't call me back, I'm never going to figure out what the hell happened."

He looked so defeated, so different from the way he was last night, Tim didn't know what to do. He wanted to take Nate back to the hotel and try to make everything all better again the best way he knew how, but he had a feeling the offer wouldn't be appreciated. "Who's Ian?" he asked instead.

"The waiter at the hotel who served me last night. I *had* to have been drugged at the hotel. I *know* I wouldn't have gone out otherwise. I was just going to have dinner and then head back to my room to work a little and sleep. That's it. Other than you, this guy, Ian, is the only clue I have."

"What about that guy you were with when we first started dancing together?" Tim asked, aching to be of some kind of help so Nate wouldn't just walk away.

Nate turned to face him again, some of the spirit Tim had seen in him before returning. "What guy?"

"I told you. You were dancing with someone before I got there. I don't know his name, but I've seen him around a few times. I think he tried to pick me up once, but he wasn't really my type, so I don't remember what his name is."

"Did you see him in there tonight?"

"No." Tim paused and bit his lip as an idea occurred to him. He didn't want to give Nate false hope, but anything that kept Nate from leaving was better than nothing. "Look. I'm here most weekends, so I know the bartenders and the bouncers pretty well. I've even gone out a few times to breakfast with a bunch of them, after hours. Why don't we go talk to them and see if they remember anything, okay? It's worth a shot, anyway."

Nate stared at him wide-eyed for a few moments before a grateful smile slowly spread across his face. "Thank you."

Tim shrugged like it didn't really matter, even though he felt ridiculously happy over that simple little smile. He was such a sap. "Wish I could help you more."

Nate would probably never know just how much Tim meant those words. It killed him that Nate looked at him like a stranger after all they'd shared—the hours of talking and loving they'd had before falling asleep in each other's arms. That night, he was so sure they'd made a deep connection, something spiritual, souls touching just like his mom used to talk about… only to have it ripped away when the sun came up.

But life wasn't fair, and he was an idiot to get his hopes up in the first place. Tim pushed his stupid romantic thoughts out of his head and led the way back to the entrance to the club.

Jana was working the front door when they got there, so Tim decided to start with her. Jana was an in-your-face and unapologetically butch lesbian with tons of tattoos and piercings. Her uniform of choice was almost always a pair of dark cargo pants, boots, suspenders, and a white tank, along with a scowl that let everybody know not to mess with her. Tonight she'd put on a coat over the tank, but she didn't look any less intimidating. When he'd first met her, it had taken Tim a while to get past the way she looked, but once he'd gotten to know her, she turned out to be pretty cool. And tonight she actually grinned and winked at them as they approached. It must have been a good night on the door—no real assholes to deal with yet.

"Hey, babe. What you been up to out in the dark?" she teased as she handed IDs back to a couple in line and waved them on to where another bouncer, Ed, was collecting covers.

Tim felt his cheeks grow hot, even though they hadn't actually been doing anything in the parking lot… unfortunately.

"Get your mind out of the gutter, Jana. We were just talking," Tim replied, purposefully not looking at Nate.

"Mmmhmm." Her smirk said clearly that she wasn't buying it, and Tim felt his neck grow hot too. That was pretty impressive, given he was still only in a T-shirt and the night hadn't gotten any warmer.

"Behave," Tim chided. "Look, Jana, this is Nate. Do you remember him from last night?"

She looked past him at Nate and pursed her lips. "Sure I do. You guys left together around one, right after I got back from my break." Without turning away from them, she held out her hand for the ID of the next person in line, glanced down at it, looked briefly at the guy's face, and waved him on.

"Do you remember who he came in with?"

She frowned in thought as she checked the IDs of a couple more people. Then she said, "Sorry, sweetie, I don't. I only noticed him later because he was with you." She leaned close and whispered, "He's not really my type. No offense." She snickered when Tim rolled his eyes, and then she put her bouncer face back on and turned back to the next couple in line.

Nate looked so disappointed Tim shoulder-bumped him and gave him an encouraging smile. "Don't worry. We still have a few other people we can ask. I don't know if you came in with the guy I saw you with. But I do know he's been here enough *someone* will know who he is."

Nate smiled back, and, without thinking, Tim reached for his hand to lead him back inside. As soon as their hands touched, Nate's eyebrows shot up and his eyes widened, but he didn't pull away. Tim's heart started to race then, like it had when Nate first agreed to dance with him last night. And despite the fact he should know better, Tim couldn't help the tiny stirring of hope in his chest. He'd had one incredible night with this man. If he could just keep Nate from leaving for a little while longer, maybe he could have another.

They walked back into the club together. Nate gripped his hand tightly but otherwise gave no sign of any upset. Tim still didn't know what the deal was with that, but he was more than happy to be the man's security blanket. Once they were past the crush by the door, Tim headed straight for the bar where he knew he'd find Josh. Josh had tended bar there almost every weekend for as long as Tim had been going to South Beach. When Tim had had a little more money and wasn't cruising for a bed every weekend, he'd even hooked up with the guy once. Josh had a really hot body he showed off to good effect, dirty-blond hair, and sweet brown eyes. They'd had a good time but no real connection. Sometime after that, Tim heard Josh had found God or something and decided to swear off dating completely, and he and Tim had remained casual friends. If anyone in the club would remember the guy Nathan was looking for, it would be Josh. Everyone hit on Josh.

"Hey, man," Tim shouted over the music when Josh moved to their end of the bar. "I need to talk to you when you got a sec."

Josh nodded and held up a finger as he quickly moved back up the bar, filling orders and collecting money. When there was a lull, he made his way back to them.

"Hey. What's up?"

"We're looking for someone who was in here last night, only we don't know his name. He was dancing with my friend here. Short brown hair, maybe five seven, a couple of studs in his ears. He's in here off and on. I'm sure he's hit on you at least a dozen times."

Josh grinned and rolled his eyes. "Dude, you're going to have to give me more than that."

Tim thought hard. "He's young, early twenties maybe, sorta cute but too much baby fat for me." Tim scrambled for something else. Then an image popped into his head of the last time he'd seen the guy dancing without his shirt on, a few months ago. "Oh, and I think he has a tattoo of a hummingbird or something on his shoulder."

"Oh yeah, I know the guy. He's a regular, but he usually comes in pretty late. I think he works most weekends, so you wouldn't have seen him much."

"What's his name?"

Josh scrunched up his face. "Ian something?"

Tim felt Nate tense beside him. "Did you say Ian?" Nate shouted over the music.

Josh nodded before looking back over his shoulder. "Look, guys, I gotta go," he yelled, waving at the people lined up by the bar and smiling apologetically as he headed off to do his job.

Nate was already moving toward the door when Tim turned back to him. He had to practically run to catch up to the man, and by the time he made it outside again, Nate already had his phone out and was halfway across the parking lot.

"This is Nathan Seward. I'm calling to find out if there are any messages for me," Nate was saying when Tim caught up to him. "No? Then can you transfer me to the hotel restaurant manager, please?"

There was that take-charge voice again. Tim shivered from more than the cold, and he felt a frustrated whine building at the back of his throat. The man was such a study in opposites—one minute vulnerable and a little lost, the next bossy and confident—Tim's heart and libido were having a hard time keeping up, even as his brain told him he was being an idiot and he was only going to get hurt.

"Closed? Dammit! Is there any way I can get a message to Candace, the manager? No, I don't want to do that. I want to get it to her now."

Nate was pacing agitatedly. It was pretty clear he was barely holding on to his temper, and Tim was glad to not be the one on the other end of the line. The man was a little scary when he was pissed—impressive and hot, but still scary.

After a few moments, Nate stopped pacing and blew out a long breath, visibly reining in his anger. "No. I understand. I'll just wait and speak to her tomorrow. Good-bye."

"What's going on?" Tim asked cautiously when Nate finally put his phone away.

Nate huffed out another breath and lifted his head to meet Tim's gaze. "It can't be a coincidence that both my waiter last night and the guy you saw me with here are named Ian. I had the restaurant manager leave a message for him to call me when I just wanted to ask him a few questions, but now… now I really want to talk to him."

Tim approached him cautiously and stopped only a few feet away. "Nate, I know this is probably none of my business, but maybe you should call the cops. You know how to find him now, and like you said, there's too much going on here for this to be a coincidence. If you were drugged, that's some heavy stuff. They can find this Ian guy for you pretty quick, I would think."

Nate shook his head vehemently. "I don't want the police involved. The minute they start asking questions, the news will get out, and that'll be it for the contract. I can't threaten whoever sent the message with going to the police if I've already gone. The only way this doesn't fuck me over is if I agree not to press charges and they agree to lose those pictures. I just wanted to know who I was dealing with so I had a little leverage, enough to let them know they could get caught."

Tim didn't understand the particulars, but he didn't really have to. A guy like Nate—silk shirt, fancy watch, take-charge attitude that screamed success—probably knew what he was doing a hell of a lot more than a guy like Tim. So he did the only thing he could think of. He reached out and put a comforting hand on Nate's shoulder. "I'm sorry, Nate. I wish I could have been more help."

Nate's expression softened, and he seemed to shake himself out of what was left of his temper. "No. Look, I'm sorry. You've been really great about all this. I should be thanking you, not bitching at you."

Tim reluctantly took his hand back and shrugged. "It's no problem. I wanted to help." He paused there and rocked on his heels a little uncomfortably, afraid to say what he really wanted to. But in his gut he knew this was it. He didn't have any more help to offer, and Nate was going to walk out of his life for good very soon if Tim didn't say something to stop him. "So, uh, what are you going to do now?"

Some of the confidence Tim so admired leeched out of Nate's posture, and he turned his head and gazed out into the darkness. "I don't know. I guess I'll have to wait until tomorrow to talk to the manager again and get her to leave a more threatening message for Ian—force him to call me back this time."

"So nothing more tonight, then?" Tim asked, allowing a hint of wistfulness into his voice.

Nate turned back and studied Tim for a few seconds before he said, "No. Nothing more tonight." He sighed and ran a hand through his thick brown hair before looking away again. "I suppose I should try to get some sleep. It's been a long day."

There it was, Tim's last opening. If he didn't go for it now, he'd always regret it. "Look. I know this whole situation is really messed up, but last night was really, *really* nice… being with you, I mean. I know you said you were straight and all, but… I don't know, maybe you wouldn't mind some company for a while?"

And didn't that sound completely lame.

*Way to go, Tim. Way to make the offer really appealing.*

The smile Nate gave him then was completely unexpected. Despite his hopes, Tim thought for sure the guy was going to blow him off, but Nate actually chuckled a little as he answered, "I never actually said I was straight."

"I don't understand. I thought you said—"

"I didn't actually *say* anything," Nate interrupted. "You said I was straight, and I was a little preoccupied at the time, so I didn't bother to try and correct you because it's... well, it's *complicated*. More complicated than I thought, actually."

That last was said more to himself, but Tim couldn't help edging closer to the man. A gust of wind found its way into every gap in Tim's shirt, and he wrapped his arms around himself as hope and dread took turns twisting his stomach. "Sooooo, is that a yes or a no to tonight?"

The regretful smile was all the answer Tim needed. His heart fell into his shoes as Nate opened his mouth to speak. But then Nate stopped before he actually said the words, and silence hung between them. Deciding to make it easy on the guy and end the torture, Tim held out his hand and said, "Can I get my keys back, please? I know you didn't have a car last night, so if you need a lift, I can take you anywhere you want to go, but I'm freezing here."

"I don't think you should be driving." Nate's expression was unreadable, but Tim supposed he shouldn't be too surprised by that. Despite the connection he'd felt with Nate, one really intense night plus a couple of hours didn't mean Tim knew the guy as well as he'd thought he did.

"I'm fine. My buzz is pretty much gone now."

*And I really just want to curl up and nurse my wounds in peace.*

When Nate frowned at him and still didn't hand over the keys, Tim started to get irritated. How long was Nate going to drag this painful and completely embarrassing conversation out?

"Look, man. You don't have to worry about me. You have your own shit to deal with. I get that. Just give me my keys, and I'll let you get back to it. I promise not to drive too far or run anyone over, okay?"

The truth was, Tim would probably only be driving far enough to find a secluded parking lot to sleep in. There were a couple around where he knew he wouldn't be hassled by the cops or towed, as long as he didn't sit in the same spot for days. He was tired, cold... and depressed. All he wanted was to pull on some of the extra clothes he kept in his trunk, wrap up in a blanket in the backseat, and go to sleep.

"I do need a ride back to my hotel. But I'm driving," Nate said firmly. Without waiting for a response, he took off toward Tim's car.

That bossy tone was back, but since Tim now knew for sure he wasn't getting any, it didn't have quite the same effect on him as it had earlier. He stomped after Nate and flopped into the passenger seat with an irritated sigh. The silence was heavy between them as Nate backed out of the parking space and pulled onto Grant. Tim stared petulantly out the window until Nate cleared his throat and said, "Uh, I don't really know where I'm going. I remember coming in from this direction in the taxi, but that's about it."

"Where's your hotel?" Tim asked, not bothering to hide his annoyance.

"Downtown. I'm at the Sorrella."

*Of course you are.*

As if Tim needed another reminder of how far this guy was out of his league.

"Turn left up there, and then take the next right. That'll get us to the freeway."

"Thanks."

"You're welcome."

And that was the end of their conversation, beyond a few clipped directions from Tim to get them to the hotel in one piece. Nate seemed preoccupied, or maybe that was just wishful thinking on Tim's part. Maybe the guy just had no interest in talking to him beyond finding out what he needed to know. And why would he? It wasn't as if Tim was educated or cultured enough to provide scintillating conversation for a guy like Nate. They had talked, Friday night, for *hours*. But that seemed like a lifetime ago now.

That oh-so-happy thought faded to background as they turned and drove down the fancy treelined drive in front of the hotel. All Tim could do after that was gape up at the place like a country boy on his first visit to the big city. He'd driven past CityCentre before on the freeway plenty of times, so he'd seen the place from a distance. But it was so far removed from the reality of his own life, it felt like he was watching it on TV. He didn't think he'd ever actually know anyone who stayed at a place like that.

As Nate put the car in park and stepped out, part of Tim wished he could get a peek inside, just once. But his more practical side told him that would be a bad idea. What would be the point? So he could torture himself later with real 3-D images of the kind of place he was never going to be able to afford?

No, thank you. That was the last thing he needed to cap off the weekend.

Tim forced himself to get out of the car and put on a brave face. But when he got to the driver's side, Nate was handing his keys to the valet waiting by the curb.

"Uh, Nate? I kind of need those."

The valet hesitated, looking back and forth between the two of them.

"Is your offer still open?" Nate asked. His voice had an odd note to it, but since it sounded like Nate was asking him to come up, Tim chose to ignore it.

Past the frantic flutter of his heart, Tim said, "Yeah, it's open."

Nate's smile was small, but it seemed genuine, and Tim's hopes for the evening did a one-eighty. He really needed to get a hold of himself, or he was going to get emotional whiplash.

"Then you won't be needing them just yet," Nate said, gesturing to the valet to go ahead.

Tim stepped out of the way, and the guy drove off with his car. He had no idea how he was going to come up with the cash to get it back, but he wasn't going to think about that now. Not with Nate and the possibility of another amazing night waiting for him.

When Nate turned and headed for the glass doors, Tim followed. Nervous and out of place in the very chic and modern lobby, Tim could feel eyes on him from the few people there at that time of night, judging his cheap clothes and ratty shoes. In truth they probably didn't give a damn enough to notice him at all, but he was self-conscious anyway. The lady behind the front desk gave him a quick glance before dismissing him altogether when Nate stopped to ask about messages. She told him there weren't any, and before Tim realized it, they were in the elevator on the way up to Nate's room.

# Chapter Five

NATHAN PUNCHED the button for his floor after fishing out and swiping his key card. He had a few moments in the quiet of the elevator to wonder what the hell he thought he was doing before the doors opened and he was leading Tim to his door. His hand shook a little as he swiped the card in the lock, but his back was to Tim, so he hoped Tim didn't see it.

Once they were inside with the door closed, Nathan had no idea what to do next. He wasn't exactly clueless about dating. He'd dated off and on over the years, though most of them had been arranged by friends or family because of that little thing he had about crowded public spaces and his awkwardness around people in general. He wasn't exactly the bar-hopping type, and although online dating would have been the perfect avenue, he just hadn't taken much time away from his business to worry about it. In fact, this was probably the first time he'd actually gone out and found someone on his own in close to a decade. Maybe that was part of his problem now.

He didn't do spontaneous.

Ever.

Well, that and the fact that this was the first time since college he'd actually been attracted enough to a guy to want to explore that side of himself.

As he scrambled for something to say, Nathan watched while Tim spun in a circle, taking in the room with obvious pleasure. To distract himself from his mounting anxiety, Nathan followed Tim's gaze, trying to see the room through Tim's eyes. The Sorella was a very nice hotel, but Nathan hadn't actually paid much attention to the details of his room, or any of the rooms he'd stayed in, in a very long time. All he cared about these days was a decent bed and room service, a place for him to work, and a fast Internet connection. The rest of it just sort of faded into the background.

Now that he was looking at it, he liked what he saw. The décor was as modern as the rest of the hotel, rich brown on the floor and furniture, lightened with cream bedding and accents. Austere but pretty, he supposed, nothing crazy luxurious or anything. He'd drawn the line at one of the penthouse suites when Sean suggested it. That would have been a pointless expense for just him, especially since he wouldn't be spending much time there if their bid wasn't the one chosen.

"Wow. This place is incredible," Tim finally said, breaking the ice before Nathan could come up with anything brilliant.

His smile was open and delighted, his feelings right there for anyone to see, and Nathan decided he was drawn to that, probably even more than the pretty package. "Would you like something to drink?"

If possible, Tim's smile got even brighter as he moved closer. "Sure."

Nathan dumped his jacket on the back of the small couch in the sitting area and went to the minibar, trying to appear more casual than he felt. "You had a rum and Coke earlier, right? You want another?"

"Just a Coke is fine."

Tim was watching him carefully now, as if he didn't know quite what to make of him, and Nathan couldn't blame him. Obviously his play at acting cool hadn't been completely successful. While he pulled the bottle from the little refrigerator and unwrapped a glass, Nathan drew in a deep breath and tried to settle his whirling thoughts. The only thing he knew for sure was, when it came time to let Tim drive away, he just couldn't do it. He clung to that fact. It was solid and real. The maelstrom of other thoughts and anxieties that had erupted since hadn't changed the feeling. In fact, now that Tim was in his room, the feeling was even stronger.

"Nate?"

Nathan looked up, still holding the glass and soda bottle he'd been staring blindly at. "Sorry." Feeling like a complete idiot, he offered the drink and glass to Tim, and Tim stepped even closer but didn't reach for them.

"Nate," Tim said, his voice more subdued than before, "why did you invite me up here?"

*Why indeed?*

"Would I sound like a complete idiot if I said I wasn't sure?"

"Not exactly."

Whether he sounded like one or not, Nathan felt like an ass as he set the bottle and glass on the desk.

"Did you want to talk some more, or did you have something else in mind?" Tim asked cautiously.

Burgeoning hope, right alongside fear of rejection, were shining clear as day in Tim's eyes. They had to be, otherwise Nathan would never have been able to see them. How long had it been since Nathan had been with someone who wore his heart on his sleeve? Had he ever known anyone like that? It was almost as intimidating as it was captivating. He wanted to taste those emotions, to feel that passion, but at what cost? He knew almost nothing about Tim. He didn't have a plan. He didn't know where any of this was going. He didn't know what happened between them Friday night, not really. Was he being fair? Would he be leading Tim on if he didn't try to think ahead, beyond what was happening between them right now?

Heat radiated from Tim's body. Nathan could feel it on his skin even though a few feet still separated them. Tim's beautiful green eyes watched him with enough emotion and need even someone as clueless as Nathan couldn't miss it. In a move so completely out of character he hardly recognized himself, Nathan threw caution to the wind and stepped into Tim's space. Unfamiliar and unsettling as everything seemed at the moment, there was no denying he wanted Tim badly. Nathan didn't stop to analyze it any more. He'd come this far, and he didn't want to back out now. He pressed a thigh between Tim's legs and slid his arms around Tim's waist to eliminate the last of the distance between them, and for the first time in over ten years, Nathan was pressed intimately against another man.

As soon as their bodies touched, Tim drew in a sharp breath, his amazing green eyes wide and searching, his lips temptingly parted. For once in his life, Nathan wanted to be the bold and reckless one. He forgot his reservations. He forgot the blackmail. He forgot his goals and his company and decided to take this one thing for himself, just for tonight.

Wrapping one hand around Tim's neck, gripping the solid column of flesh firmly, Nathan pulled Tim into what was for him their first kiss. As his lips slid tentatively over Tim's, Nathan could feel the muscles in Tim's neck tense and bunch. Tim trembled, as if he was barely holding himself back. That combined with the sexy whimper Tim made in his throat when Nathan deepened the kiss sent a shot of fire through Nathan's entire body. Tim's mouth was so sweet and responsive Nathan couldn't get enough. And Tim's shaky exhale when Nathan pulled back made Nathan tremble as well. Tim was pushing buttons Nathan didn't even remember having. His knees were weak with it, and nothing mattered but getting more.

Keeping eye contact with Tim the whole time, Nathan tugged Tim's jacket from his shoulders and tossed it on the back of the couch next to his own. After taking a steadying breath, he dragged Tim's T-shirt over his head and tossed it toward their jackets.

Nathan groaned as his cock throbbed painfully. Tim was perfect, like model perfect, every ridge of muscle in his chest and arms beautifully defined. He had to work out pretty seriously to have a body like that. Nathan felt a little niggle of self-consciousness creep in with the lust, fearing he wouldn't measure up. But Tim didn't let that last long. The way he was looking at Nathan, as if Nathan was the most beautiful thing he'd ever seen, didn't leave much room for self-doubt, nor did the firm grip Tim now had on his package through the thin wool of his pants.

"God, Nate. I want you so bad," Tim whispered shakily as he massaged Nathan's cock and then pressed his face into Nate's neck, kissing and nibbling on his skin.

Before Nathan could clear his head enough to respond in anything other than unintelligible gibberish, Tim robbed him of the power of speech completely by dropping to his knees, yanking open his pants, and stuffing Nate's cock into his mouth.

Heaven, pure, hot, wet, heaven surrounded his aching dick as Tim set to work on him, alternating between teasing licks, wet sucking kisses, and suction that threatened to end things a hell of a lot quicker than Nathan wanted. Tim was really good at this. But tempting as it was to finish in Tim's mouth, Nathan had enough pride not to let things be over quite that soon. The way Tim talked about their first night together, Nathan had a lot to live up to, and he didn't want to disappoint.

"Come here," Nathan choked out, tugging on Tim's spiky blond hair and urging him back to his feet.

As soon as Tim was upright again, Nathan mashed their mouths together, tasting himself on Tim's reddened and swollen lips. Tim hungrily kissed him back, grasping at Nate's clothes with restless and impatient hands, his body tense as if he were still holding back even though he groaned and writhed.

Nathan wasn't sure if that meant Tim was waiting for him to take the lead, but it really didn't matter. Nathan's legs were still weak from what Tim had done to him, and he needed for them to be horizontal as soon as possible, before he collapsed. He nudged forward, and Tim retreated until the back of Tim's thighs hit the bed. When Nathan pulled away enough to draw some much needed air into his lungs, Tim sprawled across the mattress, grinning up at him, holding out his arms, and wriggling his fingers in the universal sign for gimme. Tim was beautiful, vibrant and trusting, not a single sign of reserve to be found, no pretense.

Nathan kicked off his shoes quickly and pushed his pants off his hips. Tim watched for a couple of seconds before he started to work on his own clothes, undoing his shoelaces, kicking off his shoes, and wriggling out of his jeans. By the time Nathan was out of his shirt and undershirt, Tim was naked and magnificent, sprawled out on the bed like a centerfold, his cock arching hard and proud up to his navel, and Nathan's body was humming with too much need for any other thoughts or nerves to interfere.

He crawled up the bed, and Tim spread his thighs to welcome him. Nathan slowly lowered himself on top of Tim, and they both groaned as their cocks pressed together and the warm, silky skin of their torsos met. Nathan cupped Tim's chin and kissed him again, slower this time, savoring the feel of him, the taste of him, his warmth and vitality. It had been too long since the last time Nathan had been intimate with someone. Why was it that everything else always seemed so much more important than this? Why was it so easy to forget how good it felt and how *necessary* it was? Those were deep questions and probably worth further deliberation, but it sure as hell wasn't going to happen now.

While Nathan explored Tim's mouth, Tim hooked his heels around Nathan's calves and rocked against him. The sweet friction was all it took for any epiphanies he'd been having to travel right out the window.

"Fuck me, Nate," Tim whispered breathlessly against his lips.

Nathan groaned. He didn't have enough blood left in his frontal lobes to be nervous anymore, but there were a few things he needed to do to follow through on that demand. He was just having a really hard time remembering what they were with Tim's hot, horny body writhing restlessly beneath him.

Nathan pulled back for a second to clear his head, but apparently that was taking too long because Tim lunged over the side of the bed, rifled through his clothes, and came back with a couple of condoms and lube packs clutched in his fist. He shoved them into Nathan's hands before pulling him back in for another deep, full-body kiss.

When Tim relaxed back into the pillows, looking expectantly up at him, Nathan froze. It wasn't nerves. He was just feeling a little slow. Luckily, Tim didn't let him flounder long. He grabbed the packets back and tore them open, rolled the condom down Nathan's cock and slicked it up, before adding a few gratuitous pumps that definitely ended Nathan's paralysis.

"Uh, is there anything I need to—" he asked as Tim wrapped his long legs, corded with muscle and dusted with soft blond hairs, around Nathan's hips.

"I'm good. I'm ready. Please," Tim panted.

This was it: Nathan's first time going all the way with a man... or at least the first time he remembered. Despite Tim's assurances, Nathan breached him slowly at first, afraid of hurting Tim with his inexperience. But once he was assured of his welcome, Nathan slid all the way home with a groan of pure, unadulterated bliss. Tim arched and clenched around him, both the sight and the feel of him making Nathan have to fight hard not to come the second he bottomed out. He had to breathe through the first wave that threatened to crash over him, and only when he thought he had control again did he begin to thrust, slowly at first, but picking up speed with Tim's encouragement.

Tim's hands were everywhere on him, urging Nathan to go faster, harder. In the end, Tim was bent nearly in half, his knees up by his chest, pumping his cock wildly, and Nathan lost any pretense at rhythm or control over his body. He shouted out his pleasure as he filled the condom and jerked through a few aftershocks while Tim pumped himself to completion, shooting over his chest, a few streams going far enough to hit his chin.

Tim started chuckling after they both sprawled out in a sweaty tangle, and Nathan couldn't help but join in as he used a piece of discarded clothing to help Tim wipe the come from his chin.

Nathan was giddy. He was euphoric and couldn't for the life of him remember why he didn't do this kind of thing more often.

Of course, there was that little thing about being socially awkward and having a company to run, but he didn't want to think about that now.

With what little energy he had left, Nathan stumbled to the bathroom on shaky legs. He got rid of the condom, wiped himself off with a towel, and grabbed another one for Tim on his way back to bed.

Even though the high was beginning to wear off and the stress of the last few days was beginning to catch up to him, Nathan still couldn't help but take a few minutes to marvel at the strangeness in himself. While Tim snuggled up against him and rested his head on the pillow next to Nathan's, eyes closed and smiling contentedly, Nathan watched Tim's face in awe and thought about all he'd done in the space of only a few hours.

He wasn't behaving anything like the person he thought he was. All of his weirdness, his boundaries and intimacy issues, his anxieties and need for careful thought and planning, all of it was resting quietly in the back of his mind, not making a peep. He couldn't believe how comfortable he was sharing his space with a virtual stranger. He'd been drugged, blackmailed, and had his first—or second—intercourse with a man, all in the space of twenty-four hours. Instead of worrying about any of that, he was actually happy and mushy and light as a feather, as if some great weight had been lifted that he hadn't even been aware of.

How did that happen?

# Chapter
## Six

TIM WAS still wrapped in Nate's arms when he woke the following morning. Last night, he'd kind of hoped they'd both be up for at least one more round, but the weekend must have caught up to Tim because he didn't remember waking even once after falling asleep. Knowing he'd spent the whole night in Nathan's arms was better than another round anyway. And even though his bladder was screaming and his mind was telling him last night hadn't really changed anything, Tim couldn't bring himself to let it end just yet, so he stayed right where he was, reveling in the feel of Nate's skin against his, their combined scent, and Nate's gentle breaths on his neck. As completely crazy as it might sound to anyone else, Tim knew he'd be perfectly happy spending the rest of his life right where he was.

Eventually though, reality reared its ugly head, and his bladder wouldn't be denied anymore. Tim reluctantly slid out of bed, careful not wake Nate. He took care of business and washed up a little before tiptoeing back. Unfortunately, Nate woke up when Tim slid beneath the sheets, and Tim could feel the sweetness of the moment slipping away as the first rays of the sun pierced the gaps in the blackout curtains.

"Hey," Tim whispered, valiantly trying to save what was left of their intimacy before it was lost forever.

The sleepy frown on Nate's face eased a bit, and he half smiled back. "Hey."

"Thanks for letting me stay last night."

Nate's smile widened a bit more. "It was my pleasure. Believe me."

The tightness in Tim's stomach eased a little under that smile.

He could do this. Maybe there was hope for them after all.

Nate might not remember their first night together or the conversations they'd had, but that guy was inside Nate somewhere. He had to be. That incredible, sweet, strong, honest, and real person didn't come from nowhere. Tim needed to believe that, because he'd connected with that man somewhere deep. And if he was wrong and that man didn't exist....

He didn't want to finish that thought.

"I'm glad, because I'm *really* happy to be here with you like this." Tim tried to rein in his feelings, but some of it must have gushed over into his expression or his voice because Nate's teasing smile twisted into an apologetic grimace in the space of a heartbeat, and Tim's stomach twisted right along with it.

"Tim, I'm sorry. Maybe this wasn't the best idea. Not that I didn't really enjoy being with you, I did, but... I'm a bit of a mess right now. This whole situation has thrown me, and I probably shouldn't have...." Nate continued to babble, and Tim's little bubble of happiness burst.

*Shit. I scared him off. I couldn't even make it five minutes.*

"No, hey, don't worry about it." Tim scrambled for anything to say that would help. "I know you have a lot on your mind right now. I'm not pushing. I swear. I just...." Tim drew in a deep breath and let it out slowly before lifting his gaze back to Nate's. "Nate, I—"

*I what? I'm in love with you?*

Oh yeah, that would go over well. Nate would be running for the door and a restraining order before Tim even finished the sentence. And besides, Tim didn't even know if he *was* in love. He'd never been in love before, and it was too soon to know something like that anyway. Wasn't it? No matter what his mom always told him about his grandparents, people didn't fall in love over a weekend. It just didn't happen that way, not in real life. And it sure as hell wouldn't happen to *him* that way. Nothing was ever as good as he hoped, no matter how hard he wished for it.

But it felt so real.

Nate was silent as Tim struggled for the right words, but the pained expression hadn't left his face. Tim took another breath, laid a hand on Nate's bare chest, and started again. "Look. I'm not asking for anything. Honestly. I know you have some heavy stuff going down right now. I just really enjoyed spending time with you, and I know I'll regret it if I don't at least let you know that... for what it's worth."

Nate's eyes were filled with regret, but at least he didn't pull away when Tim scooted closer to him on the bed and cupped his cheek. Tim fought a shiver when Nate placed his hand on top of it. "I wish I could remember Friday night," Nate said sadly. "For a lot of reasons, obviously, but right now mostly because I feel like I'm walking in on the middle of a story. I don't want to hurt you, Tim. But I don't have much to offer you either, not right now. I'm sorry."

Tim shrugged it off even though his heart was breaking a little. "I know."

He kissed Nate then, long and slow, fighting back tears and the wishes and hopes for things he knew he couldn't have. When they finally pulled apart again, Nate pressed his forehead to Tim's, closed his eyes, and sighed. "Maybe if you told me what happened between us, I might understand a little better, even if it doesn't jog anything loose in my memory," Nate said.

Tim snuggled closer and tucked his head against Nate's neck, his heart aching for more than just himself. Nate sounded so lost, and Tim had to remind himself he wasn't the only one who'd been on an emotional rollercoaster that weekend. Tim had seen Nate's vulnerable side enough. He should show some sympathy for what he must be going through.

In an effort to lighten the mood, Tim dredged up a laugh from somewhere. It sounded weak, and it hurt a little, but he managed to get it out and to sound a bit less maudlin when he asked, "You want a blow by blow? Cuz right now, I can tell you we reenacted a lot of it last night, and I'd much rather show you than tell you about that part."

His effort paid off. Nate chuckled and gave Tim a little shake. "You know what I mean."

Tim slid lower, pressing his cheek to Nate's chest, seeking physical comfort if nothing else. Nate took the hint and settled on his back so Tim could stretch out next to him, half draped over his side. "Well, like I told you, we danced for a while at the club. By the time we got to the hotel, we were pretty worked up, so we went at it hot and heavy." Tim closed his eyes and rubbed his cheek against Nathan's chest while he absently traced patterns on Nate's belly with his fingertips, remembering. He planted a gentle kiss on Nate's collarbone before continuing. "After the first round, I was a little sleepy, but you were still awake and chatty. The more you talked, the more I wanted to listen, and pretty soon I wasn't tired anymore."

"Oh God. What did I say?" Nate groaned.

Tim's smile wasn't forced this time. "Nothing... and everything. You talked about your business, your family, your hometown, high school, college, pets. You were kinda all over the place. But it wasn't really what you talked about so much as how you said it that got me. You were just so *real* with me. No BS. No hiding. It felt like everything you said was from your heart, raw and honest. I've never been with anyone who was like that before, not someone I dated anyway. It was... really nice," he finished lamely, afraid of scaring Nate any more than he already had with the intensity of his feelings.

"Sounds like I may have shared a bit too much. The letters TMI exist for a reason." Nathan laughed uncomfortably as he said it, and Tim could feel the walls building up between them.

That's what people did. They hid behind jokes and words that didn't mean anything. They talked about movies and the weather, music and traffic, without ever talking about what was most important to them, because that made them too vulnerable. Tim was tempted to do the same, like he had before, rattle off some joke to make Nate feel more comfortable. But suddenly it all seemed so pointless, and he didn't want to belittle what they'd shared. They'd had something meaningful that night, a connection Tim wasn't ready to dismiss. Maybe he would scare Nate off, but at this point Nate was probably going to walk away soon anyway, so Tim didn't have much to lose.

He sat up and forced Nate to hold his gaze. "It wasn't TMI. It was incredible. I know you don't remember, and you might not have been completely yourself because of the drugs, but you let me see a part of you that I think few people ever get to. That was special to me, and I'll remember it always. That kind of connection doesn't happen every day, at least not to me." He wasn't saying it right. He didn't have the words to make Nate understand what those few short hours meant to him. How rare and precious they were when most of the rest of his life was shit. "It... it meant a lot," he finished lamely, suddenly embarrassed over his outburst and frustrated with his stupidity and the whole situation in general.

He made to get up, but Nate stopped him, gripped his wrists, and pulled him back down. "I'm sorry, Tim. I wish I remembered," Nate said quietly before planting a kiss on the top of his head.

Tim relaxed into his embrace and closed his eyes again, savoring these last few moments before he knew he had to leave. "Me too."

There was more Tim wanted to tell, about how they'd made love after that, gentle and sweet, how they'd just kissed and touched for what felt like hours before Nate fucked him slow and deep… about how just kissing Nate had felt more intimate than any other sex Tim had ever had, and how, afterward, Nate had listened to *him* babble for hours about his own problems and fears without judgment, with understanding and compassion. Tim wanted to, but he'd never get through all that without crying and making a bigger ass out of himself than he already had. He'd said the important parts, however badly, and they had so little time before Tim had to leave for work, he didn't want to waste it on words he knew wouldn't change anything. Instead he rose up, straddled Nate's lap, and kissed the man with every feeling raging inside him.

Their lovemaking this time was bittersweet. Tim rode him, burying his face in Nate's neck as he cried out his release. Afterward, he managed to coax a surprisingly shy Nate into the shower with him, prolonging their good-bye. But all too soon, it was time to leave. Tim's boss might give his shift away if he was late, and he needed the money too bad to risk it.

When it was time to say good-bye, things got a little awkward at the door. Tim wanted to believe Nate didn't want him to go as much as Tim didn't want to leave, but that was probably only wishful thinking. Nate probably couldn't wait to get him out the door. But before he left, Tim used the hotel notepad by the phone to scrawl his number and handed it to Nate, just in case.

"I know things are crazy. I know you have a lot on your mind. But if you have any free time after this mess is cleared up and your work is done, give me a call. I'm off Monday, so… we could have dinner or something. You know, before you go home… if you want." Tim shut his mouth before he babbled his way out of even the remote possibility of Nate wanting to spend more time with him.

Nate smiled weakly and took the paper. "Thanks."

They stared stupidly at each other for far too long before Tim dredged up the energy to walk out of the room. The door closed with finality behind him, and Tim was so busy swallowing tears and regrets that he was almost to the elevator before he realized he didn't have his car keys. He groaned aloud to the empty hall, punched the wall, and swung around, forcing his feet to carry him back to Nate's door.

"Hey, sorry, but do you know how I get my car back?" He felt like a complete asshole for having to ask, but it wasn't as if he ever had his car valet parked before.

"Oh yeah, I'll call the front desk. They'll bring it around."

As if his humiliation weren't complete enough, desperation made Tim swallow his pride and ask, "Is it really expensive? I don't, uh, have a lot of cash on me right now."

Nate's deep blue eyes didn't show any derision or pity like Tim feared, only kindness. "Don't worry about it. I'm the one who dragged you here, remember? I'll tell them to charge it to my room. Okay?"

"Okay. Thanks."

Tim quickly turned and headed back for the elevator before his face could get any redder. It was stupid to be embarrassed. Nate had already seen his piece of crap car. How could the man *not* know Tim was broke? But having to admit just how broke he was still stung a little.

Tim did manage to find a couple of bucks in his wallet to tip the guy when he brought the car around, but the valet waved him off, saying, "It's covered, man. Have a nice day."

Great. He looked so poor even the hotel staff knew he needed the money more than they did. As he drove away, Tim chose to concentrate on the sting of that rather than the pain of what he was leaving behind in the hotel, probably forever. The blow to his pride hurt less.

Oh well, maybe he should look on the bright side. Not only did he have a crappy retail job to go to for the next several hours, but after that, he got to go to Matt's place and start packing up his shit in preparation for being homeless again.

Good times. Good times.

# Chapter Seven

AFTER TIM left, the room felt strangely empty. Nathan had spent most of the last decade or so on his own, and it never really bothered him before. He was pretty sure the feeling would pass, in time. He just wasn't sure he wanted it to. But before he could ponder that too much, his phone buzzed from inside his pants where he'd left them crumpled on the floor.

*Still alive, safe, and drug free?*

It was Sean, checking up on him again. He started to push the call button but changed his mind. He really didn't want to talk to anyone right now, not even Sean. He was feeling cranky and out of sorts. His carefully ordered life and routine were in shambles, and he didn't really know what to focus on, what should take priority. He was being pulled in too many different directions.

He texted Sean back so the man wouldn't worry and decide to make good on any of his threats.

*You betcha. Will call with an update later.*

Then he plugged his cell in to charge and called for room service from the hotel phone. He needed coffee in the worst way. And when in doubt, go back to basics. He'd read that in one of his self-help books somewhere. Or maybe it was embroidered on a pillow at his grandma's house. He couldn't quite remember. But it made sense either way. He should concentrate on the basics first before tackling anything else, or he'd be running around in circles all day.

*Focus, Nathan.*

He was clean, thanks to a wonderfully long and thorough shower with Tim. But he wasn't going to think about Tim right now. Food and coffee were on their way. So the next basic item on his list would have to be getting dressed so he wasn't still in his robe when room service arrived. He liked to be fully dressed when dealing with strangers.

Nathan pulled a clean pair of slacks from his garment bag, along with a light blue crisply pressed fine cotton shirt. He was combing his hair in the bathroom when the knock at the door signaled his order had arrived. He let the waiter in, and he was just signing the slip when his room phone started ringing.

"Thanks," he said, closing the door behind the guy before hurrying to answer the phone. "Hello?"

"Mr. Seward? This is Candace from the hotel restaurant. I was given a message that you wanted to speak to me?"

And that was all it took for Nathan to go back into problem-solving mode. The crazy morass of emotions and vague, unformed realizations were pushed to the background, and he was able to concentrate again on the situation at hand.

"Yes, ma'am. I have yet to hear from your server, Ian."

She paused for a moment, possibly taken aback by the sharpness of his tone, but Nathan was done playing nice. "I am sorry, sir. He's not on the schedule to work this weekend, and since he left early on Friday, he may be ill. I could try to leave another message for him, if you like."

No matter how hard she tried to mask it, Nathan could tell she really didn't want to do that. But Nathan wasn't going to let it go until he'd talked to Ian. So despite a tiny twinge of guilt for forcing her, Nathan said, "Yes. I appreciate all you've done to help me, but I would like you to leave him another message. Don't worry. This will be the last one. I promise. I want you to tell him that if he doesn't call me today, I will be going to the police, and they will be coming to talk to him instead. If he wants to avoid that, it's in his best interests to call my cell as soon as possible."

"I'm sorry, Mr. Seward. Did you say the police?"

That got her attention. "Yes, I did. It has nothing to do with the hotel. I won't be making any complaints. I just want Ian to know I'm serious when I say I want to speak to him. He'll know what it's about."

There was a long pause on the other end as Nathan assumed she digested the information. Then she cleared her throat and said cautiously, "Uh, certainly, sir. I'll give him the message as you said it. But if there's any other way we might be of help to you, we would prefer to handle it in-house rather than involving the police. If he's done something wrong, I'd very much like to know."

"Thank you, Candace, but I'd rather speak to Ian myself. That is all I need right now." He rattled off his cell number to make sure she had it.

"Yes, sir. I'll call him right after I get off the phone with you. And please let me know if there's anything else I can do."

"I will. Good-bye."

"Good-bye."

Nate didn't have to wait long before his cell started ringing with an unfamiliar number on the display.

"Hello?"

"Is this Mr. Seward?" a strained male voice asked.

"Yes. Is this Ian?"

"Yeah."

"I will assume you got my most recent message so we don't have to mess around with any bullshit before we get down to business." Nathan was using the voice he normally reserved for salesmen and lawyers. It had the desired effect, because when he paused, he heard nothing on the other end of the line but nervous breathing. "Good. Now, I know what happened to me. I know you were involved in what essentially amounts to an assault on me, not to mention the blackmail. What I don't know is who else is involved and the details of what happened. I suggest you fill me in, because your name is the only one I have to give the police at this point, and if you make me, I will."

Ian whined on the other end of the line. "Shit, man. I didn't have anything to do with any assault. The guy just offered me a couple hundred to hit on you. That's all. I swear!"

"Don't push me, Ian. I know that's not all. Otherwise I wouldn't have ended up with you at a gay bar. You were seen there with me, so quit trying to bullshit me. My patience will only last so long."

"Dammit. I knew I shouldn't have taken it. I knew it!" Ian panted and cussed a little more before he continued, "Look. The guy only said to flirt with you a bit. When you didn't show any interest, he just said to keep trying. He was sitting at the bar where I got your drink. I didn't know he'd slipped you anything until you started acting weird. I swear I didn't know! He handed me another couple of bills and said you'd be getting sleepy soon, and all I needed to do was help get you upstairs to your room and take some pics with you while you were out. I wasn't going to do anything to you, not really. Just a couple of pics with us in our underwear, that's all the guy said. And by that time I'd already taken the money."

"How did I end up at South Beach?"

Ian groaned. "You were supposed to pass out, but you didn't. You got all hyper and started saying you wanted to go out on the town, paint the town red, and all that shit. It was crazy."

"It's called a paradoxical reaction," Nathan supplied dryly.

"What?"

"Never mind. Go on."

"Anyway, the guy started freaking out, but he promised to slip me another couple of bills if I cut out of work early and took you somewhere 'scandalous'—his word. I got you to South Beach in a cab, but it was hard to keep up with you once we got inside. By the time the guy got in to take the pics, I'd lost you altogether, and I finally just said fuck it and headed home. I didn't want any more to do with it. It was messed up from the start. I swear that's it. Don't call the cops on me, man. Please. That's all I know."

"Who's the guy? The one who paid you, who is he?"

"I don't know. I never saw him before."

"You aren't being particularly helpful, Ian. Maybe I should call the cops anyway, see if they can get anything else out of you."

"No. Wait. I don't know his name, but he gave me a number to call before I got into the cab so I could tell him where we were. It's on my phone. Hold on."

After a few seconds, Ian read out the number, and Nathan wrote it down.

"Okay, Ian. I'm going to check this out. If it turns out to be a bad number, I will go to the cops this time. You understand?"

"Yeah, I got it."

"Good." Nathan hung up without another word and dialed the number he was given.

The line rang a few times before going to voice mail. "This is Peter. You know what to do."

That wasn't exactly informative, but Nathan decided to do the best with what he had and hope Ian hadn't duped him. "Well, Peter, this is Nathan Seward. I believe we may have become acquainted on Friday night, although some of the details are a bit hazy for me. Suffice it to say, I know who you are and I know what you did." A little bluffing couldn't hurt. "I just wanted to let you know I received your e-mail, and I have a counteroffer for you. You permanently delete those ridiculous pictures and never contact me again, and I, in turn, won't go to the police with all that I know and have you brought up on blackmail and assault charges. How does that sound? I think we understand each other."

Nathan hung up and collapsed into the chair nearest him. He'd done it. He'd tracked the bastards far enough to deliver his own threat. Unless Ian had given him a bad number, and in that case he'd have some apologizing to do to whomever Peter was. But now all he could do was move ahead with his plans and his presentation and hope for the best. There was nothing more for him to do. Everything about this crazy weekend could be filed away, and he could put some much-needed order back into his life.

Except there was something about this weekend he didn't want to forget, something niggling at the back of his mind, trying to get his attention, a thought, like a wave waiting to crash down and quite possibly change everything for good, if he would only let it.

His phone beeping to tell him he had another text from Sean kept him from pondering this too closely.

*Call soon or I'm going to think you're up to something you shouldn't be.*

That made him smile. Sean knew him too well. He might as well get the call out of the way.

"Hey, man."

"Hey, man? You know when I said keep me posted often, I meant more than just a text every twelve hours or so," Sean complained.

"Sorry. I got a little sidetracked."

"Care to elaborate?"

"I don't even know where to start."

"Well, pick something before I freak out and start looking for plane tickets," Sean grumbled irritably.

Nathan huffed out a laugh. "I'm fine, Sean. I'm just... I don't know, a little off-balance right now. I have a lot on my mind."

"Well, *yeah*. That's why I'd be buying the plane ticket, dumbass. Obviously you should've never been left on your own."

"I'm on my own for this stuff all the time."

"That was before. Now you're old and getting senile. You need someone to take care of you."

Nate snorted. He couldn't help it. "If I'm old, what does that make you?"

"Ancient and wise."

"You're hilarious."

"And you still haven't told me anything."

"Okay," he sighed. "I tracked down some leads—"

"Listen to you. You sound like Perry Mason or something. Can you hear yourself?"

"Do you want me to tell you or not?"

"Spill, dammit! What the hell is going on?"

"Well, since you ask so nicely... I tracked down some leads, and I found the guy who took me to the bar, and he gave me a phone number for the guy who paid him to do it."

"Jesus, Nate. I thought you promised not to do anything stupid."

"This wasn't stupid. It's not like I'm going down back alleys or anything. I made a few phone calls. That's all. I'm still safe in my room. I just left a message threatening to call the police on them if those pictures appeared anywhere. That's all."

"So you threatened someone who was willing to drug and blackmail you with going to the police." His voice sounded even more strained now. "And you don't think that was in any way dangerous. Is that what you're saying?"

"Well, when you say it like that…. But what do you think they're going to do, come here and try to 'silence me permanently'? You've been watching too much crime TV. There's a difference between slipping someone a Mickey and actual physical assault. The waiter they paid, Ian, he said the whole thing wasn't really their original plan to begin with. It was more a quick decision that turned bad. Honestly, he made them sound like Laurel and Hardy or something. Do I really need to be afraid of that?"

"They had to have planned to drug you, though. People don't just carry roofies around for the hell of it, Nate… well, maybe serial rapists. But not your average upstanding citizen."

Nathan put a hand to his forehead and massaged his temples. Sean was starting to scare him, which he guessed was the point. But he couldn't change what he'd already done. "Look. It's done. Let me just get through the presentation tomorrow, and then we can talk about how stupid I was, okay?"

Sean grumbled, and Nathan thought he heard the words idiot and moron in there somewhere, but all he said into the phone was "Fine. But you better not leave your room tonight, and if FGE picks us, I'm on the next flight down there to keep you out of trouble until the details are ironed out and the contract is sent off to the lawyers. Got it?"

"Fine. Whatever."

They were quiet for a bit. Nathan figured neither one of them really wanted to hang up, but they were both too stubborn to be the first to break. In the end, Sean was the first to cave.

"So what else is going on, oh fearless leader? You sound weirder than normal." Sean paused there, waiting, but when Nathan couldn't even begin to figure out how to answer, Sean quipped, "Been to any more gay bars lately?"

"As a matter of fact…."

"No shit? We have *got* to have a sit-down when you get back. I feel like I barely know you. Why was I the last to know?" His last question ended on a dramatic, Lifetime channel-esque sob, and Nate couldn't help but laugh.

"You aren't the last to know, asshole. You're the first, if you don't count me, Tim, and the psycho who drugged and blackmailed me."

"Tim? Do tell."

"You're pretty pervy for a straight guy. You know that, don't you?"

"Well, up until this weekend, I assumed you were a straight guy too, so forgive me if I'm a bit curious."

"Tim's.... He's...." How could he explain the colossal tangle of emotions that one name evoked?

"Uh-oh. Sounds serious."

Nathan rolled his eyes. "How can it possibly sound serious if I haven't even said anything yet?"

"Because you always have something to say," Sean quipped back. "Something you've worked out in that complicated little head of yours or read in some idiot's guide to small talk or something. The last few times I've asked about your dates, you've been all 'She's very nice' or 'We had a good time.'" Nathan could almost see Sean's finger quotes as he spoke, but the guy had a point. Usually Nathan could come up with *something* to say, even if it was meaningless and out of a book. Nathan shook his head even though Sean couldn't see it.

"I don't know what to say yet, I guess. I like him. A lot."

"You're sure he's not involved in the blackmail stuff?" Sean asked.

"Yeah, I'm sure."

"Then go for it, dude. Live a little. You have nothing major going on beyond that goddamned presentation you've been obsessing about. Tomorrow, after the meeting, take some time off for once and see what happens."

"I don't know."

"Why the hell not?"

"Things are crazy, Sean. Do I really need any more complications in my life right now?"

"Other than the weirdness there—which could be solved quite easily with a call to the police, I might add—and your obsession with getting your foot in the door with FGE, what else is so friggin' crazy, Nate? You live the most ordered life of anyone I know." As if to accentuate that point, Nate could hear Sean's kids screaming in the background and Sean's wife, Isobel, calling for him in an angry and exasperated voice.

"Shit, hold on," Sean said before he yelled, "What?"

"Come help me with your children before I kill and eat them!" she yelled back.

While Nathan sniggered, Sean grumbled under his breath, "Yeah, yeah, yeah. They're always *my* kids when they've done something wrong and *hers* when they're being cute. How is that fair?" He sighed dramatically on the other end as the boys screeched some more in the background. "Obviously I have to go, man. But this conversation isn't over."

"Byeeeee," Nathan replied in a singsong voice, and Sean ended the call with only a disgusted huff.

He was grinning as he set the phone down, but the smile didn't last long in the emptiness and silence of his hotel room. He pulled up the slides for his presentation and tried to do a dry run, but his head just wasn't in the game. He was antsy and distracted, anxious for no reason. Sure, Sean's worries had rubbed off on him a little, but he didn't actually think he was in any kind of danger. From the way Ian talked, it honestly sounded like he'd been drugged by a moron, so what was his problem?

He tried to review his notes again, but even after two cups of coffee and a breakfast burrito, he still couldn't concentrate on his work—the whole reason he was in Houston in the first place. Frustrated with himself and about to climb the walls, Nathan decided to go for a walk to clear his head.

He walked through the plaza and past CityCentre until he moved into a residential area, ending up in a small park filled with families enjoying their Sunday afternoon together. Some were dressed quite nicely, probably just come from church, while others were more casual, bundled up in jackets and scarves. All of them seemed happy just to be there, out in the sun and the fresh air, even if it was a little chilly. A few of the parents had even put their phones down long enough to play on the slides and swing sets with their kids, and Nathan basked in the very normalness of it, even though he wasn't really a part of it. He remembered Sunday afternoons with his own family, growing up. It seemed so very long ago, though the memories were happy ones. How long had it been since he'd taken a day to sit outside and relax?

He was content to people-watch for a long time, purposefully trying not to think of much of anything so the tightness in his chest would ease and he could feel as relaxed as everyone else seemed to be. But though he didn't consciously acknowledge it, his hand frequently played with the small slip of paper he'd tucked in his pocket, the one Tim had written his number on.

Finally, when he was shivering because the jacket he'd packed for the trip really wasn't enough protection against the cold, Nathan forced himself to reengage his higher brain function and put some labels on what was bothering him. If he crystallized his feelings into a word or a phrase, maybe they'd be easier to sort through.

He'd read that somewhere too.

First, there was disappointment. For some reason, he didn't feel as triumphant with the success of his little investigation as he'd thought he would. Sean's worries aside, he should have been ecstatic at what he'd been able to accomplish on his own and at the fact that he still had a chance at the contract with FGE. After all, wasn't that what he'd been working toward for months: his shot at the big time, expansion of his company, more employees, a bigger name? He'd been thrown a curve ball with the whole blackmail thing, and he'd taken care of it quickly and quietly without an actual full-blown anxiety attack. He should be damned proud of himself.

But he wasn't. Which led to his second thought point: apathy. When it came to his proposal on Monday and his "big chance," Nathan was surprised at how little he cared at the present moment, and that was ridiculous. Here he was, on the cusp of something he'd been planning and working toward practically his whole life, and he couldn't seem to dredge up any emotion for it at all. All he could think about was a certain sweet, emotionally uninhibited blond with a gorgeous body and an even more gorgeous smile.

His third thought point had to be called "Tim," because he just couldn't crystallize all that he was feeling on the subject down to only one emotion. He was excited and nervous, guilty and off-balance. There was something poised on the edge of his consciousness, something important that his brain wanted him to realize, itching at him. Tim, Sean, the happy families playing in the park, they all wanted him to know something. He had this wild feeling that they were all connected somehow, but he just couldn't put the pieces together.

He had a headache, and his ass was numb by the time an alarm on his phone jerked him back to reality. He reached into his pocket, past

Tim's note, and pulled it out. The alarm was only a calendar reminder about his meeting the next day, as if he actually needed it. But maybe he did need it… as a reminder of who he was. He'd set the alarm because that's the kind of man he was and the kind of life he lived. He was organized, driven, and responsible. No matter where his dreams took him, he was always back to reality at the end of them, and he always finished what he started. He couldn't let them down just because he'd had an intense night with someone who lived thousands of miles away from his home, someone he barely knew.

The alarm was there to remind him he had work to do. He had people depending on him. This whole trip to Houston and the bid weren't just about him. Sean and the rest of their employees and investors were counting on him. He didn't have time to screw around right now. Maybe after he'd either won or lost the contract he could make room for something else in his life, but not now. Tim made Nathan want things he hadn't paid much attention to in years, but the timing just wasn't right. He had a life already, far away, and it was time to get back to it.

Filled with a renewed sense of purpose, Nathan stood up to put some blood back into his ass and headed back for the hotel. He had work to do.

# Chapter Eight

TIM CLOSED out his drawer and carried it to the store office on autopilot, much like he'd done his job most of the night. He felt like a complete loser—even more so than usual—but he couldn't stop thinking about Nate. What was Nate doing right now? Would he ever really call? Did Nate think he was as much of a raving lunatic as he felt?

As his angst-ridden evening progressed, Tim had no choice but to blame it all on his mom. She was the one who'd made him like this. "You'll know when you've met the right person, Timmy. You'll just know," she'd said many times when he was growing up and more often during those last few agonizing months of her life. She'd been confined to her bed, too weak to stand or do much of anything after the cancer had progressed far enough that she'd decided there was no point in chemo or radiation anymore. And during the long hours Tim had kept her company by that bed, she'd taken every lucid moment to express all of her worries and hopes for his life.

Of course, now all he could remember were those words. She was the one who'd put all those stupid romantic ideas in his head. But she'd never said what he should do if he knew he'd found "the one" but "the one" didn't know it in return. He wanted to be mad at her for that, but he couldn't. He'd loved her too much. He missed her too much. And now he was left pining for something he never should have believed in in the first place.

After everyone filed out and the manager locked the back door, Tim pulled his jacket tight under his chin, waved good night to his fellow retail slaves, and hurried to his car. It grumbled and wheezed a few times, but before panic could set in, the engine turned over and he was on his way back to Matt's apartment.

Drew should be long gone by now, on his way back to pack up his things for the big move, so Tim had tonight and the rest of the week to worry about his real-life problems that had nothing to do with romantic fantasy lands or broken hearts… like where he was going to live as of next weekend.

There was one option that he'd been avoiding, but Tim wasn't quite ready to give up hope on something better coming along yet. Instead, he pushed away the fear that his one option was going to turn out to be his *only* option, cranked up the radio, and prayed to whoever might listen that Matt and Drew would have had a fight this weekend and the whole living-together thing would be called off, at least long enough for Tim to save his pennies for first and last month's rent on a place of his own… well, his and whomever he got for a roommate.

Unfortunately, his prayers weren't answered. Drew was already gone when he got to the apartment, as Tim had expected, but Matt still looked apologetic and guilty when he let Tim in. Tim had a key, but he'd learned to knock and wait to be let in, even when he thought Drew wasn't there, after the hissy Drew threw the one time Tim had walked in on them.

"Hey, man," Matt said as he stepped out of the way to let Tim in. "I'm really sorry about Saturday, springing it on you like that. I know things are pretty tight. And I know I offered to help you out with some cash until you're settled, but I really don't have much to spare these days either, and Drew wants us to save up for a bigger place."

Tim shrugged and dropped his bag on the couch. "It's no biggy, man. I understand you guys wanting to live together. I know you love him… even if he hates my guts."

"He doesn't hate your guts."

"Yeah, he just thinks I'm a user and a leech."

"Tim."

Tim sighed and rubbed his forehead. "Sorry. You've been really great, letting me stay as long as you have. I tried to get out of your hair before this, but… well, you know what happened. I can't seem to catch a break these days."

Matt's face scrunched up even more with guilt, and now Tim felt guilty too. "Hey, man, I didn't mean you," Tim rushed to say. "I'll figure it out. You deserve to live with someone who makes you happy, really. I'm just jealous." He forced a chuckle and bumped shoulders with Matt as he passed by him on the way to the closet where he kept his blankets and sheets for the couch.

"Speaking of which, how was your clubbing as a free agent this weekend? Any hot guys you care to share the sordid details about?"

Tim paused in what he was doing and sighed. "There was one, yeah."

"Aaaaand?"

"And, it was really nice."

This was their usual Sunday night conversation. Since Matt no longer played the field, he lived vicariously through Tim's exploits, and Tim usually embellished the tales so they sounded hot and sordid, even if the reality was a bit more lackluster. But this time, even though the reality was a hell of a lot better than any of his stories, Tim couldn't bring himself to share.

"Nice? This is all you give me? Nice? Come on, man. You gotta do better than that."

Matt was trying to lighten the mood, and Tim opened his mouth to say something sarcastic, but nothing came out. He tried, but he just couldn't do it.

"Hey. Are you okay? Did something else happen this weekend? You didn't go see your dad, did you?" Matt asked, coming up to him and putting a hand on his shoulder.

"No. I didn't go see him."

*Yet.*

"Then what is it?"

Tim stepped away and started making up the couch instead of answering. He was getting a little choked up, and he felt ridiculous for it. But when Matt continued to hover over him, anxious and concerned, Tim thought he needed to come up with something. "Nothing major happened, Matt. Don't worry. I just met a guy I really liked, but it's not going to work out. That's all."

Reduced to only a couple of sentences like that, it all sounded so trite, so unexceptional. But Tim supposed that was better than admitting how torn up he was after only two nights with a guy he would probably never see again. He wanted to talk to someone about it, but he didn't want to break down and unload all over Matt, and he knew, once he started talking about Nate, he wouldn't be able to stop. Maybe a few weeks or months down the road he'd be able to have this conversation. He'd have some perspective, and everything wouldn't be so raw and new, but not now.

"Why won't it work out?"

"He's from California. He's only in town for the weekend."

"Long distance can work. Look at me and Drew," Matt said with that dopey smile he got whenever he talked about his boyfriend.

"You guys dated for like six months before he went away to school, and he's only a three-hour drive from here. I just met this guy Friday, and he lives half the country away."

Matt shrugged. "Stranger things have happened."

*Oh God, don't encourage my poor romantic little heart.*

"Yeah, I guess" was all Tim said, hoping the conversation would end before he did break down.

Matt came up behind him and gave him a quick hug. "Oh, sweetie, it's all going to be okay. You'll see. I'll help when I can… and if you can't find a place right away, I'll talk to Drew. He wouldn't want you thrown out into the cold any more than I do. Okay?"

The likelihood of Drew allowing Tim to stay on Matt's couch even one minute after he moved in was slim to none, but Tim kept that thought to himself. "Sure, man. And thanks."

"What're friends for? Oh, and I still want the dirty deets on your mystery guy, but I can be patient. I need to get some sleep anyway. You may have tomorrow off, you slacker, but I have to be up bright and early, and I didn't get much sleep this weekend."

"You don't get much sleep every weekend," Tim teased, trying to dredge up some humor before depression completely dragged him under.

"Funny guy," Matt quipped on his way to his bedroom. "See you in the morning. And don't stress. We'll figure something out."

Matt's door closed, leaving Tim alone in the quiet of the room. He was grateful for Matt's concern, but he knew he wouldn't do anything *but* stress until he figured out what he was going to do. At least being face-to-face with the reality of his situation helped Tim think about something other than Nate for a while. Even his heart had to agree that a basic need like shelter should be higher on his list of priorities than a love affair that was doomed from the start anyway.

Nate was out of his league and probably out of his life too, plain and simple. Tim had two dead-end retail jobs he hated, both of which kept him under thirty hours a week so they didn't have to offer him health insurance. He had nowhere to live. And whatever dreams or ambitions he might've had as a kid were buried with his mom, so not only was he nowhere now, but he wasn't going to get anywhere later either. Why would a guy like Nate waste his time on him?

Needless to say, thoughts like those and about his current situation turned into an all-night pity party, and Tim didn't get much sleep. When Matt's alarm went off around seven thirty, Tim already had a pot of coffee warm and waiting for him as he sat huddled in his blankets and sipping his own cup on the couch. He was exhausted, drained, and edgy, but he knew there was no hope of him getting any sleep in the near future, so he might as well give up and begin caffeinating now. At least he didn't have to work today. That would have totally sucked ass. Tired as he was, he probably would've done something to get himself fired, and wouldn't that have just been the cherry on top of his weekend?

Matt was obviously surprised to see him up so early on his day off but didn't have time to give him more than a couple of concerned looks before he was out the door. Tim was actually kind of grateful for that. It wasn't that he didn't appreciate Matt's concern, but this way he could wallow in his misery a little longer without worrying about saying something he'd regret later because he was in such a crappy mood.

After a fruitless and depressing few hours searching through listings and classifieds for somewhere he could afford, Tim had to step away from Matt's computer and go sit on the couch with his eyes closed for a while. He was fucked, and he knew it. He'd known it the minute Matt opened the door Saturday and told him the news. He had no money in the bank. He was living paycheck to paycheck as it was. The only way he could afford to share a place that wasn't so far from his jobs that gas money and car repairs would eat up what little he saved was for him to stop paying off his student loan debts and let the collection calls begin again. And any renter who was smart enough to do a credit check on him before he signed a lease with them would run screaming in the opposite direction anyway, so the point was pretty moot on whether he could afford a place or not.

If he had more time, Tim might have been able to luck into something not too scary eventually, maybe talk to some people at the club, put some feelers out there with the few friends he had. But a week wasn't much to work with, not when he had to go work every day but today. Matt had said he'd talk to Drew, but Tim didn't want to make him do that. Even though he'd paid what he could toward rent and utilities, he *had* mooched off Matt for too long. Drew would make every night Tim was there with them a misery until he left anyway, and Tim didn't want to put any of them through that if he didn't have to.

So Tim was back to that one last-ditch option he'd been trying to avoid. It didn't have to be permanent, right? He just needed a place to stay for a little while, until something came up he could afford. That was all. No problem.

Only it was a problem, a big one. But it didn't look like life was giving him much of a choice right now.

Dreading every single moment of what was to come, Tim dragged himself off the couch, took a long shower, dressed, and packed up some of his stuff. His car started right up, even though for once Tim kind of wished it wouldn't, giving him an excuse not to do what he knew he had to.

A half an hour later, Tim pulled up in front of the beat-up old yellow-sided ranch-style house that had once held many happy memories from his childhood. The small square lawn out front, once bursting with flowers and perfectly trimmed green grass, was now filled with overgrown weeds and bare spots, making it the worst in the neighborhood. The dirty siding and curled and cracked shingles made a stark contrast against his hazy rose-colored memories, and his stomach knotted as he shut off the ignition and made his way up the broken concrete driveway, past the car his dad hadn't driven more than a few miles in years, and up to the front stoop.

He still visited his dad at least once every couple of weeks, bound by promises he'd made to his mom and a sense of obligation to the man who'd been a good father to him once. But he had to psych himself up every time. The man now living in his grandparents' house was unrecognizable as the same man who'd pushed him on the swing set out back or given him piggy back rides across the hideous gold shag carpet in the living room that hadn't been changed since a decade before Tim was born.

Tim didn't bother to knock before letting himself in. Even if his dad wasn't passed out on the couch, he'd be pissed if Tim made him get up to answer the door, and the last thing Tim wanted was to give the old man an excuse to lose his temper.

"Dad?" Tim called out quietly, just in case he was awake, but there was no answer.

When he stepped into the living room, he found his dad unconscious in the recliner instead of on the couch. Tim supposed that was a step up. It meant his dad had at least gotten up from the couch at some point since the last time Tim had been there. Rather than wake him and risk putting him in a bad mood right off the bat, Tim crept into the kitchen to see about fixing some coffee and wait until his dad woke up on his own.

Tim could tell his Aunt Theresa hadn't been there in a few days, because there were dishes piled in the sink and an empty bottle of Jack on the counter by the refrigerator. There was, however, some food in the refrigerator, and he could still see most of the kitchen counters, so it couldn't have been more than that since she'd been there. Between the two of them, Tim and his aunt managed to keep his old man alive and not living in complete filth and squalor, but only just barely. Between the booze, the pain pills for his back, and the depression, James Conrad didn't do much anymore beyond collecting his disability and social security checks… oh, and drinking them away again. Luckily, the house was in Tim's grandparents' names. Otherwise his dad wouldn't have had a place to live either after the hospital bills for his mom took their house and almost everything else they owned.

Tim got the coffeepot started and then worked on cleaning the kitchen for a while. He wasn't exactly a domestic goddess, but it helped to pass the time, and he tried to make his aunt's job a little easier whenever he could. Beyond his grandparents giving his dad the house to live in, Theresa was the only one in the family who still talked to his dad—except for Tim, of course. Tim didn't blame any of them. His dad didn't make it easy to love him. In his own darkest moments, Tim wasn't even sure he did love the man anymore. He hated feeling that way, and he'd never admit it to anyone, but maybe love for your parents wasn't unconditional after all. Or maybe he was just a horrible, ungrateful son. He could add that to all of his other faults.

Tim was on his second cup of coffee when he heard a groan from the living room. A few moments later, Tim braced himself, mentally and physically, as his dad stumbled through the door.

"Hey, Dad," Tim called out cautiously.

His dad glanced blearily in his direction for a moment before a weak smile spread across his face. "Hey, Timmy. Long time no see."

Tim relaxed a little. It looked like his dad woke up in a good mood today. Maybe moving back in wouldn't be quite as much of a nightmare as he thought. "Not so long as all that, Dad," he said with a smile. "I was here last week."

"You were?" His dad looked genuinely puzzled for few moments before he shook his head and went to pour himself some coffee. "Guess I got my days mixed up."

Tim wasn't going to let a little memory lapse spoil a good visit, so he just shrugged. "Yeah, probably. So what've you been up to?"

"Oh, a little of this and that. I was going to work on the yard a bit, but my back flared up and I had to take it easy for a few days. I watched the game on Sunday. Our boys got robbed, though. That's all I have to say."

While he spoke, Tim's dad pulled a new bottle out of the cabinet and poured a large splash of Jack into his coffee. Tim pretended not to notice. History had proven there was no point in him saying anything, and it would only start an argument if his dad saw any expression on his face that might remotely be perceived as disapproval. Instead, Tim started rummaging through the fridge to see if there was anything he could put in his dad's stomach to slow the effects of the alcohol until he could bring up the subject of him moving in for a little while.

"Want me to make you some breakfast, Dad?"

His dad snorted into his coffee. "What, you cook now? When did that happen?"

Tim turned and searched his dad's face, but though his dad was smiling, Tim could tell the question hadn't been a joke. Smoothing his face so none of his concern showed, he turned back and pulled the eggs and milk out. He'd been cooking for the family, with Aunt Theresa's help, since his mom got sick the first time. His dad knew that.

Shaking it off, Tim grabbed a bowl and cracked the eggs into it. After adding some milk, he mixed them with a fork before pulling out a pan. He could feel his dad's eyes on him as he worked, but he didn't turn around, a little afraid now of what he'd see.

"Theresa was here on Friday, or maybe it was Thursday. She asked about you," his dad said, obviously uncomfortable with the silence.

"How is she?"

"Good. I guess. Still no man in her life, but I suppose that's probably out of the realm of possibility now."

Tim ignored the slight derision in his dad's voice and kept his attention on not burning the eggs. Theresa was the old maid in the family. Tim wasn't sure if she'd ever dated anyone or even wanted to. But even though she definitely didn't deserve his dad's ridicule, especially when she went out of her way to take care of him when she got no gratitude in return, Tim wasn't going to attempt to defend her, not again. Last time had ended badly.

They ate and talked a little more. And Tim turned a blind eye when his dad refilled his mug with equal measures from the coffeepot and the bottle of Jack. After shooting the shit for about an hour, Tim finally worked up the courage to broach the subject of his moving in.

"I need to ask a favor, Dad."

"Yeah? What is it now?"

Tim gritted his teeth. He hadn't asked his dad for anything in years. He'd been taking care of himself, all on his own, and taking care of his dad too for that matter. "I need a place to stay for a little while."

His dad downed what was left in his mug and went for a refill, this time skipping the coffee and going straight for the bottle. When Tim wasn't quick enough to hide his reaction, his dad's eyes narrowed at him. "What are you looking at?"

"Nothing." Tim turned his head resolutely back to stare at his plate.

"I saw that look. Don't you dare think you can judge me, boy."

Tim sighed. *Not again.* "Dad, I didn't—"

"Don't you sigh at me like that either. What? You think you're better than me? Do you?"

"No, Dad. I never said that. Calm down." If Tim had had a little more sleep and had been a little more awake, he probably would have thought of something better to say than that, but he didn't.

"Calm down? Who the hell do you think you're talking to? I'm still your father, goddammit! You will respect me in my own home. You got that!"

"Yeah, Dad, I got it." It wasn't even his home, but Tim sure as hell wasn't going to say that aloud either.

"Are you sassing me? I'll wipe that smart mouth clean off your face. Don't think I can't just because your old man's got a bum back. I can still take a skinny loser like you any day. Who the hell do you think you are, coming in here and acting all high-and-mighty when you don't even have a real job? Twenty-seven years old and still working at a goddamned Big Lots, for chrissakes. When I was your age, I was already at the factory, supporting your mom and me. What would she say if she knew what a loser you'd turned out to be?"

That one stung, more so than anything else the old man might've said, because it hit awfully close to the truth. He didn't want to know what his mom would have thought of him now. But of course, he might have been someone completely different if she were still alive.

Tim would be the first to admit he wasn't perfect, but he was tired and feeling defensive, so the first thing that came out of his mouth wasn't what he should have said. "Well, what do you think she would have said about you, huh? At least I have a job. It might be crap, but at least I pay my own way, and I don't sit on the couch all day and drink myself stupid."

"You little shit! Come here and say that to my face!"

His dad started for him then, his face almost purple with rage, but his balance and coordination were shot from all the booze and the meds, and he tripped over one of the kitchen chairs. Despite being pretty pissed off himself, Tim still leaped forward to help but ended up getting an elbow to the mouth for his trouble.

"Get off me. I can get up on my own. I don't need your goddamned pity!"

Tim tasted blood from his split lip, so when his dad got tangled in his own legs and fell on his ass again, Tim stayed right where he was, counting to ten to keep his temper in check. For a little while they stayed like that, his dad on the floor panting in exertion and Tim leaning against the counter nearby sucking on his bleeding lip. Eventually, the inevitable happened, and his dad covered his face and started sobbing softly.

"I'm sorry. I'm so sorry, Timmy," his dad sobbed out. "You're right. Your old man's useless, pathetic and useless."

Tim's anger faded quickly under a tide of pity and the same aching loss he'd felt for seven years, since his mother's death. He hadn't just lost her that day. He'd lost the man who was his father too. But Tim didn't wallow in it. He pushed the feelings away almost as quickly as they arose. His dad must not have slept off as much of his drunk from the night before as Tim had hoped, because the man had already gone past pissed and on to morose after only a few drinks. It usually took a hell of a lot more than that to get to this stage.

His dad sniffled a bit more and wiped his eyes on his sleeve, and Tim hardened his heart to it by reminding himself the pattern would play itself out over and over again until the old man either got help or killed himself with the booze or the pills, or a combination of both. Tim took a deep breath and let it out before pushing away from the counter and helping his dad to his feet.

As he got the man settled back in his recliner, his dad said, "I need my pills, Timmy. I think I twisted my back coming down in there. Can you get them for me?"

Tim went to the bathroom to get the bottle without a word. As long as the doctors kept giving them to him, there was little Tim could do to get the man to stop taking them. He'd had that fight enough times to know it was pointless to have it again. When he got back, he handed over the pills and went to the kitchen for a glass of water. His dad gave him a look when he saw it was only water in the glass, but he took it without complaint.

After his dad took the pills, he looked up at Tim with puffy, red-rimmed, and bloodshot eyes. When his gaze landed on Tim's lip, he frowned, and his own lips trembled a little. "Did I hurt you?"

Tim shrugged. "It's fine."

"Oh, Timmy, I'm sorry. You know I didn't mean it. You're right to think what you do. I'm a useless, pathetic, dried-up old man. You're right to stay away. I wouldn't want to be here either if I were you."

The words engendered more concern than pity. Tim didn't enjoy visiting his dad. It always ended badly no matter how hard he tried. But he did come faithfully every week or so. The fact that his dad didn't seem to remember that was worrying. The memory loss was getting worse.

"Don't talk like that, Dad. You could get better if you got some help. You could get out and have a life again."

"No. She's gone, Timmy. The best part of me is gone. No one can bring her back. There's no point without her."

Tim sighed and walked back to the kitchen to pick up a little before he left. He shouldn't have bothered to say anything. All it ever did was start his dad on a never-ending litany of all the reasons why he couldn't get better. Tim had already done the screaming, the pleading, and the cajoling. None of it did any good. He couldn't make his dad want to live again. No one could.

By the time Tim got back to the living room, his dad was almost asleep, mumbling and slurring the same old mournful words as always, the drugs and the drink doing their job. At least Tim had been able to get a little food in the man's stomach before he passed out. He'd have to count that as a win.

As he stepped out the door and walked back to his car, he knew he couldn't move back into that house. Even if it meant sleeping in his car for a few months and showering at the Y, he couldn't do it. He wasn't strong enough to deal with his dad every single day and not want to slash his own wrists. He had no idea why he had thought, even for a second, that he could.

He sat in his car for a long time outside the house, with the motor running and the radio blaring, but he couldn't seem to decide what to do next. He wasn't sure how long he would have stayed there like that, but the sound of his phone ringing cut through the noise from the radio and kicked him out of the daze he was in.

His heart leaped a little at the sound as he scrambled to pull his phone out of his pocket, but it wasn't an unknown number on his screen. It was Jana from the club. He couldn't remember the last time she'd actually called him.

"Hey, Jana. What's up?"

"Hey, sweetie. I just wanted to let you know I ran into Josh this morning. We stopped for coffee before he started his shift at the evil day job, and he told me something I thought you should know. That guy, Ian—I remember him now that Josh told me he was the one you're looking for—anyway, Josh said he knows a guy who's seen him waiting tables at the Carrabba's off the Katy. I don't know if that helps any, but I figured I'd let you know, just in case."

"Thanks, Jana. Thanks for calling."

"No problem, sweetie. Hey, that guy you were with, he seemed pretty classy. Did you get lucky?"

"Yes and no. I'll tell you about it next time I see ya, okay? I gotta go right now."

"Sure, babe. Maybe you can stay for early breakfast with the rest of us next weekend."

"Yeah. Sounds great. Thanks."

"Bye."

Since Nate hadn't called, Tim didn't have his number to give him the news. He supposed he could have called the hotel and asked for his room to give him the message. It would be a good excuse to talk to him again. But Tim wasn't feeling quite that pathetic yet. Besides, Nate had already said he had a call in to the guy, so maybe Tim should check it out for himself before he passed on bad information. Maybe Nate would be even more grateful if Tim got the information out of Ian himself.

After dealing with his dad, Tim could use a chance to let off a little steam, and what better way than to track down this Ian asshole and have a little chat with him? Tim would never lay a hand on a sick old man, particularly when that sick old man was his dad. But after what Ian had done to Nate, Tim would have no problem venting his frustration on the little bastard.

Tim wasn't exactly sure where the Carrabba's was on the freeway, but he asked at a gas station once he got close. Knowing he was only a little over a mile away from Nate's hotel didn't help his concentration, but he found the place easily enough. The parking lot was mostly empty that early in the day, and when Tim went inside to ask for Ian, the hostess told him Ian's shift didn't start for another hour. Instead of waiting inside and being tempted to buy food he didn't need and couldn't afford, Tim opted to wait in his car. Sitting quietly while the sun heated the interior, Tim's sleepless night finally caught up to him, and he dozed off until the sounds of at least three car doors slamming nearby and raised voices woke him up.

Despite being in the bright light of day instead of hazy club lighting, Tim recognized Ian right away—short, sort of cute, even if his face was a little too round and young looking for Tim's tastes. But Tim didn't recognize the two bigger men hassling Ian. Tim couldn't make out what was being said from where he was, but the discussion sounded heated, whatever it was about. As Tim stepped out of his car and started toward them, the shorter and uglier of the two men yelled, "Why didn't you just keep your damned mouth shut, you little cocksucker?"

The guy took a menacing step toward Ian, and Ian shrank back, looking around him desperately. Tim almost felt sorry for him... almost. He hovered nearby, not sure he wanted to get in the middle but not wanting Ian to get away either. The first guy wasn't as big as Tim, but the second had Tim beat by a good couple of inches and fifty pounds at least, not someone Tim wanted to mess with, no matter how pissy his mood was.

"What the fuck are you staring at?" the short, ugly one yelled in Tim's general direction.

Apparently he'd been discovered. Shrugging with a nonchalance he didn't feel, Tim said, "I just want to talk to Ian."

"Fuck off, asshole. He's busy."

Okay, so that didn't bode well for future conversation. "I'm in no hurry. I can wait," Tim said calmly, trying to appear as disinterested and harmless as possible.

The shorter one didn't move, but the big guy took a couple of steps toward him. "He said, fuck off."

Now it was time to make a decision. Did he walk away and leave Ian to his fate, possibly missing his only chance to get some answers out of the guy? Or did he stay and quite possibly get his ass kicked?

After that morning, Tim was itching for a fight, but he wasn't stupid. Two, possibly three, against one didn't sound like the kind of release he was looking for. There's letting off a little steam, and then there's ending up in the hospital with no health insurance to pay the bill.

Tim put his hands in the air and backed away. He considered calling the cops, but Nate had said that would ruin everything, so Tim decided to take a little drive and come back later.

He'd just turned around and started to hurry for his car when Ian squeaked out, "Hey, I know you. You're the guy! Man, this is the one I told you about, the one who went off with that Seward guy, the one who ruined everything."

*Oh shit.*

"Hey! We want to talk to you," the short guy yelled as both he and his partner came after Tim.

Tim made a break for his car, but they were on him before he could get the door open. Rather than give them an opportunity to get a hold on him, Tim came out swinging. His fist connected hard with the little guy's jaw, but the big guy got in a solid to Tim's side that doubled him over. Instead of straightening up—which Tim wasn't sure he could do at that moment anyway—he lunged for the big guy's middle, taking advantage of the guy's high center of gravity to knock him off his feet. They went down on the asphalt in a tangle of flailing limbs, but before Tim could right himself, the little guy had him under the arms and was dragging him off.

Tim struggled against the little guy's hold but couldn't break free, and his partner got in a punch to Tim's face before Tim even knew what hit him. The realization that he was pretty much screwed at this point had only just managed to make its way to Tim's scrambled brains when Tim heard shouting and the hold on him disappeared, dropping him back on his ass on the ground. By the time he finally blinked the stars out of his vision, the two men were already to their car. They drove away in a screech of tires as Ian and a somewhat rotund man in a white shirt and striped tie hurried over to him.

"Hey, are you okay? Do I need to call an ambulance?"

Tim blinked at the big man uncomprehendingly for a few seconds as he wheezed in a couple of breaths around the stabbing pain in his side. There was quite a little crowd behind the restaurant now. Tim guessed pretty much everyone from inside had come out to see the show.

"I'm good," Tim managed. The pain was easing now, and his brain didn't feel quite so rattled.

Ian hovered uncertainly nearby. He looked guilty, and he should for throwing Tim under the bus like that. Even if Tim hadn't felt like kicking his ass before, he certainly did now.

"I've called the police," the man in shirt and tie said. "They should be here soon."

*Well shit, exactly what I didn't want.*

Tim could tell Ian wasn't particularly happy about it either. The guy looked torn between keeping his job and making a run for it.

"Thank you, sir." Tim managed to sound polite at least. "I think I'll be okay, but maybe Ian can take me somewhere I can sit down until the cops get here?"

"Oh, certainly. I'm sorry. I'm Adam Trench, the manager. Ian can show you to a booth while you wait."

Adam started off toward the restaurant, dispersing the crowd to their posts while Ian begrudgingly led Tim to a booth in the back corner. When Ian would have left him there, Tim grabbed his wrist. "Why don't you sit down, and we'll have a little chat before the cops get here."

Ian's slightly chubby cheeks were red and his expression sour, but he slid onto the bench on the other side of the booth.

"Look," Tim said tiredly. "I don't know what the hell just happened out there. But if you want me to keep my mouth shut about what I know, you're going to have to do some talking."

Ian rolled his eyes and shook his head. "I knew it was fucking too good to be true. One stupid mistake and I've been in the shit ever since. Now I have guys coming after me and the cops get called anyway."

"I'm willing to hold out on the cops. But you have to tell me what the hell is going on. What happened with Nate? And who were those guys?"

The look Ian gave him was skeptical to say the least. He searched Tim's face for a while before he said, "You won't tell them why those guys were here?"

"Not if you're straight with me."

"Pfft, I'm not *straight* with anybody," Ian said with a toss of his hair. "Why do you care anyway?"

"It doesn't matter why. I just got my ass kicked out there—after you threw me under the bus, I might add—so why don't we quit with the questions and you just tell me who the hell those guys were."

Ian grimaced. "Sorry. I didn't mean to get you in trouble."

"Mmmhmm," Tim grumbled as he ran tentative fingers over the swelling around his left eye. It felt like he was going to have a lovely shiner there by morning, if not sooner.

"Really, I just panicked when I saw you walking away, leaving me with those guys, and I blurted it out."

Ian paused there. His brown eyes had gone kind of puppy dog soft, practically dripping with sincerity and regret, and Tim didn't know whether he should punch him in the face or give him a big hug. He rolled his eyes instead.

"Fine. You didn't mean it. Can we get back to the story, please?"

"Look. I told that Nathan guy what happened already. That guy, the short one, came up to me at the hotel and offered me cash to flirt. That was supposed to be all. But when Seward didn't seem interested, I guess the guy decided to drug him. I didn't have anything to do with that. I didn't know the drink was drugged until later. I swear. But by then I was already kind of mixed up in it, and then the guy offered me more money to get Seward up to his hotel room. That was supposed to be it. Just a couple of pictures. I told him all this already."

"You told Nate this? When?"

"I called him this morning after I got a message from my boss, him threatening to call the police on me. I told him what I knew. That was supposed to be the end of it. But now I got that crazy guy coming to my work and threatening me. Jesus, shit just keeps getting worse and worse. I don't know what I'm going to do."

Ian looked genuinely scared, and after what he'd witnessed in the parking lot, Tim thought he probably should be. "Who are they?"

"I *don't know*. I had a phone number. That's all. I gave the number to Seward, and I guess he must've called them because now they're coming after me. They shouldn't have even been able to find me here, except I got a call from one of the other servers that shares my shift at the hotel, telling me some guys were looking for me and she'd sent them here, thinking they were friends of mine. And now both of my jobs could be fucked. Maybe I should just tell the cops what happened. Maybe I can get off with a warning or something since I really didn't do anything but go along."

"Don't tell the cops. Not yet."

Ian looked at him like he'd lost his mind. "Dude, they're coming to my work now. At this rate they'll know where I live in no time. I don't know what else to do."

"Just keep your head down for a couple of days. Please," Tim said. He scrambled desperately for something to convince Ian to keep his mouth shut so the little shit wouldn't ruin things for Nate. "Look. You could still be in serious trouble for helping these guys if Nate decides to press charges."

Ian looked at him with that panicked puppy expression again, and Tim's guilt ratcheted up a notch. "They know we talked to the cops, so they're going to want to stay away from us unless they want to get caught. If they're smart, they'll lie low too. Just hold off a bit, and if you see them again, *then* you can call the cops. Okay?"

Tim said it with far more conviction than he actually felt. The truth was, Ian's plan was sounding pretty good to him too, but he didn't want to let Nate down. Against his better judgment, Tim continued to push Ian to keep quiet, and when the cops came and took their statements, they both played dumb about the guys who'd tried to "mug" them in the parking lot.

After the cops left and Ian reluctantly started work, Tim decided he'd had enough fun for one day and headed back to Matt's. His original plan was to work out that afternoon, but his ribs weren't particularly happy with him, and he'd probably be spending a great deal of time at the Y in the very near future anyway. He could afford to skip a day now.

After a shower and a microwave burrito from Matt's freezer, Tim sat on the couch and stared at his phone for a while, flipping it over and over in his hands. He really wanted to call Nate. He had all kinds of excuses now, and he was a little worried that the guys who'd come after Ian might actually go after Nate next. But Nate might still be at work. Today was the big presentation day, and he probably wasn't even back to the hotel yet. Besides, if Nate had really wanted to talk to him again he would've given Tim his number before letting him walk out the door like that. Right?

All of these thoughts and more were stuck on repeat in his head, but thankfully, for the second time that day, he was saved from himself when his phone started ringing. This time, the number wasn't in his contacts, and he didn't recognize the area code.

With his heart in his throat, Tim answered, "Hello?"

"Tim?"

"Nate?" Tim almost squeaked out the name. He really needed to get hold of himself or Nate was going to think he was a total spazz.

"How are you?" Nate sounded uncomfortable, and some of Tim's joy waned a bit.

"I'm good. How about you?"

Nate blew out a breath on the other end of the line, and then there was only silence for a few moments. Tim was desperately trying to think of something to say to keep him from hanging up when Nate said, "Okay. This is stupid. You said you liked it before when I was 'real' with you, right? I'm going to guess that means when I was too doped up to be anything but completely honest with you. So here goes. I thought about you all last night. When I should have been reviewing my presentation and preparing, all I could do was think about you. I'm going to go out on a limb here and guess that you might at least feel a little like I do. Otherwise you wouldn't have given me your number. Right?"

"Yes. Yes, I do," Tim choked out breathlessly when Nate paused.

"This is crazy," Nate said. "Despite all the weirdness that happened this weekend, I just had an awesome day. I nailed it. I know I did. Everyone at that meeting was excited by what I had to offer, and even though I have friends and family waiting to hear from me, I can't think of anyone I'd rather celebrate with right now than you."

The wonder and confusion in Nate's voice did nothing to take away from the impact of his words, and all the crap Tim had been through that day faded away under a rush of joy. "Yeah?"

"Yeah. So, uh, how about it? Can you come out and celebrate with me?"

"Hell yeah I can! Where?"

Nate laughed at him. "Can you come to the hotel again, and we can decide once you get here?"

"I'll be there in half an hour."

Tim heard a shaky indrawn breath on the other end and then Nate said, "Great. See you soon."

"Okay." Tim ended the call and jumped off the couch to rifle through what little he had in the way of clothes. His ribs protested the sudden move, reminding him about the black eye that was going to be hard to hide, but Tim didn't care. Nate wanted to see him again. Nate had been thinking about him. Of all the people Nate probably had in the world, he wanted to share tonight with Tim. He'd said so.

Realistically, Nate probably didn't have many other *local* options, given that he wasn't from Houston, but Tim wasn't going to let reality ruin his happy, not yet anyway. Tomorrow would take care of that all on its own. At least he'd have tonight.

# Chapter Nine

NATHAN PACED the confines of his hotel room like a caged animal after he hung up with Tim. Now that he'd finally made the call, after agonizing over it for far longer than it warranted, he was incredibly impatient to see Tim again. It was crazy. He'd finally accomplished what he'd been working toward for months. The presentation was done, and he'd nailed it. He'd cleared his head long enough to do the best he possibly could. He thought he'd gotten his priorities straight. But instead of feeling like he owned the world, he'd walked out of the FGE building feeling like something was missing.

He was almost back to the hotel by the time the realization finally hit. What was missing was someone to share it with. He'd called Sean, of course. And Sean had been his usual enthusiastic, supportive, and encouraging self. But after he'd gotten off the phone, he'd been alone, facing another dinner alone and another night in his great big fancy hotel room alone. What little enthusiasm he'd had waned pretty quickly after that, and all he could think about then was Tim's number on a crumpled piece of paper, still in his pocket.

Now half an hour had never seemed so long in Nathan's entire life, and he ended up making a plan for the night without waiting for Tim just so he had something to keep him busy. By the time Tim knocked on the door to his room, Nathan had already had room service up with a bottle of wine and candles, and dinner was ordered for both of them, to be delivered later.

Romance wasn't exactly something Nathan had taken much time to read up on, but he figured a few of the standbys like candles, wine, and quiet music couldn't hurt. They might not be particularly original, but they were clichés for a reason, right? Did guys even go in for romantic things like this?

His palms were actually sweating as he reached for the door handle, and he had to wipe them on his slacks before he could open it. He took a breath and then another for courage, deliberately straightened his shoulders, and opened the door.

"Hey," Tim said with that thousand-watt smile.

He was dressed in a pair of tight jeans and a dark green dress shirt that looked new enough to still have the creases from the store. The shirt accentuated Tim's stunning green eyes so well, it took Nate a lot longer than it should have to notice the swelling and darkening of the skin around Tim's left eye, partially covered by what looked like makeup. A closer look at Tim's mouth showed his lower lip looked swollen too, and there was a split in it just visible beneath the sheen of lip balm.

"Are you okay? What happened?"

Tim's smile faded into a grimace. "I was hoping it could wait until later. But I guess it's hard to miss, huh?"

"Come in." Nathan stepped out of the way and then closed the door and followed Tim into the small seating area. Tim spun around in a circle in the middle of the room, taking in the lit candles and the wine bottle and glasses, and his smile came back. "Did you do this for me?"

Nathan waved it off impatiently. "With a little help from the hotel. But I want to talk about what happened to you."

"I don't want to ruin your big night, Nate. Can't we talk about it later?"

Nathan stubbornly folded his arms across his chest and waited.

Tim's pretty green eyes pleaded with him for a short time before he sighed and shook his head. "Fine. I went to see that Ian guy this afternoon. Jana from the club called me and told me where I might find him. So, since I knew you had your big thing today, I figured I'd go and talk to him, ask him what the hell was going on."

"You did what? Tim, why would you do such a thing?" Nathan cried.

"I wanted to help."

Nathan's whole body tensed, and he had to force his muscles to relax. Whatever happened was in the past. It did no good for him to freak out about it now. Tim was safe and sound in front of him. "So what happened?"

"These two guys were arguing with Ian when I found him. I tried to get away, but they jumped me after Ian recognized me. I think they were the guys who drugged you. Anyway, they got in a few good ones before the restaurant manager came out. I'm okay, though. I'm tougher than I look. I promise."

"Holy shit."

"Yeah," Tim agreed. "The manager called the cops. But don't worry. I didn't tell them about you or what happened Friday night."

"What? Why the hell not?"

"I thought… you said you didn't want to go to the police. You said it'd ruin everything if the cops started asking questions."

"Well *yeah*. But that was before they started beating people up. Jesus, Tim. They hurt you. Do you really think I care more about some stupid contract than the fact that you got hurt trying to help me?" Nathan cried.

In an unusual, blinding moment of insight, Nathan was pulled up short by the sudden realization that this must have been how Sean felt on Saturday when he'd been trying to talk some sense into Nathan about going to the police.

*I am such an idiot.*

He groaned inwardly just thinking about the apology he'd have to give Sean, but he wasn't going to worry about it right now.

"I'm calling the police," Nathan said firmly, and he headed for the hotel phone.

Tim rushed after him and grabbed his arm. "No! Don't do that. Nate, the last thing I want to do is ruin this for you. You were so happy on the phone. I don't want to be the one who fucks it up."

Nathan was about to shrug off Tim's arm and keep going. He even had the phone in his hand before a second unprecedented flash of insight hit him and he realized how insensitive he was being. Tim was the one who got hurt, and here Nathan was upsetting him even more by blabbing on about what he should do instead of comforting him. Everything didn't always revolve around him. He had that printed out and tacked up somewhere in his office to refer back to periodically. If he continued to have these epiphanies, he might actually be able to move up from beginner's self-help books to advanced someday…. And Sean would have to take back the "Socially Challenged" plaque he'd given Nathan as a gag gift their second year of working together. It also held a place of prominence on one of his walls at work.

Of course, Tim made it pretty easy. Nathan really would have to be as clueless as Sean joked if he couldn't read him, which kind of made Tim perfect for him. So instead of brushing off Tim's concerns, Nathan set the phone back down, turned, and cupped Tim's cheek in his palm. He leaned in slowly, giving Tim plenty of time to object, but when Tim's eyes went wide and he gasped a little but didn't pull away, Nathan was pretty sure of his welcome. He closed his eyes and touched their lips together, slow and tender, careful of Tim's injury. Through the palm on Tim's cheek, Nathan felt Tim give a full-body shiver, and he smiled and kissed him again.

Tim really made this so damned easy.

Nathan pulled back and rested their foreheads together. "Thank you for trying to help," he whispered into the closeness between them. "But this has gone too far. I don't want anyone hurt because of me. I don't want *you* hurt. I'm going to call the police now, like I probably should have done from the start. Okay?"

Tim didn't open his eyes, but his Adam's apple bobbed as he swallowed. "Okay," he whispered back.

Nathan gave him one last quick peck on the lips, picked up the phone again, and dialed the front desk. "Yes, this is Nathan Seward. Would you please connect me with the police? The nonemergency number? Thank you."

After a short conversation with the detective he was eventually transferred to, it was decided he and Tim needed to go down to the station and give their statements in person. Nathan reassured Tim a few more times that he hadn't ruined anything and then blew out the candles and called room service, postponing his dinner order.

The ride to the police station was quiet. Nathan could tell Tim was anxious, but since Nathan was pretty riddled with anxiety himself, he didn't have a lot of attention to spare for more reassurances—big building, lots of people, not his favorite thing in the world. Luckily it didn't take long for them to be led upstairs, and once they were in a quiet room, Nathan was able to relax some.

Detective Jimenez was an average-looking man in his midforties. He was professional and efficient. He didn't laugh at Nathan or make any snide comments about how stupid he was for not calling them earlier. He took both of their statements and contact information and had Nathan forward the e-mails from the blackmailer and Nathan's doctor to him. He'd taken the phone number Ian had given Nathan, the one for the mysterious Peter, when Nathan had talked to him earlier, and he had some news on that front already.

"We checked into it, and it's a cell number for Peter Vold. Does that name mean anything to you?"

Nathan shook his head. "Sorry. Not ringing a bell."

They both looked at Tim, but Tim shook his head too.

"Well, it seems Mr. Vold has a record," Jimenez continued. "Minor assault, trespassing. From his file, I take it he styles himself as a bit of a private detective. I'd like to show Tim here some mug shots, see if he recognizes anyone."

"Okay," both Tim and Nathan said at the same time.

While Nathan waited in the little room, Jimenez took Tim to a desk and had him scroll through pictures on a monitor. In the end, Tim picked one man out, and it was indeed Peter Vold.

"We have enough to pick him up on the assault charges, so I'll get a warrant drawn up tonight, and we'll have a little talk with him once he's in custody to see what we can find out about the drugs and the blackmail."

"You don't sound very optimistic," Nathan pointed out.

Jimenez sighed and gave both Nathan and Tim a regretful smile. "The assault charges are pretty straightforward. I don't think we'll have too many problems making that stick, especially if the other witness, Ian, cooperates. We'll talk to the rest of the staff at the restaurant to see if any of them can also make a positive ID. The rest of it...?" Jimenez shrugged. "People use anonymizers for a reason. Most are out of the country, so there's no subpoenaing their records. We might be able to find his payment history to link him to the site, but that's about all. And if no one actually saw him put anything in your drink, a good lawyer could probably weasel him out of that too. I'm not trying to discourage you or anything, Mr. Seward. We'll do everything we can. But getting him on the rest of this isn't a sure thing."

Nathan sighed and nodded. "I understand. Thank you."

In all honesty, Nathan just wanted it done and over with. He wanted the man behind bars so he couldn't hurt Tim again. But when it came to the rest, he'd be more than willing to forget about it if it meant he wouldn't have to deal with this mess ever again.

The entire process at the station seemed to take forever, and by the time they returned to the hotel, both of them were starving. They could have stopped somewhere on the way back, but Nathan really didn't want to. He wanted their perfect evening together, just how he'd planned, even if it was a little late. And now that everything was in Detective Jimenez's hands, Nathan could finally relax and enjoy it.

Once they were back in the room, he told Tim to make himself comfortable on the couch. He relit the candles, filled the wineglasses, and called to place his order again. Tim accepted his wineglass with a shy, happy smile, and Nathan felt like he was on top of the world again. That was all it took.

"To us," Nate said as he clinked their glasses together.

Tim's glass froze halfway to his mouth, and he stared at Nathan. "Us?"

*Oops.* Nathan barely restrained a full-body cringe as he realized his mistake.

Tim's eyes were so hopeful. Nathan immediately regretted getting carried away with the moment. It was a stupid thing to say when he didn't know what the hell he was doing. He wasn't being fair, saying something like that. He'd meant to toast the contract.

*Idiot.*

With a sigh, Nathan set his wineglass down and took one of Tim's hands. "I guess I need to be *real* and *honest* with you again now, huh?" At Tim's wary nod, he continued, "Okay, then, I don't really know what I'm doing here, Tim. I haven't thought anything through, not enough anyway. I like you. I really do. But I've been acting kind of crazy since I met you, and I still can't make any promises. I don't want to hurt you, and I'm probably doing this all wrong."

"You haven't. It's okay." Tim sighed and looked away. "I really like you too. But I guess I've been pretty obvious about that." When he turned back to look at Nathan, his eyes were wide. "I hope you don't think I act like this with every guy I meet, because I don't. And I'm not stupid. Like I said before, I know you're leaving soon. You have a whole life far away from here to go back to. I know that. But I'm willing to take whatever you have to give right now." He stopped there, chugged about half of what was in his wineglass, and took a long, deep breath. "You were honest with me, so I'll be honest too and just hope I don't scare you away…. Even as weird and crazy as these last few days have been, I feel better being with you than I've felt in a really long time. It's not crazy to want more of that, is it? Even if it can't last?"

"No. It's not crazy."

Or it might be, but who was Nathan to judge?

Nathan took Tim's glass and set it on the counter by the minibar. When Tim looked up and met his gaze, Nathan cupped his jaw as he had earlier and pulled him in for a kiss. It started out sweet and teasing. He plucked at Tim's lips gently with his own. But soon Tim was making soft whimpering noises at the back of his throat and pushing into Nathan's kiss, and Nathan let himself get swept away again. He didn't worry about the future. He didn't worry about Tim's injuries. He let Tim take over so he wouldn't do any more damage to Tim's lip, but beyond that, he was lost in the taste and heat of the man in his arms. That feeling of something missing was gone.

Nathan cursed when the knock sounded on their door, announcing the arrival of their dinner, but he really was starving and they both managed to control themselves long enough to get through at least half of their food before Tim pounced on him and picked up where they'd left off. Before Nathan knew it, they were naked and in bed together. There was laughter and passion, deep intimacy and playfulness, tenderness and wildness. Tim provided the condoms and lube again because Nathan was an idiot and hadn't even thought to take care of that in his attempt at romance. Little things like that reminded him how long he'd been out of the dating game. But Tim didn't let him dwell on any of his shortcomings for long. Soon enough he was spooned against

Tim's back, inside of him again, and Nathan couldn't think of anything at all beyond wanting to stay right where he was forever.

Tim arched into him, moving with him, urging Nathan on with his movements and words. Nathan's arms were wrapped tightly around Tim's chest, squeezing him, wanting to be even closer though not a millimeter of space was left between them. And when Tim fell apart in his arms, crying out Nathan's name, his muscles clamping down on Nathan's cock and squeezing the orgasm out of him, Nathan could only hold on and ride the wave they'd built until they both slumped to the mattress, spent and breathless.

It took all the energy he had left to get rid of the condom and give them both a quick wipe down, but Nathan was fastidious enough he wouldn't be able to sleep if he was still sticky. He'd let a lot of his intimacy issues fall by the wayside where Tim was concerned, but there was a limit to how laid back he could be. Tim just watched him with a sleepy smile while Nathan fussed, and once he was clean enough, Nathan spooned up behind him, closed his eyes, and buried his face in Tim's neck, happy to just be *happy* for a while. Tim snuggled against him and made a few quiet contented noises before his soft snores filled the room, and it wasn't long before Nathan drifted off as well.

He woke quite pleasantly to Tim's mouth on his cock sometime in the night. That was another first, and Nathan definitely hoped it wouldn't be a last. Tim's enthusiasm for him didn't seem to have waned in their time together, and apparently it included every inch of Nathan's body, because he worshipped Nathan's cock for a good long time, drawing out the pleasure until Nathan was positively shaking with it before allowing him to come down his throat.

When Nathan could string two thoughts together again, he reciprocated with fully the same amount of enthusiasm, if perhaps not the same amount of skill. But Tim didn't seem to be complaining. Using a few of the tricks Tim had used on him only a few minutes before, even being so bold as to slip a wet finger inside Tim's ass to stroke him on the inside as he sucked the orgasm out of him, Nathan put his all into giving the best blowjob he could and was rewarded when Tim arched off the bed and cried out his name in release.

When they were cuddled up together again, Nathan was riding high on a sense of accomplishment and wasn't really ready to fall asleep again. Tim's head rested on his chest while Nathan lounged on his back, absently playing with Tim's surprisingly soft blond spikes. Tim purred like a cat when Nate dragged his fingernails across his scalp. "You like that, huh?"

"Mmmhmm," Tim hummed against his chest.

"Well, I'll make you a deal. I'll keep going as long as you do some talking."

"About what?" Tim said sleepily.

"About you. You said you told me things our first night together after I apparently blabbed my whole life's story to you. But that's not really fair since I can't remember any of it. I don't know that much about you, and I want to know more."

Nathan kept scratching Tim's scalp, but he could feel Tim tensing up with each word that came out of his mouth.

"There's not much to tell," Tim said evasively, but Nathan wasn't going to let him get away that easy.

"Tell me anyway. Where are you from? Let's start there."

Tim was quiet for a while, and Nathan wondered if he was going to have to make good on his threat and stop petting. But eventually Tim started talking.

"I'm from here, Houston. I grew up in the burbs."

"Do your parents still live here?"

"My dad does. My mom… my mom died about seven years ago."

"Oh, Tim. I'm so sorry." Now Nathan felt guilty for bringing it up.

"Thanks." Tim shrugged against his chest. "She got sick. There wasn't much anyone could do. Cancer."

Nate pulled him closer and rested his chin on Tim's head. "That must have been hard," he said, because he couldn't think of anything else.

Tim was quiet for another long time, long enough for Nathan to regret asking even as little as he had. Everything had been so easy up until then. He'd obviously gotten a little overconfident. But then Tim cleared his throat and said, "It was. I miss her every day. But life goes on, right?"

"Yeah. I suppose it does. Why don't we talk about something a little less painful? How about where you work? What do you do for a living?" Nathan asked, trying a tack he thought would have to be foolproof.

He was wrong. Tim's muscles had just begun to relax again, and then Nathan had to open his big mouth and suddenly Tim was stiff as a board in his arms.

*Shit. What now?*

Nathan was starting to feel like he was walking on a minefield he didn't even know was there.

He let his arms relax a little and drew back, trying to make out any of Tim's face he could in the darkened room. "Obviously I'm not doing this very well. I'm sorry, but I don't know how else to try to get to know you. Maybe if you tell me which subjects are the safe ones?"

There were a couple of seconds of heavy silence, and then Tim snorted. "I'm sorry. It's not your fault. It's me."

"I'm not too good at this, but I think the 'it's not you, it's me' speech is reserved for breaking up," Nathan said, only half joking. "Is that what we're doing?"

Tim's eyes were wide when he lifted his head to stare at Nathan. "No! No. I only meant, I'm the one who's being stupid. Your questions are perfectly normal, Nate. I just...." Tim pulled away and sat up. "You're a really great guy. You're successful and smart. You're only like five years older than me, but you've got all your shit together. I mean *really* together, like your own company, your own house, retirement plans and investments, and all that. I can barely manage my checkbook, and I'm nowhere near having any of the rest of that stuff. It's embarrassing."

Nathan felt his cheeks flush under all the praise, and he laughed uncomfortably. "Wow. You make me sound a hell of a lot more on top of things than I feel most of the time."

Tim gave him a little shake before dropping his cheek back down to Nathan's chest. "Don't joke. I wish I had even a tenth of the passion you have for your business. I've never felt that way about any job or class I took—*ever*. I'm twenty-seven years old, and I still have no idea what I want to do when I grow up. It's pathetic."

Tim fell silent after that, and when Nathan tried to pull him up to meet his gaze, Tim resisted. They wrestled until they were both laughing, and they ended up lying on their sides facing each other, legs entwined. Nathan couldn't see every detail of Tim's face in the weak light from outside the windows, but he could see enough. Despite their teasing, Tim was obviously upset, and Nathan was at a loss as to what to do about it. People really needed to come with manuals. That was the only way Nathan thought he'd ever be able to figure them out. The only thing he could think of to do was kiss Tim until that frown disappeared, so that's what he did.

When Nathan finally pulled away, a thought occurred to him, and he said, "What did I say to you Friday night? You told me we had this conversation before, and you obviously still liked me afterward, so I must have said something right."

Tim snorted again. "You didn't say much, really. You just didn't judge me. That's all. You were sympathetic… understanding."

Nathan frowned, reviewing what he'd said earlier. "And I'm not any of those things now?"

"No. You *are*."

"Then…?"

Tim sighed and kissed Nathan's chest. "Then I'm being stupid. Okay? You're right. I just didn't know you quite as well, then. I was caught up in the moment, and I didn't have time to really think about it, so it was easier."

"I don't want easy. I want real. That's what you said, right?"

"Yeah."

"Then be real with me. Talk to me. The more time you spend with me, the more you'll realize how hopeless I actually am at this kind of thing. I was probably real with you that night because I have no talent for anything else. I suck at interpersonal stuff most of the time. Ask any woman I've ever dated. Or, uh, wait. I guess you wouldn't want to do that, would you?" Nathan paused and thought about it for a second. "Ask Sean, my business partner. He'd take great joy in telling you how bad I am when I'm out of my comfort zones. Believe me. I have no room to judge anyone."

At least Tim was smiling at him now. Nathan had managed that much.

# Chapter Ten

TIM DIDN'T know whether to laugh or cry. Here he was, in the exact same place he'd been with Nate only two nights before, about to have nearly the exact same conversation, and he couldn't seem to go through with it. Last time, he was kind of drunk. That probably made it easier. For a few seconds, he thought about going for the wine bottle again, but he was so warm and comfortable, curled up with Nate, he didn't want to ruin the mood by getting up. He just needed to cowboy up and do it.

*Okay. Here goes nothing.*

"The truth isn't very pretty, and I can't think of a way to spin it to make it sound better right now, so, if you promise you won't run away as soon as I finish, I'll tell you."

Nate squeezed him tighter and kissed the top of his head. "I promise."

Tim took a deep breath, lifted his head, and rested his chin on Nate's chest so he could watch his face. "Okay. I work two part-time retail jobs that I hate most of the time, but I can't afford to quit. I have student loans from the one year I was able to go to college before my mom got sick, and even after all these years, I can't seem to make a dent in them. I've been couch surfing at a friend of mine's for about a year now because I couldn't afford a place of my own after my last roommates broke up and wouldn't live together anymore at my old apartment. My credit sucks, so there aren't many places that'd let me sign a lease anyway, even if I could afford it. And every time I think I might be digging myself out of the hole I'm in, something comes along and wipes me out again. Last time, it was a trip to the dentist, about six months ago, and a new fuel pump and tires for the piece of shit car you rode in…. There you go. That's the truth. Now do you understand why I didn't want to tell you?"

Tim closed his eyes then, in part because he was afraid of what he'd see on Nate's face, but also because he was afraid he might actually start to cry, and he had no idea where that was coming from. He never cried, especially not over something that had been going on for years. That would be just stupid.

Instead of saying anything, Nate pulled Tim closer, hooked a leg over Tim's hip, and wrapped his arms around Tim's back, holding him tight. Tim didn't care how hopeless Nate insisted he was. The man was goddamned perfect. Tim buried his face in Nate's neck and just held on.

Eventually Nate's voice rumbled through his chest. "I'm sorry, Tim. I'm sorry for all your hurt and disappointment. Everybody should have a chance to follow their dreams."

Tim groaned and pulled away. "But that's the worst part. The part someone like you couldn't possibly understand. I don't even know if I *have* any dreams. I'm not like you, Nate. You love your work. I can tell even from the few conversations we've had. You're passionate about it. You had a dream and you went for it. Look at you." Tim shrugged and looked away. "I've never felt that strongly about anything."

Nate was silent for long enough Tim began to worry he might have sold Nate a little too hard on how pathetic he was, so he backtracked a little. "Don't get me wrong. I'm not lazy. I don't mind hard work, and I've always worked hard at the jobs I've had. But my bosses can usually tell I have no real love for it, no drive to be promoted beyond the fact that I'd get more money. I was close to getting promoted to management at my last job, but the store went out of business. And it's hard out there right now, with so many people looking for work. I took what I could get."

That didn't sound as pathetic as he thought, did it?

Nate chewed on his lip a bit, seeming to ponder Tim's words deeply. Eventually he asked, "You said you went to college for a year, right? What was your major?"

"Graphic design."

Nate smiled triumphantly and gave Tim a little shake. "See. That's somewhat specific. You must have had some reason why you chose it."

Tim didn't want to contradict him, but it would have been dishonest if he didn't. "I chose it because of my mom. She loved art and design and stuff like that. At the time, I thought it was what I wanted, but now I know I only picked it because it was her dream, not mine… to make her proud of me. And now she's gone, I don't really have a direction to go." Tim sighed and shook his head. "I'm sure I'm not saying this right. You probably think I'm a big loser right about now. Way to kill the mood."

"I didn't say that. When did I say that?"

"You don't have to." Tim climbed out of bed and started to look for his underwear.

"Hey, come here. Come back to bed." When Tim hesitated, Nate lifted his arms and pouted his lower lip. "Please?"

Since there wasn't any other place Tim wanted to be, it didn't take much convincing to get him back in bed. And when they were curled up together again, Nate said quietly, "I'm not judging you. I only want to help. You helped me, remember? Besides, you can't go until you help me figure something out, because I'm a little confused, and it would be cruel of you to leave me like this."

"Figure what out?"

"Well, I'm confused. You say you're not passionate about anything. But ever since I met you, I've felt like you were one of the most passionate people I've ever been around. It's all right there in your eyes and on your face, out there for anyone to see. You helped me even though you barely knew me, and you got hurt doing it. So I don't understand how you can think that you're not passionate. You're going to have to help the socially handicapped person figure this out."

Tim chuckled and squeezed Nate a little tighter. Walking away from him was really going to suck. "That's not work," he answered. "That's you. I'm not a stone. I can love *people*. I've just never found any *thing* that I loved that could actually be turned into a career. You know, something I could be proud of when someone asks me what I do for a living, something that would make me enough money that I wouldn't be next door to homeless most of the time."

Nate's arms jerked around him, and Tim realized with chagrin that he'd said too much. He cringed inwardly as Nate drew a breath, afraid of what he was going to say.

"The pillow and blankets in the backseat of your car," Nate murmured as if to himself. "Do you actually have to use those?"

"Sometimes," Tim mumbled, feeling like he couldn't sink any lower.

"Oh, Tim, I don't know what to say."

"Don't say anything." Tim kissed Nate's neck and forced himself to sound more upbeat than he felt. "I'm okay. *Really*. I'll be fine. Look, I'm kind of tired. Can we just go to sleep for a while?"

Eventually Nate sighed and said, "Yeah. Okay. Good night."

"Good night."

It took forever, but the stress of the last few days caught up with Tim and he passed out. Nate was still snoring softly beneath him when he woke in the morning. But when he got back from the bathroom, Nate was already up and on his cell phone. He hadn't taken the time to pull on anything but his boxers, but that was just fine with Tim. All that lean ivory perfection was definitely worth watching, and Tim flopped down on the mattress to do just that.

"Hey, what's up?" Nate said into his cell. There was a pause, and Nathan frowned. "No, I haven't checked anything yet. We are in different time zones, remember? Oh. Well yeah, of course I knew it's actually later here than it is there. So I slept in a little." Nate moved over to the coffee table by the couch and opened his laptop. "Okay. Okay, I'm checking it now…. Yes, I'm sitting down. Why?" Nate tapped on the touchpad of his laptop a couple of times. "Oh shit. Son of a bitch!"

Worried by the sudden anger in Nate's voice, Tim hesitantly rolled off the mattress and walked over to where Nate had slumped into the couch cushions. The e-mail he had up on the screen was filled with pictures of the two of them together at South Beach—*lots* of pics.

Nate groaned. He lifted the cell back to his ear and said, "Did it go to everyone? *Fuck!*"

With a sinking feeling in the pit of his stomach, Tim just stood behind the couch uselessly while Nate listened to whoever was on the other end of the line.

Eventually Nate said, "Yeah, man. Thanks for the call. No. Don't worry about it. Not much we can do now anyway." Then Nate laughed, surprising Tim. "I actually went to the cops last night, smarty-pants. So there." Nate opened his eyes and locked gazes with Tim. "Look, Sean. I'll call you later, okay? I'm fine. Really. Yeah. Bye."

Nate's expression was unreadable as he turned away and set the phone down. Tim wanted to say something, but he didn't even know how to start. It was fairly obvious what had happened. The asshole had sent the pics out, and now all Nate's hard work was probably for nothing. Tim felt sick.

When Nate continued to sit quietly with his elbows resting on his thighs and his head down, Tim couldn't take it anymore, and he hurried around the couch and sat down next to him. "God, I'm so sorry, Nate. I can't even begin to know what you're feeling right now. But I'm so, so sorry."

Tim was actually on the verge of tears himself. It seemed to be a recurring theme lately, one he wasn't sure he liked. He felt so useless, and the more he thought about what happened, the guiltier he got. If Tim hadn't gone after that Ian guy, Nate wouldn't have insisted on going to the cops last night, and maybe they wouldn't have sent the pictures out. Maybe it was all his fault. The thought didn't help the tightness in his chest or the prickling in the corners of his eyes. But before he could work himself up into a real puddle of angst, Nate's arms were suddenly around him, and Tim was being kissed to within an inch of his life. He had to gasp for air when Nate finally let him go. And to his utter shock, Nate was actually smiling and laughing when Tim's vision cleared.

"Nate? Are you okay?"

Nate's grin only grew wider. "Yup."

Now he was really confused. "Uh, I don't get it. I thought the e-mail meant your chances at the contract were screwed."

"Oh, I'm sure they are," Nate answered with a grin.

"And you're not upset about that?"

Nate sobered a little. But even though he wasn't grinning like a lunatic anymore, he was still smiling pretty wide. "Let's just say I'm not as upset as I'd thought I'd be."

"Okaaaaay?" Tim replied warily.

"Look. I'm starving. Why don't we go get some lunch? I'd say breakfast, but I think we slept past that."

Nate hopped off the couch and headed for the bathroom while Tim lingered uncertainly by the couch. After only a few moments, Nate's grinning face popped out of the bathroom door, and he crooked a finger at Tim. "Come on, slowpoke. You can't expect me to wash my own back, can you?" And with that, he disappeared back into the bathroom, and the sound of the shower being turned on came from inside.

Tim had no idea what was going on. Nate was acting a little like the drugged, manic Nate he'd met at the club that first night, all teasing energy. But Tim didn't think drugs were involved this time. He just couldn't figure out exactly what was.

Not wanting to pass up a chance at a couple more hours of happiness, Tim decided he didn't need to understand, and he went for it. He climbed into the shower with Nate, and they spent a lovely half hour washing each other. No nook or cranny was missed, and a few got some extra attention.

Afterward, they dressed, and Tim followed Nate out of the hotel, feeling bemused but happy. He only had two hours before he had to leave for work, and he wasn't going to waste a single minute. But when they were seated at a nice little brew pub in CityCentre and Nate was still acting like he'd won the lottery, Tim couldn't take it anymore. He had to know what Nate was thinking.

"Nate, what's going on?"

# Chapter Eleven

NOW THERE was the question of the hour, and Nathan wasn't sure how to even begin to answer it. Over the past few days, he'd been drugged and blackmailed. He'd had his first real full-on gay sex. He'd decided for some crazy reason to become an amateur detective—which he'd turned out to be pretty good at… at least insofar as he'd gotten most of the answers he was looking for. He'd been given what should have been crushing news only a short time ago. And now, he felt like a million bucks.

*Crazy.*

But Tim really looked worried, and Nathan didn't want that, so he took his head out of the clouds, reached across the table, took Tim's hands, and said, "I'm happy. That's what's going on."

Tim gave him an uncertain smile, and Nate couldn't help himself, he leaned forward and kissed that smile until Tim was laughing. "You're not going to freak out on me at some point, right?" Tim asked.

Nate chuckled and squeezed Tim's hands. "Nope."

Or at least he didn't think so.

He took a deep breath and let it out before continuing. "I don't know how to explain it, but I feel… good. Call it an early midlife crisis. Call it whatever you want. But I've spent the last ten years of my life building my company. I've worked nights and weekends, not only making sure the clients got what they wanted but drumming up sales and studying management and business books until my eyes crossed.

And then there I was, on the verge of making it into the big time—expansion, getting our name out there so clients would start coming to us instead of the other way around—and one stupid e-mail from a guy I've never even met cuts it off at the knees... and honestly, I don't care. Now, it is still possible FGE might surprise me and not give a rat's ass about the pics at all. We could get the contract anyway—although I doubt it very much. But I'm good either way. I feel... *good.*"

Tim continued to smile as he listened, but Nathan could tell Tim didn't quite believe him. He looked like he was waiting for whatever high Nathan was on to wear off any second now, and he would just humor crazy Nathan until it did.

That wasn't going to happen.

Sean had been trying to tell Nathan something for months now, hinting here and there that he should take a break. He'd said it again on the phone yesterday, but Nathan hadn't been listening. And now it finally dawned on him what Sean was talking about. It was like a lightbulb had finally been turned on... or more accurately, his blinders had finally been taken off.

Nathan stared deeply into Tim's concerned green eyes and willed him to understand. "Look. Remember what you said about me being passionate about my company, about it being my dream?" At Tim's nod, he continued, "Well, it is. It has been for over ten years. I wanted it to succeed. I wanted to show the world what I could do. But I got so caught up in that, I kind of forgot about a lot of other important things, like people and relationships and *life*. I'm thirty-two years old, and my business partner is the only person I've formed a meaningful relationship with outside of my family in nearly a decade. And the only reason I have that is because he's tenacious and made friends with me. I don't think I actually had much to do with it, at least in the beginning. Does that make sense?"

"I think you're too hard on yourself, but yeah, it makes sense. Sort of."

"Sean's been trying to tell me some things, and I've been too stubborn to listen. He was right. The only one really depending on me to get this contract was *me*. The rest of the guys at the company are happy where we are. He's been trying to tell me to stop and smell the roses for months—*years* maybe—but somehow I got it in my head that dream was the only one I had, and I focused so close on it, I think I missed a lot of good things along the way."

Tim was quiet as he seemed to absorb this. But at least some of the don't-spook-the-crazy-person look was fading from his face, and by the time their food arrived, they were both relaxed enough to enjoy it. Unfortunately, all too soon, Nathan noticed Tim glancing at his phone more and more often, and Tim's happy smile faded a little with each time he looked.

"What's wrong?"

"I have to go to work soon. I'm sorry, but I can't afford to call in."

Nathan struggled to hide his disappointment. Just because he'd had a life-changing epiphany didn't mean that the rest of the world stopped. "Oh yeah. Work. That thing I should be doing today too. I guess."

Tim's laugh was subdued and his smile sad. He looked like he was gearing up for a good-bye speech, and Nathan's heart clenched in sudden panic. He didn't want to say good-bye.

Feeling reckless and crazy and romantic, Nathan cut Tim off before he could say anything too irrevocable. "Come with me," he said in a breathless rush, surprising himself.

"What?"

"Come with me." It came out stronger, more sure the second time.

Tim frowned at him in confusion. "Where? Somewhere close? I really do need to leave soon or I'll be late."

"No. I mean to California. Come back with me."

"Be serious," Tim scoffed.

Nathan squeezed Tim's hand and held his gaze. "I am being serious."

"You *can't* be serious."

"Why not?"

Nathan wasn't sure how anyone could look so hurt and hopeful at the same time, but somehow Tim managed it.

"Nate, I told you. I don't have any money. I can't just pick up and fly halfway across the country on a whim. You don't get vacation working part time."

"I'm not asking you to do it on a whim. I'm asking you to move out there and stay with me. I've got enough that you can take some time, find a job, figure out what it is you want to do. You've got a dream in there somewhere, whatever it might be. I know it sounds a little crazy, but I'm feeling a little crazy… and happy, and romantic, and all that stuff I've forgotten about. I don't want this to end, and you said yourself you don't either. You hate your jobs. You made it sound like you didn't really have a permanent place to live right now. So what better time for a fresh start?"

It was perfectly logical to Nathan.

"I…." Tim trailed off, seeming at a loss, and Nathan's happy little bubble returned. He was winning Tim over. He could tell by the way Tim's eyes had gone wide and wondering.

Deciding to press his advantage, Nathan kept going. "I have a spare bedroom. In fact, you could have most of the lower level of the house, if you wanted. You could pay rent, if you really feel like you have to, whatever you can afford. We wouldn't have to shack up overnight if you weren't comfortable with that. And if you really didn't like it out there, I wouldn't leave you hanging. You could have a ticket home whenever you wanted. I promise."

Nathan stopped there and waited a few breaths, but it seemed like he'd left Tim speechless yet again. He watched Tim's face closely, but when the answer came, it wasn't the one he was hoping for.

Tim's face closed off, and he turned his head away. "I can't, Nate. I'm sorry, but I can't."

The last words were barely above a whisper, and Tim sounded like he was on the verge of tears. Nathan quickly dug a couple of twenties out of his wallet and left them on the table. Then he tugged on Tim's hand and led him out of the restaurant. Tim was silent on the walk back to the hotel, but Nathan wasn't ready to give up yet. But they needed privacy, so he waited until they were back in the room to try again.

Once the door was closed and they were both seated on the couch, Nathan asked, "What is it, Tim? What's wrong?"

Tim drew in a long shuddering breath and buried his face in Nathan's shoulder. "I'm sorry," he whispered. "I want to. Believe me, I do."

"Then why?"

"It's more than just me. It's my dad. I can't leave him. I promised my mom I'd take care of him. And even though I'm doing a pretty crappy job of it, at least I'm trying. If I left…."

Tim didn't finish, and Nathan didn't try to force any more out of him. Maybe it had been too crazy to think he could just ask and Tim would drop everything to come with him. He'd felt a real connection to someone for the first time in possibly ever, and maybe he'd gotten a little carried away because of it. It wasn't all about Nathan. The printout on his office wall said so.

Nathan sighed and wrapped his arms around Tim's shoulders. "I understand. It was a lot to ask." He rubbed his face into Tim's hair and inhaled his scent, taking what comfort he could from it. After a few more breaths, he said, "I wish I could stay longer, spend more time with you, but I have a lot of work waiting for me back home. And while they may not have been depending on me to succeed down here as much as I thought, they do depend on me for a lot of other things I've been putting off to pursue this contract. It wouldn't be fair to them to have to keep taking up my slack."

He felt Tim nod against his shoulder. "Yeah, I know. I don't want to say good-bye, though."

"I don't either. So why don't we say 'until next time' instead. I've got your number. You have mine now. And I haven't actually heard anything definite on the contract yet. If I do get it, by some miracle, I'll have to come back to iron out the details, and I'll have to come down from time to time to work with the client as well. And even if I don't get it, the cops are going to want to talk to me again, and I can always fly back for more personal reasons, right?" Nathan tugged at Tim's shoulders and forced him to meet his gaze. "This doesn't have to be good-bye."

But despite his words, the kiss they shared sure felt like good-bye, bittersweet and full of longing. And when Tim walked out the door only a short time later, it hurt like it was forever. Nathan had never really considered himself an emotional man before, and he was pretty sure he didn't like the feeling now. The highs were wonderful, but that made the lows almost crushing. Maybe his epiphany wasn't such a good thing after all.

# Chapter Twelve

TIM WALKED out of Nate's hotel with his heart in his shoes. It was one of the hardest things he'd done since watching his mom get lowered into the ground, because he wasn't just walking away from the guy who could have been the one. He was walking away from the promise of a better future that Nate was offering him on a silver platter.

Was he an idiot to turn that down? Was he completely out of his mind?

He drove to work on autopilot. He didn't even remember the trip there, which was pretty scary when he thought about it later. As he'd been the night before, he was completely useless at work. Luckily, he was at his other job, so hopefully his manager wouldn't notice until it became a pattern.

When the store closed and everybody headed out, it took all of his willpower to turn his car in the opposite direction from Nate's hotel and head back to Matt's. He still had a couple of nights to figure out what he was going to do about a place to live, which was a good thing because he wasn't in any kind of shape to deal with it tonight. Hopefully, after a good night's sleep, he could handle the necessities of life, because right now he wasn't sure he cared.

"Hey, man," Matt said as Tim walked in the door.

"Hey."

"Jesus, Tim. You look like shit. What the hell happened to you?"

Tim had forgotten about the black eye and the split lip. "It's a long story."

He sank onto the sofa with a defeated sigh and let his eyes close.

"Are you sure you're all right?" Matt asked, hovering anxiously.

"No."

And there were those tears again, threatening to fall if he let them. Tim rubbed at his eyes and stubbornly refused to give in. He hadn't truly cried since his mom's funeral, and he wasn't going to start now.

"Hey, man. I don't know what's going on, but I'm your friend. You know that, right? I'm here if you want to talk."

"Thanks, man. This whole weekend has been pretty fucked up. I'm not sure I can take much more right now."

"You gonna tell me what happened? That guy you were talking about didn't do this, did he? If he did, I'll kick his ass."

Tim smiled in spite of himself. "No. Nate didn't do this. Nate was…. God, he was perfect." Tim choked a little on that last.

When Matt still hovered over him, vibrating with concern, Tim started with Friday night and gave an abridged version of the story, including getting his ass kicked in a parking lot and Nate offering him the moon.

"Holy shit," Matt breathed out when Tim had finished.

"Yeah."

"That's…. Wow."

"Yeah."

"So this Nate guy, you really like him, don't you?"

"Yeah. I really like him." That was the understatement of the century.

"I think you should go for it," Matt said, as if it were that easy.

Tim grimaced and punched his friend lightly on the arm. "You just want me out of here so Drew doesn't throw a shit-fit. Don't worry. I told you I'd be out."

Matt punched him a little less than lightly back. "I am still your friend, asshole. I didn't say it because of that. It sounds like this guy is pretty cool. Maybe a sugar daddy is what you need right now."

Tim punched him back, and they started wrestling and slinging insults until Tim got a knee in his sore ribs that sent him curling up in the fetal position on the floor.

"Sorry, man. I didn't mean to get you that bad."

"No. It's fine," Tim managed after the rush of pain receded. "You didn't do it. That's where the bastard got me. That's all. You couldn't beat up a ten-year-old girl."

While Matt huffed in mock offense, Tim climbed slowly back up onto the couch with an arm wrapped around his ribs. When he looked up, Matt was watching him with concern again.

"I said that before, about going for it, as your friend, man," Matt said earnestly. "I know about your dad. I know you don't want to leave him. But you've been trying to take care of the guy for like seven years now, right? He's not going to get any better unless he chooses to. You know that. Nothing you do is going to fix him unless he *wants* to be fixed. You can't throw your whole life away fighting that battle. I'm sure your mom wouldn't have wanted that."

"But how can I just leave him? He's still my dad, even if he hasn't been the guy who raised me for a long time. How can I just walk away?" Tim cried, hoping desperately that Matt would have an answer he could live with.

"Look, man. I'm not sure I can say anything that's going to be of much help here. I can't know what you're going through. But maybe you should talk to your dad about it. You never know. It might help."

Tim had an idea of how helpful a conversation with his dad was going to be, and some of that must have shown on his face, because Matt rolled his eyes. "Dude, you're already planning on staying, right? So if he guilts you about it, at least you'll have already made the decision to do what he wants. But maybe he'll surprise you. You never know. And if he's the whole reason you're holding back—not because you're just chickenshit or something—then you should at least give him a chance to weigh in, right?"

Matt got another punch on the arm for the chickenshit comment, but he had a point. Maybe Tim should talk to his dad about it. He'd have to be careful what time of day he called. The middle of the afternoon would probably be best, maybe.

"I'll think about it. And thanks, man."

"What're friends for?" Matt said before patting Tim on the shoulder and ambling off to bed.

Tired in both body and spirit, Tim curled up on the couch and passed out shortly after Matt turned off the lights. He desperately needed to get some sleep. He had the late shift at his other job again tomorrow, but he had to squeeze in some apartment hunting before that, and he couldn't afford to show up as a zombie for the same job twice in one week.

He woke later than he'd wanted, but he felt a little more like himself in the morning. After a few hours of fruitless hunting for a place to live online, he started his shift at work. But Matt's advice was heavy on his mind. Twice during lulls in between customers, Tim managed to talk himself out of making that call to his dad. But then he'd think about Nate—wondering what he was doing, if he'd already gotten a flight home—and that would convince him yet again that he needed to at least try. Nate had said they weren't really saying good-bye. He wasn't giving up on them. But long distance wouldn't last. It might work for people who'd been together a long time, but they barely knew each other. They couldn't keep that intense connection going over the phone. They needed to see and touch.

After the manager let them out the back, Tim said his good-nights, climbed into his car, and pulled out his phone. He wasn't thinking about the call to his dad this time. He was thinking about Nate. He wanted to call just to hear the man's voice, to hear his assurances that he hadn't forgotten about Tim already.

It was stupid. That's why Tim didn't actually hit send. But he really wanted to.

When he got back to Matt's place, Matt was on him as soon as he came in the door.

"So, did you call your dad?"

"No."

"No? Why not? Dude, seriously, what's stopping you?"

Tim slumped onto the couch and sighed. "I'm tired, Matt. Give me a break."

"Did you at least call your boyfriend?"

When Tim didn't answer, Matt groaned. "Oh, come on. I can understand wanting to put off talking to your dad. But the way you talked about this guy, obviously you really like him, so why not call him?"

"He's probably back in California by now and tired from traveling. He said he had a ton of work to do once he got home. I just figured I'd give him a day or two to get settled. That's all." His voice sounded whiny even to himself, so he stopped there before it could get worse.

"You're an idiot."

"Yeah, well… I never said I wasn't," he grumbled petulantly.

"The dude offered for you to come live with him. I think maybe he'd be okay with calling to say hi."

"Or maybe, now that he's had a day to think about things, he's regretting making the offer and relieved I didn't take him up on it."

There it was. The real reason he hadn't been able to dial Nate's number the hundred or so times he'd thought about it over the last day and a half.

"You won't know unless you call," Matt said with an irritating amount of wisdom.

It was Tim's turn to groan. "I *know*. That's what I'm afraid of. Maybe I don't want to know the answer."

"You're a mess," Matt grumbled.

"No arguments there."

Matt went into their little kitchenette and pulled a Coke out of the refrigerator. He took a swig before he asked, "Did you have any luck finding a place today?"

"No. But don't worry. I'll find something."

Matt was quiet for a while before he sighed heavily and shook his head. "You can stay here until you do, man. I won't just kick you out into the cold."

Shocked and hopeful, Tim sat up and stared at his friend. "Dude, what about Drew?"

Matt grimaced and shrugged. "I'll talk to him. He's moving in this weekend, no matter what, but giving you only a week's notice was just shitty. He'll have to deal. That's all."

Feeling like at least some of the weight had been lifted off his shoulders, even though he dreaded the misery Drew would probably put them through, Tim was suddenly weak with relief. He jumped off the couch and threw his arms around Matt, hugging him hard before slapping his back a couple of times. "Thanks, man. I can't tell you how much this means to me."

"I'll remind you of that when you're about ready to kill Drew," he laughed. "But I have a couple of conditions."

*Uh-oh.*

"What?"

"First, you gotta promise me you'll call your dad and tell him what you want to do. And second, promise you'll call your man, too, none of this waiting for him to call you first bullshit. Got it?"

"Okay. Deal."

God, he was going to miss Matt when he did move out. He wasn't going to miss Matt's crappy, lumpy couch, but he would miss his friend.

Since he had the early shift the next day, Tim said good night not long after that, and Matt went to his room. He was a little less useless at work the following day. Since he'd already given his word he'd make the calls, he didn't spend his shift arguing with himself about it anymore. And by the time three o'clock rolled around, he'd almost psyched himself up enough that he didn't feel like he was going to throw up either.

After he clocked out, he headed for his car. His phone had a full charge and he still had plenty of minutes left, so there were no more excuses. If he was going to do it, it needed to be now. He brought up his dad's number, sucked in a deep breath, and hit send.

"Hello?" his Aunt Theresa answered on the second ring, and Tim smiled in relief.

"Hey, Aunt T, it's me."

"Hi, Timmy. How are you, sweetie?"

"I'm okay. I didn't know you were going to see Dad today."

"I had a doctor's appointment near here, so I decided to stop by."

"The doctor? Everything okay?" Even after all these years, Tim always had that strange plummeting feeling in his stomach whenever anyone in his family talked about going to the doctor.

"Oh, I'm fine. It was an annual checkup. That's all. Healthy as a horse, as always."

His stomach settled, and he felt the tightness in his chest ease. "Okay, good. How's he doing today?"

She sighed into the receiver. "He's asleep now. He was a bit grumpy this morning, but I managed to get some food in him. Other than that, pretty much the same as always."

"I know he doesn't say it often enough, but he really appreciates all you do for him. I do too. I want you to know that. I wish I could be more help," Tim said, suddenly realizing he wouldn't just be leaving his dad if he went with Nate. He'd be leaving her too.

"Oh, sweetie, you've got plenty of problems of your own. Your momma wouldn't have wanted you to have to worry so much. She asked me to look out for both of you, and that's exactly what I'll do. Don't you worry about me."

"I know he doesn't make it easy on you," Tim said quietly.

"Pfft. I work in home care, darlin'. I deal with more cantankerous old birds than him every day of the week. At least your dad's family. I can tell him to go to hell whenever I feel like it."

Tim laughed because he knew she wanted him to, but his smile didn't last long. "So he's asleep?"

As if on cue, Tim heard his dad's voice hollering in the background. "Who the hell are you talking to?"

"It's Timmy, and you don't have to be so loud," she hollered right back at him while Tim cringed on the other end of the line.

His dad didn't sound like he was in one of his better moods. That didn't bode well for their conversation.

"Here you go, sweetie. I'll talk to you soon," Theresa said. And then there was a pause as the phone was handed off.

"Tim?"

"Yeah, Dad, it's me."

"Decided to call instead of coming to see your old man this time, huh? I don't blame you."

They were going to start out with the guilt right away. Fabulous.

"I might still come by this week, Dad. I just had something I wanted to talk to you about."

"What now?"

Tim almost didn't do it. He was this close to chickening out, making up something stupid, just so he could get off the phone. But the thought of what would—and wouldn't—happen if he didn't at least try stopped him.

"Timmy? You still there?"

"Yeah, Dad, I'm here. I called because I wanted to tell you I might be going away for a little while. I have an… opportunity, and I want to take it."

"An opportunity? You mean a job?" The honest surprise in his dad's voice stung.

"No. Not yet, anyway. I… I met someone, Dad, someone special, and he lives in California."

"California? You mean a guy, right? You can't be serious." Disapproval and derision were a hell of a lot worse than surprise, and Tim dropped his head against the steering wheel as he tried to think of something to say to save the conversation.

He took a breath, cleared his throat, and tried again. "Look, I know you haven't exactly been overjoyed with my job situation. This is a chance for me to start over somewhere, maybe find something better… better money at least. Nate's a really great person, Dad. I think you'd like him if you met him." His dad was actually quiet on the other end of the line, and Tim had no idea whether that was a good sign or a bad one. He started babbling then just to fill the silence. "You remember Mom always said when I met the right person, I'd know? Well, I think this is him, Dad. I've finally met—"

The yelling started before Tim could finish that thought. "I don't want to hear any more. How dare you bring your mother into this? You want to do something completely stupid and irresponsible, it's all on you. Don't you use her as an excuse!"

"I only meant—"

"I don't give a rat's ass what you meant. If you want to go to California and leave us all behind, then go! But show some balls for once and own up to it. Hell, I should be grateful. At least you're doing something besides pissing your life away here with no rhyme or reason, no drive. Who knows? Maybe this guy'll take care of you so you don't have to work at all, be your sugar daddy. That's what they call it, right? You go on out there to California and make your momma *real* proud."

The man couldn't have hurt Tim more if he'd been there in person to deliver the backhand across his face.

"Dad, it's not like that. If you'll just listen for second—"

"I don't need to listen. You want to go, then go. I don't need you. I don't need any of you!"

Tim had to assume that last was shouted at his aunt, because a moment later, after the sound of the phone landing loudly on a hard surface, she was there. "Timmy? What's going on?"

"I'm sorry, Aunt T. I guess I should have tried to talk to him face-to-face, but I figured the conversation wouldn't have gone any better that way either. I hoped it would, but I didn't really expect it."

"What was he hollerin' about you leaving? Are you going somewhere?"

Tim's chest hurt. He couldn't leave her to deal with his dad on her own. How selfish would that be? "I was just thinking about it. I met someone really nice, Aunt T. I think you'd really like him. He wanted me to go back to California with him, to have a fresh start out there, but... but I told him I couldn't go."

It was hopeless. He couldn't do that to her.

"Why not? Don't you want to go?" The honest confusion in her voice surprised him.

"No, I want to go."

"Then I don't understand. If he wants you to go and you really want to, then what's stopping you?"

"I can't. I can't leave Dad. I promised to help take care of him."

*And you, not that I'm doing a bang-up job of it or anything.*

"Oh, sweetie, your momma made us all promise to take care of each other, but I'm sure she didn't mean for you to throw your whole life away in the process. I know she would've wanted the best for you."

Tim sniffed and rubbed at his eyes. He wasn't crying. His eyes were just a little itchy... allergies or something.

He wanted to believe her. God, he wanted to. But he wasn't sure if he could handle the guilt in the long run. "I don't think I can do it, T. What if something happens and I'm not here?"

Theresa let out a tired sigh, and then Tim heard the sliding glass door open and close. She must have moved outside to the deck.

"Timmy, I'm going to say something now that's going to sound pretty harsh. Don't get me wrong. I've loved your dad like family from the moment your momma brought him home to meet us. But you can't make a man get help if he doesn't want it. Both of us have spent years coming by to make sure he eats and to help out where we can. But in the end, it's up to him to get better. We can't do it for him... and sweetie, I don't think he wants to."

She paused there, and Tim tried to come up with a response but couldn't. Eventually she cleared her throat and said, "There comes a time when you have to start living for yourself too. If something happens, it's not your fault. You hear me? A man has to take some responsibility for taking care of his own damned self. He's your dad, not the other way around. He should have been there for you, and I may never forgive him for not doing right by you. I know for a fact he made the same promises to your mom we all did, and he's the only one of us not trying to keep them. It makes me so mad sometimes."

She sniffed on the other end of the line, and Tim's throat tightened a little more. Before he could force any words past the lump, she went on. "You listen to me, Timmy. You do what you need to. I think this might be the first time I've heard you get excited about anything since... well, in far too long. You do it."

"But Aunt T, if I leave, you'll be the only one left taking care of him. I can't ask you to do that."

"Sweetie, no one's asking me to do anything. Besides, you're not going to like what I have to say now either, but it needs to be said, okay?"

That sounded ominous. Tim wasn't sure if it was okay, but he murmured an assent anyway.

"You know I've worked in home care a long time. I've taken care of a lot of people near the end of their lives, and I've learned a thing or two along the way. Honey, you weren't born until your dad was over thirty. That means he's pushing sixty now. Ordinarily he'd have decades more to go. But, sweetie, he's been hitting the pills and booze real hard for a real long time. You and I both have tried to get him to the doctor, and he won't go. If I'm as brutally honest as I can be, I don't expect to be taking care of your daddy for much longer."

Her words landed heavily on his chest, but it wasn't as if they were a shock. Much as he hated to admit it, he'd thought the same things himself from time to time. No one could expect to go on forever like his dad had for the past seven years. Even before that, his dad had been a drinker, the fun kind who got a little loopy every night after work and on weekends. And now, since his wife died, he was never far from a bottle. But just because Tim realized these things in theory didn't mean he was ready to face them in reality.

"Sweetie? I'm sorry," Theresa began hesitantly. "I shouldn't have said that. I just don't want you to pass up an opportunity if it's what you really want. I wouldn't be keeping my own promises to my sister if I didn't look out for you too."

"I know. It's okay."

"I just want you to be happy again, darlin'. That's all."

"I think Nate's the one, Aunt T. The one Mom always talked about. Like with Grandma and Grandpa," Tim blurted out.

"Then don't let him get away. Don't let your life pass you by while you're waiting on the curb. Don't do what I did. Don't regret the chances you didn't take."

"Aunt T?" This was the first time Tim had ever heard his aunt talk about regretting anything.

But she didn't go into detail. "Listen to me rattling on. Just do what your momma always told you, sweetie. Follow your heart. She never had a regret a day in her life, and that's how it should be."

"Thanks, T. I love you so much."

"I love you too, honey. And when you make it big in California, you better fly me out there to see you. You hear?"

He laughed. "Yes, ma'am. I hear. I gotta go now. Will you tell him I love him for me? I don't think he wants to talk to me right now."

"I will. And remember what I said. You deserve to be taken care of too."

Tim ended the call and slumped back in his seat, feeling drained. Why did everything always have to be so hard? He was in love… or as close to it as he'd ever been in his life. Wasn't everything supposed to sunshine and roses now? He must have heard his mom tell the story of his grandparents falling in love at first sight and living happily ever after a hundred times growing up. Why wasn't it like she'd always made it sound?

He knew the answer to that. He wasn't a kid anymore and he wasn't stupid. But he wanted to wallow in self-pity a little longer, to stomp his feet and whine about how unfair it all was, so he could get it out of his system and then finally make a decision as to which choice he could live with.

Putting off agonizing over it a little longer, Tim stopped at the Y on the way home to take his frustrations out on the exercise machines. The place was a little crowded, and he had to wait a few times, but it was nice to just let his mind go blank and sweat for a while, even if his bruised ribs complained pretty loudly. The pain helped distract him, though, and that was a good thing.

By the time he got back to Matt's, he was no closer to making any kind of decision, but at least his body felt pleasantly tired, and the endorphin rush helped his mood a little. Matt wasn't there, so Tim took a long shower and then microwaved something out of the freezer again for dinner. He turned on the TV because the apartment was too quiet, but it didn't help. Now that he was out of distractions, his brain was so full of his dad and Nate and what the hell he was going to do about a place to live, he felt like it would explode at any second.

He was worked up and anxious, and despite feeling exhausted, he paced in front of the couch until he was sure he was wearing a trench in the cheap carpeting. Thankfully, for the sake of Matt's security deposit, salvation came at about ten that night, in the form of a call from Jana.

"Hey, sweetie!" she yelled over the club music in the background.

"Hey!"

If she had any idea how happy he was to hear her voice, she'd swear he'd gone straight.

"I wasn't sure if I'd get you on a weeknight, but I thought I'd let you know. We're working a special event at the club, and a group of us are going out for breakfast after we close. You said you'd be up for it next time we went."

Tim heard angels sing, and he was already rummaging through his bag for something to wear as he cried, "God yes! Meet you at the club?"

"Yeah, Josh and I are here. Come on over! I gotta go. They need me at the door. See ya!"

He needed this, a little space from his thoughts, or he was going to go batshit. His car was still warm, so it started up without any complaints, and Tim hoped that was a good omen for the night. When he pulled into South Beach's parking lot, the place was pretty full, but he lucked out with a spot at the far end of the lot, a definite benefit to going on a Thursday. The cover was pretty steep because of some special feature DJ, but Tim sure as hell wasn't going to wait around the apartment or in the parking lot. Familiar surroundings, casual friends, and a dance floor full of hot guys were the best distractions he could think of. The money would be well spent.

Jana waved him in without making him wait in line, and Tim felt his first real smile since he'd walked away from Nate. Was it pathetic that a club felt more like home to him than anyplace else right now?

Yeah. It probably was.

Josh was as gorgeous and unattainable as ever, holding court behind his bar. He brought Tim a drink early on but was too busy to chat. Tim was happy enough to simply watch the man work, flirting his way to good tips but deftly fending off any serious come-ons. All the other nights he'd spent at the club, Tim had been too busy scoping out his own prey to truly appreciate Josh's skills. It was like watching a master at work. The guy was Teflon. Nothing stuck to him, but he still managed to send his customers off with a smile.

The show at the bar and people-watching in general helped entertain him for a couple of hours at least, until Tim got bored and ventured out on the dance floor. He wasn't looking for anyone this time. He just wanted to lose himself in the music for a while. Keeping his eyes closed, he flowed with the crowd, feeling his body loosen up from any stiffness left over from his workout and the amount of stress he was under. He felt a few gropes and questioning brushes up against him, but he ignored them, and they soon faded away, seeking more enthusiastic prey. The thump of the bass and the rhythm of the music were his whole word, and he let his mind go blank. It was amazing what a little sweat, a little alcohol, and a bit of club energy could do to lift his spirits. It wouldn't last, but it helped.

Unfortunately, as the crowd got drunker, the press of bodies got a little too tight and the groping a little too distracting, bringing Tim back to himself, and he decided it was time to take a breather.

He was back at Josh's bar, joking around with him between customers, when he noticed a familiar face in the crowd, and his whole forget-about-Nate plan went up in smoke. When Ian spotted him too, the guy looked about as happy to see Tim as Tim was to see him. They were probably both hoping to get away from their problems for the night. And even though Tim didn't exactly feel any sympathy for the guy, he definitely understood the sentiment. Ian ducked back into the crowd, but not before Josh saw him.

"Hey. That's the guy, right? The one you were looking for?" Josh yelled over the music.

"Yeah. That's him. I caught up with him already at his job. Thanks for that, by the way."

"No problem. Though I'm not sure I did you any favors, judging by the bruises. Was that the 'disagreement' you were telling me about earlier? That little fucker didn't do that to you, did he?"

Tim snorted. "Not hardly. I think I could take Ian without this much damage, thanks."

Josh grinned and held up his hands. "No offense, dude. But it had something to do with it, right? You—shit, I gotta get back to work. You're going to tell me, though," he yelled over his shoulder as he moved to the other end of the bar.

Tim spotted Ian once or twice more, but he didn't bother to seek him out. They'd said all they needed to say the other day. Tim would let the cops decide what happened to the little shit.

Unfortunately, putting Ian out of his mind was a hell of a lot easier than getting Nate out of there, now that Ian had reminded him, and the rest of Tim's evening was spent wallowing in indecision while he threw back another two rum and Cokes. It was just as well he couldn't afford to buy any more, or he would've been plastered by the time last call came over the sound system.

For once in his life, Tim was actually relieved as the lights came up. He waved Josh over and told him he'd wait for them outside before making his way to the door with the rest of the stragglers. He was a little buzzed, so he wouldn't be driving to breakfast, but he figured he had another half hour at least to kill before Jana and Josh got out of there, and one of them could take him to the restaurant and back.

He'd just wait in his car until they were ready. But as he made his way to the back of the lot, a dark shape stepped out of the shadows right in front of him, and Tim jumped back, his heart in his throat.

"Hey," Ian said with a little awkward wave.

"Fuck, man. You nearly gave me a heart attack," he whined as he tried to get his breathing under control.

"Sorry. I was leaving, but then I saw your car, and I thought I should at least say something before I went."

"Okay." Tim was a little wary, but he honestly didn't think he had anything to fear from Ian.

"I felt like I should apologize again for what happened the other day… in the parking lot. It really was a shitty thing to do, telling them who you were, but I hope you know I didn't mean to get you in trouble with those guys."

Tim shrugged, so very ready for all of this to be done and over with. "Whatever. I'm not the kind who holds a grudge. Don't worry."

Ian smiled. "Thanks. Hey, that guy? Seward? I guess you're still talking to him?"

"Yeah?" Tim responded suspiciously.

"He's okay, right? I haven't been able to think about anything but that night for days now, and the more I think about it, the shittier I feel about what I did. It wasn't just stupid. It was *wrong*. He could have really been hurt by those guys, and I just panicked and went along with it instead of doing the right thing and calling the cops after things got crazy. That's not me. I swear."

Maybe Ian was a salvageable human being after all. Maybe not. Tim didn't actually care one way or the other. He just wanted to stop talking about it right now.

"I'll tell him," Tim said.

He was trying to come up with an excuse to send Ian on his way and get into his car when he caught movement out of the corner of his eye. Too slow, he ducked to the side as a fist came at his face, but the sucker punch only clipped his chin instead of laying him out. He heard Ian start to protest behind him, but the words ended in a grunt as he was knocked to the ground with a fist to the gut.

Tim had only a couple of seconds to realize how screwed he was before both guys were coming after him. Ian was currently useless on the ground, they were in the darkest corner of the parking lot, and Tim had had a hard enough time holding his own with these two even when he wasn't buzzed and sporting a set of bruised ribs. He backed away from the two men with his hands up, trying to get a car between him and them.

"Hey, guys! I'd say it was good to see you again, but Momma always told me not to lie."

They didn't laugh, but Tim hadn't really expected them to.

The little ugly one, Peter, glowered at him as the two men advanced. "Because of you and your little bitch friend here, I spent last night in jail, faggot. You won't think this is so goddamned funny when we're done. You're gonna learn to keep your fucking mouths shut— you two cocksuckers and that fucking suit—if we have to make it so they wire your goddamned jaw shut at the ER."

Oh, wonderful, not just revenge but also some incentive not to talk to the cops, a perfect cap to a stellar week.

Tim kept backing up until his ass hit the door of his car. He had nowhere else to go. There was no way he'd be able to get inside before they were on him, and the smiles on their faces showed they knew it too.

"When we came back here looking for that little cocksucker," the short one said, pointing to Ian, still wheezing on the ground, "who knew we'd get two for the price of one? Must be our lucky night."

Tim sent a little prayer heavenward, straightened, and fisted his hands. They may kick the ever-loving shit out of him, but he sure as hell wasn't going to make it easy. They both took another step toward him, but a sudden shout from across the lot made everyone turn in that direction. Tim nearly swooned in relief as he saw Jana, Josh, and one of the other bouncers running across the lot.

"Hey! What the hell's going on?" Jana shouted in her butchest crowd-control voice. Tim had only ever heard it once before, when a fight broke out inside the club, but he had to admit it was effective. The two assholes looking to kick the shit out of him took about two seconds to weigh their chances before it appeared they decided to make a run for it. Jana and the others didn't give chase. Not all the streets around there had good lighting, and only an idiot would go running out into the dark.

"Fuck! Thanks, guys. You saved my ass," Tim said as he slumped against his car in relief.

"Who the hell were those guys? What's going on?" Josh asked as he bent down to help Ian to his feet.

"It's a long story," Tim said wearily. He'd really had enough of this bullshit. Was it ever going to end?

"Well, Freddie called the cops when he saw you guys from the door, so you've got some time to tell it, if you want," Josh said.

"You think Freddie would mind if we did it inside?" Ian wheezed. He had an arm across his stomach, and he didn't seem to be able to stand up straight. They all shared a look, and Tim rolled his eyes.

Josh helped Ian inside and into a chair while Ian gazed up at him adoringly, clearly enjoying the attention. Tim followed not far behind, starting to feel a little drained now that the adrenaline rush was wearing off. At least he didn't have to do much except sit there, because now that Ian had Josh as an audience, Ian was the one telling their story, embellishing his side of the tale just a bit and gesticulating wildly. Freddie, the manager, joined them not long after they came inside, and they all listened raptly to Ian's tale. Unfortunately for Ian, as soon as he was done, Josh didn't coo and fuss over him as he'd clearly hoped. Instead, Josh moved closer to Tim and squinted at the spot on his face where the bastard had gotten in the sucker punch.

"Damn, Tim. Sounds like you're on an episode of *Dallas* or something," Josh said, and everyone cracked up, even Ian.

"Tell me about it, man."

He didn't even want to think about what would have happened if they hadn't come to his rescue. He might have gotten his reunion with Nate, but it would have probably been at a hospital after the cops called him, not exactly the romantic scene Tim had pictured in his mind.

Nate.

"Shit." A surge of panic made Tim's stomach drop to his shoes, and a sudden memory of those guys saying something about shutting up "the suit" popped into his head.

"What?" Jana asked.

"I gotta make a call. Hang on a second." Tim pulled out his phone and dialed Nate's cell with shaking fingers. As it rang, Tim tried to calm the panic by telling himself Nate was already in California, safe and sound. Tim just needed to check and make sure. By the fourth ring, though, Tim was having a hard time convincing his racing heart of that. But then, *finally*, a very sleepy sounding Nate mumbled, "Hello?"

"Oh good," Tim breathed out. "You're okay. Right? You're good?"

"Tim?" There were rustling noises. "Tim, is that you?"

"Yeah, it's me." Tim's voice wobbled a little, and he cleared his throat to cover it up. It was a reaction to the adrenaline rush from earlier. That was all.

"What's going on? What time is it?"

"Late... or early, actually. It's probably closer to two there maybe. I'm sorry for waking you. I just wanted to make sure you were okay."

"What's wrong?"

Tim closed his eyes and breathed through some of the panic, forcing himself to relax. "I'm sorry I woke you. I just saw those guys again, the ones we talked to the cops about, and I was worried. But of course you're safe at home, and they wouldn't be able to get to you there, right?"

"Where are you?" Nate's voice was sharp with worry, and Tim cringed. He hadn't meant to do that.

"I'm at the club. I had a lot on my mind, and Jana and Josh invited me to breakfast, so I decided to get out for a while." Tim wasn't sure why he felt the need to defend his going to the club, but he did. He didn't want Nate thinking he was out tricking so soon after all they'd shared.

"Tim—"

There was a commotion at the door, and Tim couldn't hear whatever else Nate said. When he looked up, he saw a couple of uniforms talking to Freddie. He really didn't want to hang up with Nate, but it was the middle of the night, and he'd already obviously woken the guy up from a dead sleep. Whatever else he needed to say could wait until morning. Maybe he'd figure out what it was he wanted to say by then.

"Hey, Nate, I gotta go. The cops are here. I just wanted to make sure you were okay. I'll call you later."

"Cops?"

"Okay, bye." Tim hung up and braced himself for another interrogation.

BY THE time the police officers were done with him, Ian, Jana, and Josh, Tim no longer felt like going to breakfast. He was exhausted, and for the first time ever, crashing on Matt's lumpy couch sounded like heaven. Besides, if he chose to stay in Houston, this would be one of the last nights he could do that before Drew moved in and things got ugly. He should probably take advantage of the peace and quiet while he still could.

"Hey, guys, I'm sorry, but I think I'm going to bug out. I've had enough excitement for one night," he said as he walked over to where Josh and Jana were sitting and talking.

"Sure, sweetie, we were just thinking the same thing. Maybe next time," Jana said before she yawned hugely.

Ian, who'd been watching Josh with a focus that bordered on creepy, finally seemed able to tear his gaze away when Tim walked up. But whatever he'd been about to say died on his lips as his gaze suddenly shifted over Tim's shoulder and his eyes bugged out. When Tim swung around to see what Ian was looking at, he found Nate standing just inside the club's door, searching the place. Tim's feet were moving before his surprise even registered.

Nate was here?

Tim didn't run to him, he had a little more pride than that, but it was a near thing. He was smiling so wide his face nearly cracked by the time he pulled up short, only a couple of feet from him.

"Nate?" he breathed out. "I don't understand. I thought you were going back to California."

Nate closed the distance between them and touched the sore spot on Tim's jaw with gentle fingers. "Are you okay? I got a cab down here as soon as I could. You don't need to go the hospital, do you?"

"No. He only got in one good punch before my friends helped bail me out." Tim's voice shook with everything he was feeling, and he was afraid of embarrassing himself if he tried to say anything more, so he just wrapped his arms around Nate's back and buried his face in Nate's neck, breathing him in. A moment later, Nate's arms came up and hugged him tight. And as Tim continued to cling to him, Nate began rocking them just a little bit.

"It's going to be okay," Nate whispered against his hair as he squeezed Tim tighter. Tim was embarrassed by his own clinginess but not enough to let go.

"Tim?" Nate murmured.

"Mmmmmm?"

Nate's chuckle vibrated through his chest. "Will you come back to the hotel with me?"

"Oh God, yes."

But Tim couldn't bring himself to release his grip on Nate until he heard Jana say from somewhere close, "Hey, sweetie. We're going to hit the road, now that we see you'll be taken care of."

The laughter in her voice finally broke the spell, and Tim was able to step back from Nate's embrace long enough to hug her and Josh good-bye.

Ian hovered just beyond their little group, and Tim felt a little sorry for him as Ian waved awkwardly at them and followed the other two out. When Tim turned back to Nate, Nate was staring after Ian with a frown on his face.

"What was he doing here?"

"I don't know. I guess just hanging out. This is one of his regular haunts, according to Josh. The guys that jumped us tonight actually came here looking for *him*. I was just a bonus."

Nate's expression softened as he turned back to Tim. "Come on. Let's go. You look like you're dead on your feet."

"I am a little. But it's so good to see you, Nate." He was exhausted, and he was gushing. He really needed to stop now.

They walked to Tim's car, and Nate insisted on driving. Tim wanted to talk once they were on the road, maybe say something a little more cool and dignified to salvage his pride, but the heater in his car was on full blast, and he kind of passed out until Nate shook him awake in front of the hotel. He revived a little on the elevator. But as soon as Nate had him stripped down and underneath the blankets in his room, Tim couldn't keep his eyes open anymore. The hows and wheres and whys could wait until morning. The important part was Nate was there, warm and solid, spooned against his back. If that was all he had for the rest of his life, he'd die a happy man.

# Chapter Thirteen

NATHAN WOKE the following morning to a very horny Tim. Somehow Nathan had ended up on his back, and Tim had crawled on top of him and was now rubbing their morning wood together. Tim was grinning down at him, his green eyes filled with heat and mischief, and Nathan couldn't help but laugh. It bubbled out of him even as his blood heated. It was a wonderful thing to wake up feeling happy, not just content or determined or pleased but *happy*, joyful. How many people in this world had a chance to wake up this way every morning?

They still had a lot to talk about, and Nathan didn't know how long they would have together beyond today. But Tim was now draped over Nathan's chest, sucking on his earlobe and whispering dirty things in his ear, so Nathan sure as hell wasn't going to stop and have a conversation now, even if he could pull enough brain cells together to manage it.

They didn't have any condoms or lube this time because Nathan was still an idiot and still hadn't thought to go shopping for them, and Tim didn't have any with him either. Nathan could have called the concierge, but he probably would have been too embarrassed to even get the words out, let alone face whoever came to the door with them, and Nathan sure as hell wasn't leaving the room any time soon.

Tim seemed a little disappointed by the lack of supplies, but he gave Nathan one outstanding blowjob anyway. And afterward, Nathan did his best to return the favor while Tim whispered tons of filthy words of encouragement. Nathan had been a little embarrassed by it at first, but the more Tim talked, the hotter Nathan got. This was another first, being with someone who liked to talk dirty during sex, but he liked it as much as everything else Tim had shown him. He probably wouldn't ever be able to join in on the sexy talk without blushing and stumbling over his words, but Tim didn't seem to need any help.

After a little post-orgasmic nap, Nathan awoke to find Tim gazing up at him with a contented smile but eyes full of questions.

"I'm definitely not complaining, but how come you're still here?" Tim asked quietly.

Nathan propped himself up on an elbow so he could see Tim a little better and trailed his fingers along the stubble just starting on Tim's jaw, still a little in awe that he could reach out and touch him any time he wanted. "I couldn't quite bring myself to leave. I know I said there's tons of work waiting for me back home, but…." He shrugged. "After being with you and having everything I'd planned fall apart, I realized I didn't actually know why I was pushing myself so hard anymore. Sean encouraged me to take a few days, since I'd probably be fairly useless at work right now anyway. I'm not feeling particularly focused."

"Why didn't you tell me you were still here? I would have come to see you last night instead of going to the club if I'd known."

Tim's eyes were a little hurt now, and Nathan kissed him and pulled him closer. "I'm sorry. I thought you needed a little space. Maybe I needed a little space. I was disappointed you couldn't come with me, but I understood. I love my family very much too. And if one of them needed me, I'd want to be there for them. I didn't want to pressure you, and I knew I would if I saw you." Nate laughed a little ruefully. "I've actually spent the last couple of days just walking around and thinking about things."

"What kind of things?"

"You, for one," Nathan said with a grin. "And my business… my personal life—what there is of it—my family. I haven't gone home to see my family in forever. I was always too busy with work to take the time, always saying next year, next year I'd go. So yesterday, I called my mom and dad and then my sisters. We had some really nice conversations, and I promised to take some time to visit them really soon." Nathan gave Tim's shoulders a little shake and kissed him again. "They have you to thank for that, you know. *I* have you to thank for that. Even with all this craziness, I don't know that I would have figured it out on my own."

Tim blushed, but Nathan could tell he was pleased. "I think you don't give yourself enough credit, Nate. But, thank you. I don't think anyone has ever told me I made a difference in their life before. You... you've made a big difference in me too. I—" Tim cut off there and shook his head.

When it seemed as if he wasn't going to complete the thought, Nathan touched his cheek and said, "Hey. What is it?"

Tim swallowed and lifted his gaze to Nathan's again. "I want to come with you." The words were rushed, and Tim seemed a little breathless. Nathan was feeling a little out of breath himself.

"Are you sure?"

"Yes, I'm sure."

"What about your dad?" He didn't really want to ask, but he felt like he should so everything was out on the table, no surprise changes of heart later.

Tim looked away from him. "I've thought about this a lot since the last time we talked. I love him, and I want to help. But I don't think I can anymore, not really. My aunt and I have been checking up on him for *seven years*, and he's only getting worse. He won't get help. He won't listen to us. I don't know what to do for him anymore. I just... I just want to be with you and start over somewhere else so much." Tim stopped and took a few breaths. "I don't want to leave him behind, but I can't go on like I have been. I'm afraid I'll end up just like him someday if I do."

Tim fell silent then, and Nathan wasn't sure what he should do to help. He petted Tim's hair and kissed his temple because it was the only thing he could think of, and Tim sighed and buried his face in Nathan's neck. "I love you," Tim whispered against his skin. "I know it's probably too soon—and crazy—but I do."

Nathan closed his eyes and squeezed Tim tighter. "Then we're both crazy, I guess," he whispered back. "This is real. We're going to do this," he said louder, as much to reassure himself as Tim. His heart was racing and his stomach was full of butterflies, but he wanted this more than anything else right now.

Tim drew in an unsteady breath and pulled away enough to look him in the eye. The smile he gave Nathan was watery as he nodded firmly and said, "Yeah. Let's do this."

After a quick breakfast and a slow shower, they headed off in Tim's car to his friend's apartment to collect his things, grinning like fools. Tim assured Nathan he didn't have enough stuff to bother having it shipped, so they made a quick stop at a department store to buy a few large suitcases instead. Nathan would happily pay the extra baggage fees to have everything finished by the time they got on that plane.

But on the way back to the car from the store, Tim was unusually grave and silent, and Nathan started to worry that Tim might be having second thoughts already. Nathan had almost gotten up the courage to ask him what was wrong when Tim said, "I'm sorry about the money. I'll pay you back as soon as I can."

More than a little relieved that that was all it was, Nathan lifted a hand to wave away Tim's concerns. But then he remembered their previous conversations and the insecurities that Tim had been brave enough to share with him, and he stopped. He might not know all he needed to make a relationship work yet, but there were a few fundamentals that were mentioned in nearly every book he'd ever read about interpersonal interaction, like listening, paying attention, and showing respect for other people's perspectives. He let his hand drop back down to his side and said, "You can pay me back later, if you want to, when you get settled and figure out what you want to do. I'm not in a hurry."

The smile Tim gave him was a little mollified, but not as much as Nathan had hoped. He thought he'd picked the right thing to say, but now he wasn't so sure. Reviewing some of their earlier conversations as Tim pulled out of the parking lot, Nathan tried a different approach, the unvarnished truth Tim seemed to like so much. "Tim, I'm the one asking you to uproot your whole life and move with me to somewhere you've never even been before, remember? It's not like you aren't making any sacrifices here. Let me help. Please?"

After a few tense moments of silence, Tim gave him a lopsided grin, leaned across the seat, and kissed him quickly before turning his attention back to the road. "Thank you."

Nathan slumped back in his seat, relieved. "You're welcome."

The apartment Tim took him to was tiny and not much to look at. Nathan couldn't imagine being crammed in there with another person, sleeping on the couch every night. He kept his observations to himself, though. Tim might prize honesty, but even Nathan knew there could be too much of it. Despite the weirdness that was his family, Nathan's mom had at least taught him a few things about being a guest in someone's home.

"Nate, this is Matt, the most generous friend a guy could ask for. Matt, this is Nate," Tim said by way of introduction.

"Nice to meet you," Nathan said, shaking Matt's hand.

Matt's smile was broad as he looked between Nathan and Tim. "So you're really going to do it?" he asked Tim.

Tim drew in a shaky breath and nodded. "Yup. I'm here to pack my things, and we're off tomorrow." Tim winked at Nathan before moving with Matt to a hall closet and pulling a couple of bags out.

Matt was a little shorter than Tim, with dark wavy hair and smiling brown eyes. Nathan thought he was pretty good looking, even if the man didn't ring any of Nathan's bells, and a slight twinge of jealousy popped up out of nowhere as he watched the two men pack up Tim's things.

After they'd wheeled the suitcases full of Tim's few belongings out to the taxi they called so they could leave Tim's car with Matt, Matt stood awkwardly nearby while Nathan and Tim and the cab driver squeezed them into the trunk and back seat of the cab.

"I guess that's it," Tim said as he approached Matt and stood uncomfortably in front of him.

"Yeah, I guess it is. Good luck, man," Matt said, rocking on the balls of his feet.

"Thanks for everything, Matt. I owe you, big time."

Nathan hung back a little, giving them a chance to say their good-byes. Matt seemed like a nice guy. He'd certainly been a good friend to Tim. Looking at the two of them together, Nate wondered absently why they'd never hooked up. He'd have to ask Tim more about the guy later, only because he was curious, not because he was worried or anything.

They spent that night in the hotel together again. Tim seemed nervous and a little withdrawn, so Nathan didn't push for any deep or intimate conversation. They'd have plenty of time for that later. While Tim made a few calls, finding people to cover his shifts and officially resigning from his jobs, Nathan kept himself busy with work e-mails, reluctantly prioritizing them for when he got back to work.

He'd talked to Sean a few times over the past few days, and he knew his friend was worried, but he hadn't felt like spilling the beans just yet.

"You have until next Monday to either get your ass back here or tell me exactly what the heck is going on. Otherwise, I'm coming down there myself to put you on the flight home. Got me?" Sean had said before they hung up the last time.

Nathan smiled just thinking about it now. He considered giving Sean a heads-up that he was coming home with Tim but decided against it. He was pretty sure Sean would be at Nathan's house the second they got off the plane to find out what was going on, and Nathan wasn't quite ready for that yet. He had Tim all to himself until Monday, and he wanted every second of that to get them both settled before the rest of his life came rushing back in to distract him.

After their phone calls and business were done, Tim and Nathan curled up on the couch together, watched a movie, and sampled whatever sounded good from the room service menu. They both had a bit too much wine, but Nathan figured they needed it. Nathan dozed off during the movie, and when he woke, Tim was gone. Before he could panic, Nathan got a happy surprise when Tim came back to the couch naked and holding condoms and lube with a sexy smirk on his face. And then Nathan was naked on that couch, and Tim was riding him, providing a show Nathan hoped he got to see as often as humanly possible in the future. He came, shouting Tim's name, and luckily his vision cleared quickly enough to watch Tim jerk his own cock until he shot all over his hand and Nathan's chest.

"God, that was hot," Nathan gasped after Tim flopped bonelessly on top of him, apparently without a thought for the mess between them.

Tim started giggling for no reason Nathan could figure out, but eventually, Nathan couldn't help but join him. They giggled their way through cleanup and all the way to the bed, and Nathan fell asleep thinking this was how life was supposed to be and hopefully would be from now on.

They next day was a blur, up until the plane took off. Hungover as he was, Nathan still managed to get them on a decently early flight so they didn't have long to wait. Tim was a nervous wreck because this was his first time on a plane *ever*, and he hadn't felt the need to tell Nathan that until they were about to take off. Nathan would have yelled at him, but Tim looked like he was having a hard enough time keeping his breakfast down as it was, so he decided to keep his irritation to himself... at least until they were safe at his house. Then all bets were off.

Tim clutched Nathan's hand like a lifeline during takeoff, nearly squeezing all the blood out of Nathan's fingers in the process. But once the plane was in the air, he seemed to settle down and actually enjoy the flight. Nathan had given him the window seat, and Tim spent most of the flight with his face practically plastered to the glass, watching the world go by.

"Looks like I may have created a monster. You're going to want to fly all the time now," Nathan joked after about the fifth time Tim told him to look at something amazing outside the window.

Tim grinned sheepishly and shook his head. "Let's get the landing over with before we go all crazy. Baby steps, baby steps."

Tim needn't have worried. The landing was a little bumpy but otherwise flawless. The airport was another matter. God, Nathan hated airports, people everywhere, feeling like he was in everyone's way. It was Tim who got his hand squeezed bloodless during that part of the trip, but he didn't seem to mind as Nathan dragged him through the terminals until they were outside in the open air.

Unfortunately, once they were in the taxi on the way to Nathan's house, Nathan's nerves kicked in for an entirely different reason. They were about five miles out when Nathan suddenly felt feverish and sweaty, much worse than he'd felt in the airport.

This was it.

They were almost home. There was no going back now. There was probably no going back for several days now, but being home just made the finality of it more real. Nathan really hoped Tim liked his house. He hoped everything was as perfect as it seemed. He hoped he hadn't made a mistake choosing to be this impulsive for probably the first time in his entire life. He hoped Tim didn't stay with him for a week and then decide Nathan was too much of a freak to live with.

*Okay, maybe it's more than a "little" attack of nerves.*

The sweats only lasted long enough for them to pull up in front of his somewhat ordinary two-level beige stucco house, because as soon as Tim got out of the car, he turned to Nathan with his eyes round and the biggest smile on his face. "Wow. God, Nate, your house is great."

Then the warm fuzzies started in Nathan's chest again, and he felt like everything was going to be all right. Tim was wonderful and sweet and so goddamned open it was heart wrenching. They were going to be okay. Nathan just knew it.

After hauling all their bags inside, they both collapsed on the couch. It didn't seem to matter that all he'd done was sit on his ass on a plane and then in a taxi, traveling was always exhausting. Nathan had enough energy to call for a pizza, but that was about it. He'd have to give the nickel tour later, when he wasn't half-asleep.

Thankfully, Tim seemed just as exhausted by his ordeal as Nathan and was content to cuddle with him on the couch until the pizza arrived. Once they'd scarfed down every slice, they napped for a couple of hours on the couch. And when Nathan opened his eyes again, the house was dark and quiet but for Tim's breathing. Nathan smiled happily down at Tim's sleeping face and would have been content to just listen to the man's heartbeat alleviate the aching quiet that usually pervaded his home. But his bladder had other ideas, and eventually Nathan had to give in and take care of it.

Tim was sitting up and rubbing his eyes when Nathan came out of the bathroom, so Nathan turned on the light in the kitchen so he could see a little better but wouldn't blind Tim.

"Hey there," Nathan said happily, stealing a kiss from Tim after he plopped down on the couch beside him.

"Hey," Tim said, a little shyly. "What time is it?"

"Nine thirty I think. Ready to go to bed?"

At Nathan's grin, Tim laughed and waggled his eyebrows. "I'm ready if you are."

"We can worry about the rest of this stuff tomorrow. We have the whole weekend to get you settled," he said as he stood up and held out a hand. "Sean's promised not to send out the cavalry until Monday."

Tim took the offered hand and pulled himself up, but the look he gave Nathan wasn't amused or happy. It was worried. "I'm not screwing things up with your job or anything, am I? I mean, I can unpack my own stuff and get settled if you need to go into work. Just show me where I should put it."

Nathan shook his head and gave Tim a peck on the lips. "No. It's fine. Besides, I *want* to spend the weekend with you. I'm looking forward to it."

That must have been the right thing to say because Tim's smile was radiant. He stepped in close to Nathan and hooked his fingers in Nathan's belt loops. "I'm really happy to be here, Nate. Despite all the guilt and everything about my dad and being a little worried you'll wake up at any minute and decide you've made a huge mistake, I don't think I've felt this right about a decision I've made since before my mom died."

"It feels right to me too. I'm not going to change my mind. Come on. Let's see if I can make a few other things feel right as well."

Tim snorted at Nathan's corny joke, and Nathan took his hand and led him upstairs to the bedroom. The room was just as he'd left it, although it looked a lot colder and more austere than he remembered, for some reason. Maybe it was seeing it through Tim's eyes that made the difference. He noticed things he never paid much attention to on his own, like there were no pictures on the walls. There was a rug on the wood floor at least, blinds on the windows, and blankets on the bed, but everything was solid and dark, no prints anywhere to make things a little more interesting. He felt kind of self-conscious about his place now. But when he turned to see Tim's reaction, Tim only had eyes for him. He wasn't even looking at the room. And the heat was enough to make Nathan forget all about his decorating shortfalls. His bed was comfortable and worked just fine, whether it was bland or not.

Tim backed Nathan toward the bed as he undid the buttons on Nathan's dress shirt. But Nathan wasn't going to let Tim have all the fun, and he tugged Tim's shirt out of his jeans, skimming his fingers over the soft skin of Tim's belly, teasing along his light treasure trail. Tim dove in for a kiss, and they tumbled onto the mattress, laughing. Nathan couldn't remember sex ever being this much fun. They were still laughing as they both kicked off their shoes and shimmied out of their pants. The process involved a great deal of wrestling, as neither one of them seemed to want to lose contact with the other for long enough to get the job done. Nathan almost got an elbow in the face when he tackled Tim to the bed and pinned him down, but he was pretty sure he wouldn't have minded. He felt joyful and lighthearted, like the crazy Tom Cruise on *Oprah*. Sean would probably send him to the doctor again if he could see him now, but Nathan didn't care. He grinned like a fool and kissed Tim's lips until Tim suddenly pulled away and groaned... and not a happy groan.

"What? What did I do?"

Tim pouted at him. "Do you have any stuff? Lube and condoms?"

Nathan shook his head. "Sorry. I haven't been that optimistic about my chances of getting a date back to my house in a long time."

Tim rolled his eyes and sniggered. "I think your chances were better than you realized. But that doesn't help us now. Damn.... Oh, wait. Duh. I have some in my stuff." Tim hopped out of bed and hurried to the door, apparently completely unconcerned with the fact that he was stark naked, not that Nathan minded or anything. The view was quite spectacular. He guessed it was just one more thing he'd have to get used to.

He'd suffer through somehow.

After only a few moments, Tim came rushing back, the condoms and lube held triumphantly in his hands and a happy grin on his face. He hopped back on the bed, and Nathan was wrapped in all that tanned skin and muscle. He couldn't have been happier.

They made love twice that night and once more first thing in the morning. After a shower, Tim cooked them breakfast, working miracles with the odd assortment of baking supplies and whatever Nate had in his freezer from the last time his mom had come to visit. Nathan originally offered to order in, but Tim had obviously wanted to show what he could do. And what he could do was damned impressive, especially to a guy who ate most of his meals out of a box when he was home.

"Oh my God. That was good," Nathan groaned as he patted his full belly. "You do realize this means you're going to be doing the cooking from now on, since my idea of preparing a meal is digging through the drawer of take-out menus."

Tim flushed a little at the compliment and shrugged. "I don't mind. I have to earn my keep somehow until I can find a job."

That sobered Nathan up a little, and he reached across the table and took Tim's hand. "I don't want you to feel like you need to earn your keep, Tim. You don't have to rush anything. From all you've told me, you've been pushing yourself pretty hard for a long time, the same as me. Take a little break. Relax and get your bearings."

Tim shook his head stubbornly. "Thanks. But I can't just sit around while you're at work all day. That wouldn't be right."

Even with his minimal experience in relationships, Nathan had a feeling money was going to be a difficult subject for them going forward. He didn't want it to be. He didn't see what the big deal was, but he was smart enough not to pick a fight about it now. "Okay, sure. I just wanted you to know it's okay to take some time for yourself, if you need it."

The smile Tim gave him was grateful, but he still looked determined. "Matt's agreed to sell my car to his uncle, but that money isn't going to last long. I'm gonna need to get a job soon, just to keep up with my student loan payments, even if I'm not paying rent here right away. It's very generous of you. But I got bills to pay."

"I could help you out with those until you've found something."

Tim's chin jutted out and he looked like he was getting upset, so Nathan held up his hands in surrender.

"Okay. I'm not trying to insult you. I just want you to be happy."

The frown Tim was giving him eased into a half smile. "I know, Nate. I'm sorry. I am happy. I'm just used to taking care of myself, and I don't want you to think of me as a charity case or anything. I know you have your shit together a hell of a lot better than I do. And maybe that doesn't make a difference to you, but it does to me."

"I guess that's one of the things we should maybe talk about, huh?" Nathan let go of Tim's hand and stood up. "Why don't we go somewhere a little more comfortable?"

Tim was a little tense when he joined Nathan on the couch in the living room, but Nathan wasn't having any of that. He stretched his legs out across the cushions and pulled Tim down until his head was resting on Nathan's chest.

"So obviously, I'm new at this relationship stuff," Nathan began as he ran his fingernails over Tim's scalp. "I'm going to make mistakes, I'm sure, until I figure out what I'm doing."

In the back of Nathan's mind, he was already scheduling time to go shopping online for self-help books on relationships to add to his rather impressive library on business management, interpersonal communication, and team building.

Tim sighed heavily and ran a hand over Nathan's chest. "Nate, I'm not exactly an expert either. I'm not mad. I promise." Tim rose up on his elbow and held Nate's gaze, nothing but earnestness and sincerity radiating from his eyes. "I just don't want to be a burden. My bills are my fault, my responsibility. It wouldn't be fair to make you pay for them. And I don't feel right about being in debt to you any more than I already am."

Nathan opened his mouth to argue, but Tim put his fingers to Nathan's lips, shutting him up. "I know you said you were the one asking me to leave my whole life behind and travel to a new place. But it isn't as if I didn't want to do it. I feel like you've given me the opportunity of a lifetime here, a new beginning. I can find my dreams and do all the settling in I need to while I work. The job I get doesn't have to be anything major, just something to keep a little money coming in while I figure out what it is I really want to do."

Nathan smiled against Tim's fingers, wrapped his hand around them, and drew them away from his lips. "Okay. I just want you to be as happy with me here as you possibly can so you'll never want to leave. You've done more for me already than I think you know. I don't want to lose that."

"Believe me. You won't. I'm not going anywhere," Tim said before snuggling against his chest again.

They took a little morning nap but were woken by Nathan's cell phone not long after. He didn't have the number in his contacts, but he recognized the area code.

"Hello?"

"Mr. Seward, this is Detective Jimenez."

"Oh, yeah. Hello, Detective."

"I've been trying to get in contact with your friend, Mr. Conrad. I've left messages, but I haven't received a reply. Do you happen to know where he is?"

Nathan looked down at Tim and smiled. "Yes, he's here. Maybe he hasn't turned his phone back on from the flight. Hold on."

Nathan gave Tim a little shake and handed him the phone.

"Hello. Yes, this is Tim." Tim listened for a minute, and then his face broke out in a relieved smile. "Oh, great. That's great news." Tim pulled the phone away from his face and said to Nathan, "They got him, Peter. They found him and his friend. He's been arrested again."

Nathan was relieved too. Even though they were far away now, it still worried him that Peter Vold was out there and probably more pissed off than he'd been before.

"I'm still here," Tim said back into the receiver. "Yes. I'll be back to testify when the time comes. Wait. Hold on." Tim pulled it away from his face again and pressed the speaker button. "You're on speaker. Nate should hear this too."

"Okay. As I was saying"—Jimenez's voice came out a little hollow but clear—"we followed up on the information Mr. Seward provided and looked into Mr. Peter Vold a little closer, and we believe we found the connection. Peter's dad just so happens to own a small computer contracting company, like yours, Mr. Seward. I don't know the details, but it appears as if he's done work for Frontier Global Energy before. I talked to some employees at FGE, and they remember him. He still has some friends there apparently."

Nathan didn't understand. "I don't remember hearing about any other small companies in the running, though, so why would his son target me?"

"We picked Mr. Vold Sr. up for questioning, but he denies being involved. He did give up his son's location pretty quickly, however, to show he was cooperating with us, which I thought was a bit odd, but he says he has no knowledge of his son's activities." Jimenez paused there to give them time to digest that bit before he continued. "I will tell you what some of the employees at FGE had to say regarding this whole contract thing you were trying for, and maybe it will make a little more sense. One of the VPs I spoke with said FGE was actually looking to give your contract to a smaller company this go round. Apparently what started all this is the company's desire to distance themselves from some bad PR, environmental screwups and stuff like that. The whole 'creating a new company to put their green research programs into' is smoke and mirrors, a shiny new coat of paint, and with the new company, they were leaning toward little companies like yours to contract with because I guess it sounded better than just the same old dinosaurs they've been using. You know, fresh, new, exciting, supporting small business, yadda, yadda."

"Okay," Nathan replied. "I guess I get that. But where does Vold's dad come in?"

"Seems he had a little inside information about this plan and was going to make a last-minute bid. The people I talked to said they thought he might be in a little financial difficulty and couldn't beat your bid. But if you were out of the running…."

Jimenez didn't need to finish. Nathan got the gist. "You think he was that desperate?"

"To tell you the truth, I've seen people do a lot more for a lot less, Mr. Seward. But unfortunately, proving any of this is going to be next to impossible. I talked to the other witness, Ian, and while he backs up your story, he never heard Peter Vold actually admit to drugging you. He says Mr. Vold 'expected you to get sleepy,' but a good lawyer would only argue you were drinking wine and he was waiting for you to get drunk. Also, Ian never actually saw Mr. Vold at the club that night taking pictures. The only thing he can say is Vold paid him to take you to a club and call him when you got there. I'm sorry, but we have a lot of circumstantial but not a lot of concrete evidence, and juries today like everything tied up in a nice little bow for them."

Tim looked angry, but Nathan only shrugged. "I understand. I'll be happy if he goes away on the assault charges. I'd be happier, of course, if he went away on all of it, but I'll take what I can get."

"Well, we have him now. We'll lean on him some more, and we'll talk to the DA's office about it, see if it's enough to build a case for the rest. I'll keep in touch."

"Thank you."

"Thanks," Tim said before hanging up. "I'm sorry, Nate."

Nathan shook his head. "Don't worry about it. I was more concerned about what he did to you anyway. If you want the absolute truth, I'll be glad to let it go as long as he goes to jail for something."

Tim kissed him and gave him a hug before climbing off the couch and wandering into the kitchen for a snack. That afternoon they spent some time shuffling Nathan's stuff around to make room for Tim's. Despite his offer of a room of his own, Tim opted to share Nathan's bedroom, and Nathan wasn't exactly disappointed by that. All he had to do was move a few clothes he rarely wore into one of the other bedrooms and Tim's entire wardrobe fit into a few drawers in the dresser and a small part of the closet. The process gave Nathan tons of ideas of gifts to buy Tim, but it also made him realize he didn't have very much stuff to move around.

When he gave Tim the tour of the house, most of the rooms were empty. He remembered having good intentions when he bought the place. He'd just had his first million-dollar year with his company— even if all of it had to go to loans and employee salaries—and he'd wanted to celebrate with a little slice of the American dream. It didn't have a white picket fence, but it was close enough to work, and he'd liked it on sight. Now he was wondering why he'd spent so much only to rattle in a big empty place the few weeks of the year when he wasn't off traveling. In all, he probably only used three rooms in the entire house. But Nathan had a feeling Tim would help him change that. Tim had already asked if there was a YMCA nearby, and Nathan started thinking a home gym was a great idea, now that there would be someone to actually use it. A few fantasies of watching Tim work out may have contributed to that idea, but Nathan was really starting to get into this nesting thing.

That night, while Tim was cooking dinner for them—after a trip to the grocery store, because even Tim could only do so much with Nathan's mostly empty refrigerator—Nathan unpacked his laptop, went to his home office, and bought the first five books that showed up when he typed "gay relationship books" into his search engine. There were actually a surprising number of books out there on the subject, but Nathan figured he'd start with the first five and then branch out if necessary. E-book copies would have been faster, but for a techie, Nate actually liked his self-help books to be in hardcopy, lined up neatly on his shelves. Of course that meant he'd have to wait a day or two to get them, but he figured even he couldn't screw up too royally between now and then.

They ate dinner by candlelight—Tim's idea. They had to use some holiday candles Nathan's mom had bought him a few years back because that was all he had in the house, but the pine-scented atmosphere was still romantic, and Nathan made a note on his phone to order more from Amazon the next time he was in his office.

When it was time for bed, Nathan figured they should sort out who got which side, but it took a lot longer than he'd expected. Nathan had always slept in the middle, so it honestly didn't matter to him, and Tim was being way too accommodating and wouldn't make the decision.

"It doesn't matter to me either. You pick. It's your bed. I'm just happy I'm not on a lumpy couch," Tim said with a laugh.

"It's your bed now too," Nathan corrected him. But when Tim still wouldn't choose, Nate lost patience, crossed his arms over his chest, and growled, "Pick one."

He expected Tim to either roll his eyes or throw up his hands and say "Fine!" What he didn't expect was the sudden flare of heat in Tim's eyes or the sexy smirk Tim gave him. Nathan's cock immediately stood up and took notice, and eventually Tim ended up on the right side of the bed after some rigorous physical negotiations.

"You know, I'll be perfectly happy if this is the way you want to resolve any disputes in the future as well," Nathan said as he spooned against Tim's back—in the middle of the bed. Tim only chuckled sleepily and then drifted off.

Sunday, Nathan took Tim out exploring. They did a little sightseeing, but Tim wouldn't let him take them to any of the big attractions like the zoo or any of the museums. He mostly wanted to get familiar with the area immediately surrounding Nathan's house so he could start job hunting as soon as Nathan went to work on Monday. Nathan had to admit he was a little disappointed—not about the sightseeing, because he hated the tourist crap and the crowds would make him a nervous wreck—but he'd hoped Tim would relax his timetable enough they could spend the day together without stressing over his job situation.

Before they went home, Nathan insisted on taking Tim shopping. The stores weren't too crowded in the evening in January, so now was probably the best time to do it if he was going to. Knowing from the look on Tim's face that he wasn't going to be able to buy anything solely for Tim, Nathan settled for looking at stuff they could buy together to make his home more… *homey.*

Unfortunately, it turned out Tim was as clueless about the whole home décor thing as Nathan was. They both stood in the middle of the home department like a couple of lost children until eventually they were overwhelmed enough to leave. Apparently Tim didn't actually see anything wrong with Nathan's bland and Spartan style. But Nathan still felt like something was lacking, and he'd set his mind on fixing that. They were probably going to have to enlist some female aid to get it done, though. Maybe Isobel, Sean's wife, might help. She'd done most of the decorating in their house, and Nathan had always liked it. He might be able to con her into it if Tim cooked for them one night. That could work.

"Whatever you want, babe," Tim said with a laugh as they climbed back into Nathan's car. He was being way too accommodating again, and that wasn't helping at all. But Nathan liked being called babe, so he didn't grumble too much. It felt a little weird, but it was good weird.

Tim made them steaks, mashed potatoes, and salad that night, and Nathan forgot about grumbling altogether. He was going to get fat if he kept eating like that, which of course reminded him of his home gym idea. But then they went to bed early for some fairly rigorous sex, and Nathan thought maybe he wouldn't have to worry about getting fat after all.

Monday morning came all too soon. And even though a large part of Nathan didn't want to go and leave Tim's side, another part was actually looking forward to talking to Sean about everything and exploring this new vitality and energy he seemed to have acquired along with his boyfriend.

Boyfriend. It seemed like such an odd word, but he was getting used to that too.

Only a couple of minutes after Nathan arrived at his office, Sean walked in and closed the door behind him.

"The prodigal boss returns," Sean quipped. He was wearing an impressive scowl as he flopped into one of the leather chairs in front of Nathan's desk, and Nathan was pretty sure he wouldn't be getting much work done for a while.

"Yup. You said Monday, and here I am, hale and healthy."

"And looking pretty pleased with yourself," Sean mused as he searched Nathan's face. "I have to tell you, I was expecting to have to pick you up from the depths of despair, no matter what you told me on the phone."

Nathan couldn't help it; he grinned like a fool. "Nope. No despair here."

"I can see that." When Nathan didn't do anything but continue to grin at him, Sean finally threw up his hands, hopped up, and came around the desk. He gave Nathan a quick hug and then shook him a few times by the shoulders. "You scared me, you stupid bastard—all that craziness and not really telling me what was going on in that head of yours. Do that again," he warned, wagging a finger in Nathan's face, "and I'll quit. I swear it."

Nathan sobered a little then. That was a real threat. Nathan knew he couldn't keep things running without Sean. "I'm sorry, Sean. I should have kept you more in the loop. But I wasn't sure what I was feeling most of the time, so I couldn't have explained it to you if I tried."

"Well, try harder next time," Sean relented begrudgingly. "Have you checked your e-mail yet?"

"No. I just got here, and I was otherwise occupied before I left the house." Nathan's grin was coming back, and Sean gave him a curious look.

"We'll get back to that in a minute. I don't know if it makes much difference, but we got the official word this morning. FGE has gone with one of our competitors."

Nathan wasn't surprised; maybe a little disappointed, but he'd expected it, and it definitely didn't come as the blow it might have only a couple of weeks ago.

"Did you tell anyone else?" Nathan asked.

"Nothing official. After the, uh, e-mail they got last week, courtesy of your blackmailer, they aren't quite sure what to expect from us."

Nathan sniggered. He couldn't help it. Just imagining some of his employees opening that ridiculous e-mail of him, their fearless leader, cutting loose at a gay bar was enough to crack him up. The looks of confusion and bewilderment must have been priceless. His giggles started Sean laughing, and they were in tears by the time a thought occurred to Nathan and he sobered.

"Did anyone, you know, have a problem with that e-mail? Did we lose anyone because…?" Nathan left that hanging when Sean shook his head.

"If they did, they didn't say anything to me. And honestly, if we lose anyone because of what you do on your own personal time, they weren't SDS material anyway."

Nathan didn't know how this "coming out" thing actually worked. He wasn't submerged in gay culture. He wasn't even sure what gay culture was exactly. He'd always known he was most likely bi, but given how much time he'd put into his personal life in the past, he'd never really worried about it much, figuring he'd cross that bridge if he came to it… and now he had.

"I won't insult you by asking if you have a problem with it," Nathan said cautiously.

"Thank you," Sean replied primly after he perched on the edge of Nathan's desk. "Now, I'm done being put off, so how about you tell me everything you haven't told me already?"

Nathan had to take a few seconds to figure out where to start, but Sean knew him well enough to wait for him to order his thoughts. That wasn't an easy task these days, given all Nathan had swirling giddily around in there, but he did the best he could.

"You'll be happy to know Peter Vold, the guy who blackmailed me, was arrested—not for the blackmail, unfortunately, but I'll take what I can get. Actually, the full story is he was arrested on Wednesday, got out on bail, went after Tim again, and then he was picked up this weekend."

"He doesn't sound too bright."

"No, he doesn't. In the end, the detective told me his dad ratted him out, hoping to convince the police he had nothing to do with the whole mess." Nathan filled Sean in on the rest of what Jimenez found out while Sean shook his head in amazement.

"You said these guys went after Tim twice? Is he okay?"

Nathan smiled. He hadn't expected any less from Sean, but it still warmed his heart to know Sean was concerned about Tim when they hadn't even met yet.

"Yeah, some friends of his scared them off before they could do too much. He's got a few bruises, but he'll be okay. We're taking it easy."

"We?" Sean asked, drawing out the word suggestively and cocking one eyebrow.

Nathan couldn't help the goofy grin that spread across his face. "Yes, we." Nathan cleared his throat and pushed on with the part that he was the most nervous about telling Sean. "I asked Tim to move in with me, and he said yes."

He peered over at Sean cautiously to see his reaction, and at first, Sean's face was completely blank. Then both his eyebrows slowly lowered into a *V*, and he frowned in confusion, or possibly disbelief. Nathan wasn't sure which.

"Are you serious?" Sean asked.

"As a heart attack," Nathan replied, trying to lighten the mood a little.

"I don't—" Sean began, and then he paused and took a breath, rubbing his temple as if he was getting a headache. "Let me see if I can wrap my head around this. You get drugged and taken to a gay bar. You end up spending the night with a guy you don't remember. Then someone blackmails you and you find the guy again? Then while you're tracking down bad guys, you hook up with this guy and invite him to move in with you? You do realize how crazy this sounds, right?"

"Well, when you put it that way," Nathan grumbled, only partly in jest.

"I need a drink," Sean said as he got up and headed for the door.

When Nathan just sat there staring after him, Sean rolled his eyes at him. "Are you coming or what?"

Sean went straight to a little restaurant down the street from their offices. It was a favorite among the employees, not a place to wine and dine clients but a place to kick back and shoot the shit, which was exactly what Sean did after downing half his Scotch and soda.

"Okay, forget about all the crazy blackmail stuff and talk to me about the guy—Tim."

Nathan sipped at his "froufrou girly drink," as Sean called it, before answering. "I know you think I'm crazy, but I'm not."

"Isn't that what all crazy people say?"

Nathan smacked him on the arm. "Shut up. I'm opening my heart to you, and you're ruining the mood. Now, as I was saying, I'm not crazy. Tim is a wonderful person, and you'll realize that as soon as you meet him. Until then, there's not much I can tell you about him that you'll likely believe. The only thing I can say that might convince you of anything is that he, and this whole situation, opened my eyes to some things that I've been ignoring for way too long, things you've been trying to get through my head but hadn't quite made it yet."

"Like what?"

"Like why am I doing what I'm doing? Why am I working so hard? What's the outcome? What's the end result I'm shooting for? You've been working right alongside me for years, Sean. And I think, if I asked you to tell me why, you could come up with a whole list of reasons, right?"

Sean shrugged. "Sure. Of course. My wife, my kids, you, our employees."

"Exactly," Nathan agreed. "But if you'd asked me the same question and forced me to stop and think instead of just rattling off the first thing that came into my head, I can honestly tell you, beyond you and the company itself, I'm not sure what my answer would have been. I probably would have just said 'success,' success for the business, the investors, to *say* I was a success. But then what? What happens after I'm a success, after we're a success?"

"Retirement on a beach somewhere," Sean answered and then toasted the sentiment with his glass and downed the rest of its contents.

Nathan smiled and shook his head. "Yeah, except I didn't have anyone to share it with. What the hell would I do with myself if I retired? I'd go crazy in a week... or at least I would have before. Now I've found someone, Sean. And I know it's really fast and kind of weird, but he makes me happy. Every minute I'm with him I just feel great. And today, knowing he'll be there when I get home, I feel like nothing is beyond my grasp. I feel energized and ready to move on from what happened with FGE to something bigger and better."

"You left him at your place by himself?" Sean asked. His expression was truly pained as he waved at the bartender for a refill.

Nathan didn't dignify the question with a response. It wasn't as if Tim was going to rob him blind.

"Well, at least you don't have dick to steal in that big empty house," Sean said before taking a gulp from the glass the waiter brought him. Then Sean seemed to realize the double meaning in his choice of words, and he tried to laugh but ended up choking and coughing instead, snarfing his Scotch.

Nathan frowned at his friend and mopped up the spewed Scotch from the table. "Funny."

When Sean finally got hold of himself, he said, "I'm sorry. That was bad. I'm just trying to be your friend, Nate. I'm allowed to worry about you, especially after all that happened last week."

A little mollified, Nathan nodded. "Just trust me when I say I know what I'm doing. I'm willing to take the risk if I get to wake up feeling like I did this morning every day. I want you to meet him."

"Oh, you bet your ass I'll meet him. Tonight. You guys. Over at our place. Dinner. Eight o'clock," he said with finality.

"I don't know. I need to call Tim and make sure that's okay with him."

Sean leaned back in his seat with the first genuinely happy smile he'd had since starting this conversation. "Look at you, being all domestic and stuff already. Have to call the wife before you make any decisions."

Nathan gave Sean the finger. "It's the polite thing to do in any situation, smartass. And if you call him my wife again, I'll have to kick your ass on principle, so he won't. He's kinda buff. I don't think you'd last long."

"Yeah, yeah. I'll lay off for tonight and be on my best behavior. God, since you've gone gay, who knew you'd get all sensitive."

Sean got Nathan's napkin in the face for that crack, and they both laughed.

"But seriously, call him. And I'll call *my* wife to make sure it's okay with her."

# Chapter
## Fourteen

AFTER NATE went to work, Tim didn't waste any time starting his job hunt. He only waited long enough to give Nate a good-bye kiss at the door before going to find his best pair of khakis and a polo. They were both a little wrinkled from the trip, so he did delay getting dressed until he figured out the steam cycle on Nate's incredibly fancy—and obviously rarely used—dryer. But when he thought he looked respectable enough, he pocketed the extra set of keys Nate gave him, his phone, his jacket, and his wallet and headed out for the bus stop.

The shopping area Nate took him to the night before was probably a little high-end, but it was close by, so Tim started collecting applications there. He'd move farther out later, if he needed to. As Tim expected this time of year, most of the shops were only looking for part-time help, if they were looking at all, but he took the applications anyway, just in case. He wanted full time. His schedule was going to be crappy enough compared to Nate's. He didn't want to make it worse by doing two jobs like he'd done in Houston. But he would if he had to.

By the time Tim made it back to Nate's, it was late in the afternoon, and he didn't have much to show for how much his feet hurt. The only full-time job he'd found was at a restaurant, and he cringed just thinking about working in food service. He knew plenty of guys who did it, but he really didn't think he had the personality for it. That didn't stop him from taking the application, of course, but he put it on the bottom of the pile.

That morning Nate had told him he'd be home around six. Tim had been a little surprised by that, considering the amount of work Nate said he had waiting for him. But Nate only grinned and said it was a perk of being the boss, before kissing him good-bye.

After a quick shower to wash away the long day on his feet, the clock told him it was still only four in the afternoon. That gave Tim a good couple of hours to figure out what he was going to make them for dinner. He had to admit he was looking forward to it. Nate's kitchen was a dream, all dark granite counters and pristine stainless steel appliances. The only bad part was that Nate only had two pots and one pan, and though they were brand new, they didn't give Tim many options for cooking methods. He hadn't wanted to say anything about it while they were out—still feeling a bit weird about the money situation—but now he was kind of wishing he had.

Tim was staring into the refrigerator at what they'd bought the night before and trying to decide what he was going to make when Nate's house phone started ringing. Tim wasn't sure if he should answer or not, so he let it go to voice mail. But when it started ringing again, he went to check the caller ID in case it was important. It was Nate.

"Hey."

"Hey? God, Tim, where were you? I've been trying your cell all afternoon. I was starting to get really worried," Nate said in a rush.

Frowning, Tim pulled his cell out of his pocket. The screen was blank. "Shit. It looks like my piece of crap phone died on me." Tim carried it to the charger and plugged it in. It came back on right away, displaying three texts and four missed calls from Nate, so maybe that meant only the battery was shot. He'd gotten the phone secondhand from a pawnshop, and it was way past time for a new one. He guessed he'd have to add that to the list of expenses he couldn't afford.

"Hey, sorry. My phone was dead, and I was out job hunting. I'm okay."

Nate blew out a breath on the other end of the line and said, "It's okay. I probably overreacted a little. But after the last two weeks, all kinds of crazy things were going through my head."

Tim smiled. He didn't like to think he'd scared Nate, but it was nice to have someone worry about him. "I'm fine. I'm back at the house now, obviously. I was just about to get started on dinner if you have any suggestions or requests."

"That's actually why I was calling. We've been invited to Sean's house for dinner. He wants to meet you."

Tim's stomach did a little flip, and he had to clear his throat before he answered, "Oh, sure. What time?"

"I'll pick you up at six. You're going to love them. I promise."

"I'm sure I will," Tim said. Nate seemed so happy and excited that Tim didn't have the heart to sound anything but positive about it.

They hung up, and Tim was left at loose ends. He had two hours of anxious waiting ahead of him and nothing to do to keep himself busy. Nate's house was pristine, so it didn't need any cleaning. Tim could do a little laundry maybe, but that only required a few minutes to get the machine going, and then what?

Tim wandered around aimlessly for a while. He didn't snoop in drawers or closets or anything, but he checked out the few family pictures Nate had up and the couple of knickknacks he found on tables and shelves. Maybe Nate had a point. The house didn't really look lived in at all. It certainly didn't represent Nate's energetic and complex personality, except for maybe the home office. That appeared to be the only room in the house that Nate spent any time in. The large dark oak desk along one wall had three monitors on it and a rack of computer towers and printers next to it. Nate had offered him free use of it and set him up a log-in on the desktop, but Tim had been a little daunted by all the hardware and hadn't used it yet without Nate's supervision.

Turning away from the technological monstrosity, Tim smiled as he read the titles of all the books on his office shelves. There was a whole bookcase of programming reference books on one side, but the bulk of the shelves were taken up with self-help books. Titles like *Shut Up And Talk: An Effective Guide to Communication* and *The Solution Within Yourself* as far as the eye could see. It was adorable, mostly because Tim didn't understand why Nate thought he needed them. Nate did just fine as far as Tim could tell, more than fine.

When Tim had wandered through every room in the house and still had an hour and a half to kill before Nate arrived, he decided to bake some cookies to take with them to dinner. Not only would that give him something to do, but they'd have a gift to give their hosts as well, earn him a few brownie points with Nate's friends. At first he'd wanted to do muffins, but Nate didn't have a muffin pan, so cookies it was. Nate didn't actually have a cookie sheet either, but he had the bottom part of the broiler pan that came with the oven, so that would work.

Tim got busy, and before too long the house smelled like peanut butter cookies, and Tim's nerves were a little soothed. He could do this. He could meet Nate's friends. The way Nate talked about Sean, the guy sounded really nice. There shouldn't be anything for him to worry about… at least that's what he kept telling himself until Nate arrived home and came bursting into the kitchen with a huge smile on his face.

"Are those peanut butter cookies I smell?"

Tim couldn't help but return the grin. This playing-house stuff was pretty cool when he had someone who actually appreciated his efforts.

"Yup. But you can't have any. We're taking them with us."

Nate snuck one anyway while he was kissing Tim hello or shortly thereafter. Tim knew this because Nate's mouth was surprisingly sweet and peanut buttery the second time Tim dove in for a kiss, after pulling the last batch of cookies out of the oven. To stop any more from disappearing, Tim quickly packed up the rest, and all too soon they were climbing into Nate's beige Lexus to go meet his friends.

Dinner was a little uncomfortable to start. Tim could tell Sean and Isobel weren't sure what to make of him. And Tim didn't exactly hang out with a lot of married couples with children, so he was just as lost. It felt like a long way from microwave burritos on the couch with Matt. But Nate's friends were nice people and polite hosts, and Nate seemed so utterly thrilled to have all of them there together, Tim did his best to fit in and enjoy himself.

At least the cookies were a hit. There was a little tense moment at the start because one of Sean's kids was allergic to peanuts, but both parents were delighted to scarf them down since they almost never got to eat them anymore… all in the name of protecting their child, of course.

The worst moment of the night was when the subject of Tim's "career" came up. He knew they'd ask at some point, but he still tensed anyway when Sean turned to him and asked, "So what do you for a living, Tim?"

"He just got into town, Sean. He hasn't had time to do anything yet," Nate answered for him, a little defensively.

Tim knew he was just trying to help, but it almost made things worse because now everyone was staring at him—Nate anxiously and

Sean, Isobel, and their kids with even more curiosity than before. He felt like he had a spotlight on him.

Cringing inwardly, Tim said, "I'm looking for a job now. I went out today."

"Oh yeah, sure. Of course. Well, good luck to you," Sean said uncomfortably, exchanging a look with Nate before changing the subject.

Tim didn't feel like talking much after that. He was embarrassed and upset, but he knew Nate hadn't done it on purpose, so he didn't want to say anything until he had a little distance from it, a chance to calm down. But Nate wasn't as clueless as he seemed to think he was, and as soon as they were in the door to Nate's house, he asked, "Did I do something wrong?"

"What?" Tim asked innocently as he shrugged out of his jacket and went to the kitchen for a glass of water.

Nate followed close behind. "Don't do that. You said you wanted honesty. So do I. You've been really quiet, and if something's bothering you, I wish you'd tell me."

Tim drank his water, giving himself time to decide how to answer without overreacting. "You embarrassed me," he said finally.

Nate seemed a little taken aback, but he recovered quickly. "Okay. How?"

"When you answered for me about the whole job thing."

Nate looked really confused now. His eyebrows were all scrunched together, and he was chewing on his lower lip. It was actually pretty adorable.

"I just thought... I know when we talked about it before, the subject upset you, so I didn't want Sean pushing you on it. That's all. I didn't mean to embarrass you," Nate said.

"I know," Tim sighed. "That's why I'm trying not to be mad."

Nate seemed to take a moment to digest that before asking, "Is it working?"

Tim couldn't help himself. He snorted, set his glass down, and walked over to where Nate stood, watching him uncertainly.

"Yeah. It's working," Tim said just before he fisted a hand in Nate's shirt and pulled him in for a kiss. "Although your friends probably think I'm a loser now," he continued after letting Nate go.

"They don't. They like you. I can tell."

"Yeah?"

"Yeah."

Feeling a little mollified, Tim kissed Nate again and said, "Let's go upstairs and you can show me how sorry you are."


THE REST of that first week flew by. Nate went off to work each morning, and Tim continued his hunt for a job. Every night Tim would cook dinner, and then they'd cuddle on the couch and watch some television or just talk until bedtime. When the TV was on, Nate spent more time looking at his laptop or one of the new books that were delivered on Wednesday than what was on the television, but Tim didn't mind. Not only could they spend time together while doing different things, but Nate was getting back to work and seemed excited about it again, full of ideas… even if Tim didn't actually understand what most of those ideas were.

Finally, on Thursday, after visiting dozens of stores, Tim lucked into a full-time position at a men's clothing boutique. He was pretty sure the manager only hired him because he liked the way Tim filled out his polo shirt, but Tim didn't care, whatever got him the job. He'd have to go back to working a lot of evenings and weekends, but that couldn't be helped. It was retail. And he didn't have to be there forever, just until he figured out what he wanted to do when he grew up.

Nate wasn't exactly thrilled about the prospect of Tim working nights and weekends, but he made an effort to sound supportive when Tim told him about it. Tim had a feeling it was because Nate had been reading all those gay relationship books, and he was really tempted to give Nate all kinds of shit about them. But he knew Nate was making the effort for him, so he didn't have the heart to make fun of him for it. The man was just adorable, and Tim was so besotted he could hardly stand himself.

Tim's first day on the job wasn't until Monday, so Friday night, after gorging themselves on a five-cheese mushroom lasagna Tim made, Nate wanted to plan something special for them to do together, since it might be the last full weekend they had for a while. They'd just sat down on the couch with a couple of beers when Tim's cell started ringing. It was plugged in by the front door, where he left it most of the time since he couldn't afford a new one just yet. But no one had actually called him on it since he'd gotten to California.

The screen told him it was Theresa, and Tim felt a sudden stab of guilt. "Hey, Aunt T. What's up?"

"Tim, honey…." Her voice was shaky and obviously upset, and Tim's stomach plummeted with dread before she even said the words. "Your dad's in the hospital, sweetie. I went over to check on him today, and I couldn't wake him up."

Tim swallowed before he asked, "Is he… is he going to be okay?"

"I don't know, honey. They said they have him stabilized, and he did wake up for a little while. But they've been running all kinds of tests on him, and we won't know anything until they come back."

Tim just stood there frozen, his mind blank. He didn't know what to do or say next. Then Nate was in front of him, watching him with concern etched deeply in his handsome face. "What's going on? Are you okay?" Nate asked.

Tim shook his head and closed his eyes. "It's my dad," he whispered

"What?" Theresa asked.

"Sorry, T," Tim said, "I was talking to Nate. I'll… I'll get there as soon as I can, okay? I'll call when I know about my flight and when I'll be there."

"Okay, sweetie. I won't try to tell you not to come. If he is sick, he'll feel better with *you* here more than me, I'm sure. I'll stay at the hospital as long as I can. Do you need me to pick you up from the airport?"

"I, uh, I don't know. Let me call you back once I know what I'm doing, okay?"

"Yeah. Okay. Talk to you soon."

"Bye."

Tim ended the call and stood with his phone held loosely in his hand until Nate's arms pulled him close. "You need to go home?" Nate asked.

Tim could only nod. His chest felt like an elephant was sitting on it. He couldn't breathe under the weight of all the emotions roiling inside him, the fear of what he would find when he got back to Houston, fear that he wouldn't be able to handle going through this again. The first time with his mom had been enough to almost crush him. Pain, old and new, twisted inside him so tightly he couldn't tell one from the other.

"Go upstairs and get a bag packed. I'll go online and see about getting us tickets for the earliest flight we can," Nate said in his take-charge voice as he gave Tim a shove toward the stairs.

Under the circumstances, Nate's bossiness didn't have its usual effect. Tim was simply flooded with relief and gratitude that someone else was making decisions—that he had someone to lean on—all he needed to do was go upstairs and pack. He'd have to thank Nate later, when he could do it without bawling all over him.

"Hey," Nate said from the doorway to their bedroom a little while later, breaking Tim out of the trance he'd been in. Tim didn't know how long he'd been staring at his empty suitcase. "They don't have anything tonight that won't involve us going all the way to Atlanta and back to Houston, not arriving until tomorrow anyway, so I booked us on one leaving first thing in the morning. Is that okay?"

Tim looked at the clothes in his hands as if he hadn't seen them before and then up at Nate. "Yeah?"

Nate came into the room and took the clothes out of his hands. He set them on the bed before wrapping Tim in his arms and whispering, "It's okay. It's going to be okay. We'll get a bag packed for each of us tonight, and I already called to schedule a taxi to pick us up. All you have to do is try to sleep tonight so you're rested for tomorrow. Okay?"

Tim drew in a long, shuddering breath and blew it out before saying, "Okay." He buried his face in Nate's neck and squeezed the man tight. "Thanks, Nate. I don't know what I would have done without you."

"Come on. Let's finish packing and go to bed. The taxi is going to be here at o'dark thirty tomorrow."

Tim dreamed he was back at his mom's bedside, in their old house, watching her waste away before his eyes. Only this time, it was his dad's pale, gaunt face staring up at him from the pillow instead of hers. He woke up sweating and shaking, and it was a long time before he got his breathing under control.

God, he couldn't go through this again. He wasn't strong enough. The last seven years he'd been able to lock the pain away in a little box inside him because he'd had to. There was no one else to take care of him. The rest of the family had made promises of help at the funeral, but they'd slowly faded away, one by one, either chased away by his dad or simply swallowed up in their own lives. Tim couldn't really blame them. They'd helped all they could through the months and months of his mom's illness. There was only so much they could give before the well ran dry.

And now it was starting all over again. Tim closed his eyes and relaxed back into the pillows, just listening to Nate's quiet breathing for a while and trying to calm down. He was jumping to conclusions. He didn't know anything yet. His dad might be okay after a few days in the hospital. And who knows, maybe they'd be able to get him into a rehab program, where Tim and Theresa had failed. This might be enough to scare his dad into taking care of himself again.

It could happen.

Even as these thoughts ran through his head, his Aunt T's words to him before he left whispered in the background. *"I don't expect to be taking care of your daddy for much longer."* The tightness in his chest was back, making it hard to breathe again, so he slid out of bed as quietly as he could before he woke Nate up with his freak-out. It was still pitch black outside, and the alarm would be going off soon enough without Tim making it worse.

He wandered into the kitchen, turned on Nate's coffeepot, and sat at the island, counting to five between each inhale and exhale so he wouldn't hyperventilate while it brewed. Maybe he should have gone to see that therapist Theresa suggested after his mom died—no matter how much it would have cost—because obviously he hadn't dealt with things as well as he'd thought he had. And maybe he and his dad had more in common than Tim wanted to admit.

As he sat and sipped his second cup of coffee, a pair of strong hands landed on his shoulders and squeezed, startling him out of his downward-spiraling thoughts. "Hey. You okay?"

When Tim couldn't clear the lump out of his throat quickly enough to answer, Nate came around the table and gave him an apologetic grimace. "Sorry. That was a stupid question. How about, why didn't you wake me?"

"No reason for both of us to lose any more sleep than we already have to." Tim finally found his voice. He gave Nate what he hoped was a reassuring smile, but Nate didn't appear to be buying it.

"Except you're obviously upset," Nate said. He took one of Tim's hands in his own and squeezed it. "I may be new at all this, but I think that's what boyfriends are supposed to be for."

Tim smiled for real this time. It wasn't just the boyfriend comment either. He didn't know how he'd gotten so lucky, but every day with the man was more proof that maybe his mom had been right. When he found the right man, he would know it. He *did* know it.

"Thanks, Nate. For a beginner, you're a natural."

"You make it easy," Nate replied, and then they grinned sappily at each other until Tim couldn't take it anymore and he laughed.

"It's too early in the morning for this much sap," he said as he got up and went to the coffeepot. "How long until the cab gets here?"

"We have about an hour and half."

"Then you get a cup of coffee and wake up a little while I take a shower." Tim gave Nate a peck on the cheek and headed for the bathroom. He needed to do something mindless for a little while, and hopefully a hot shower would ease some of the tension in his body as well as the beginnings of the stress headache he'd started.

Unfortunately, the headache didn't vanish with the shower, and Tim had to make do with the incredibly expensive pills they bought at the airport during Nate's mad dash for the gate. Tim had experienced Nate's discomfort with crowded spaces the last time too, but this time it didn't seem quite so adorable. His head was pounding as he continually reminded himself how grateful he should be for all Nate had done for him, but the hurry up and wait hadn't improved his mood any, and he was pretty cranky by the time they got on the plane.

The trip back to Houston was a blur. He dozed for most of the ride, not even bothering to look out the window, and after a few failed attempts to make Tim feel better, Nate got the hint and left him alone. Tim wallowed in as much guilt as any other emotion, especially when Nate pulled out his laptop and started working, reminding Tim of all the trouble he'd already caused. But he couldn't dredge up the energy to apologize at that moment. Maybe after he'd seen his dad and had a chance to sleep off his headache, he'd make it up to Nate. Anything that came out of his mouth right now would only make things worse or have Tim blubbering all over Nate in a public place.

As he had up until that point, Nate took care of everything once they landed too. He dragged Tim through the airport in Houston, just like he'd done in San Diego. He stuffed Tim into a cab and told the driver what hospital to take them to. He paid for the cab and talked to the woman behind the welcome desk at the hospital to figure out where they were supposed to go, while all Tim did was stand like a bump on a log and let it happen. He was going to regret that later, when his pride reminded him of who he was, but at that moment it was so nice to let someone else deal with it.

Then he was standing in front of a waiting room, and his Aunt T was there, and Tim couldn't hide in the background anymore. Nate couldn't do this part.

"Oh, honey. You made it," Aunt T said before she wrapped her arms around Tim and squeezed him tight. Theresa was about the same height as Tim, though a bit rounder in the hips and tummy and almost broader in the shoulders. Growing up, Tim had always wondered how his petite, slender mom and his Aunt Theresa could have come out of the same womb. Aunt T was more linebacker than delicate flower, but Tim was really grateful for that now. She was solid and strong in his arms, and Tim thought he might just be able to make it through whatever came next if he had both T and Nate at his back.

"Aunt T, this is Nate. Nate, this is my Aunt Theresa," Tim said after pulling back and waving Nate forward.

Theresa smiled at Nate and held out her hand. "It's a pleasure to meet you, Nate."

"You too," Nate replied.

"So what did the doctors say? Have they found anything yet?" Tim asked as he reluctantly stepped back and shoved his hands in his pockets.

The expression on her face wasn't at all comforting as she said, "Sit down, honey."

They moved to the boxy vinyl-covered waiting room chairs and sat down, Nate on one side of him, T on the other.

"They're still running tests, but so far it doesn't look good."

"What doesn't look good?" Tim didn't really want to know, but he supposed he needed to.

She patted his hand and opened her mouth to answer, but then she closed it again and blew a breath out her nose, making Tim's stomach knot in apprehension. "Honey, you know your dad hasn't taken care of himself for a while now. We talked about that before you left, right?"

She was being so careful in her word choice it was making him even more nervous than if she'd just come right out and said it. Tim fidgeted in his seat, part of him wanting to shake it out of her and be done, but he nodded.

"Well, sweetie, the doctors aren't very optimistic. Your dad's got a lot going wrong inside. The booze and the pills have done quite a number on his liver and his heart. And while they're still doing some more tests, with the high blood pressure and everything else, it doesn't look good."

Both Theresa and Nate were watching him closely for some sort of reaction, but Tim didn't know what to give them. What she was saying hadn't quite sunk in yet.

"So what does that mean exactly?" he asked numbly.

"It means, I don't think he's going home again any time soon."

She still seemed to be beating around the bush, and Tim was getting annoyed.

*She's trying to help,* Tim reminded himself. *She's hurting too.*

He repeated that to himself a few times so he wouldn't do or say anything he'd regret. But he really needed a straight answer.

"Excuse me, Ms. York?"

A pretty blonde woman in a white coat stood in the doorway.

"Doctor Baker," Theresa breathed out, sounding relieved.

Tim stood up and followed Theresa over to the woman. "Doctor Baker, this is my nephew, Tim, James's son."

"It's nice to meet you, Tim. I'm in charge of your father's case." She held out her hand, and Tim shook it automatically.

"Is there any news?" Tim asked, fearing the answer.

"Can we sit down?" Dr. Baker said, motioning toward the chairs.

Tim didn't want to sit down again. He wanted this conversation to be over with. His headache was getting worse, and all this tiptoeing around was setting his teeth on edge. He just wanted to find a dark corner to hide in and pray that all of this was just a nightmare and he'd wake up any minute back at Nate's, ready to start a new life.

"The news isn't good, I'm afraid," Dr. Baker started, once they'd all taken their seats. "We're managing his withdrawal with benzodiazepines, keeping him sedated, but with all of the other issues we're finding, there isn't much we can do in the long run. In his current state, his body can't take much more stress. The most we're able to do is keep him comfortable for now."

Tim frowned.

*"Not good?" "Other issues?" "There isn't much we can do?"*

He couldn't make the phrases mean anything in his head. Tim rubbed his temples. He didn't want to sound like an idiot, but he had to ask, "But what does that *mean*? Plain English, please."

The doctor sighed, and the look she gave him was full of pity. "It means he's dying. I'm sorry, but that's as plain as I can make it. The liver damage is extensive. We can manage some of the symptoms of that, but we can't reverse it. His heart is severely weakened. He's probably been experiencing symptoms for a long time: fatigue, stomach pain, shortness of breath. The painkillers your aunt told us about may have masked some of it, but… maybe if he'd come in sooner we could have done more. I'm sorry."

"What about a transplant?" Nate asked when Tim simply stared at her in shock.

The doctor shook her head. "I'm afraid, with all his other issues, he's not a good candidate. There are hundreds of people in front of him on the donor list. But even if we found a donor, his chances of surviving the surgery are slim. I wish I could be more optimistic."

His dad was dying.

Somehow, when Theresa made her predictions before he left, it had been easier to dismiss, probably because they'd only been hypothetical at the time. Now the words echoed in his head with a finality he couldn't quite wrap his brain around.

That wasn't exactly true. His head was getting the gist of it. It was his heart that didn't know what to do about it.

"What happens now?" Theresa asked into the heavy silence that hung in the air.

"Now we try to get him stabilized and keep him comfortable. We'll need to get the edema, the swelling, down and manage his symptoms until the worst of the withdrawal has passed. But after that, once he can be moved, I believe he will need to go to hospice. He'll have a caseworker assigned to him soon, and they'll work with all of you on the rest."

"How long?" Tim croaked out the question. He didn't know why he asked. Everyone always asked, and no one really had the answer. They'd asked enough times when his mom got sick, and nothing the doctors ever said made a damned bit of difference. Yet here he was asking anyway.

She gave him an apologetic smile. "It's hard to say. We don't like to put a number on things like this. Sometimes people surprise us. Maybe after this crisis is over, his numbers will improve, and we might have a better idea. But, in the end, it would only be a guess on my part." She shrugged.

"But what's your guess, ballpark, anything," Tim pushed.

She looked pained, but she answered, "Weeks… months maybe. If we can get him through the worst part now."

"Thank you," Tim said hollowly, and the doctor nodded to each of them and left them alone.

"Tim? Honey?" Theresa asked cautiously.

Even though Tim had closed his eyes, he could still feel her, practically vibrating with concern. Nate's hand was on his back now, but rather than comforting him, it felt like a lead weight pressing down on him. The ugly bluish light from the florescent bulbs above his head hurt his eyes, even through his eyelids, and the buzzing from the drink machine outside the waiting room was becoming almost deafening. He had to move. He had to get out.

Tim practically jumped out of his seat. "I gotta go. I'll be back," he said as he rushed for the door.

"Tim?" Nate called after him worriedly, and Tim paused in the doorway.

"I just need to be alone for a minute. I'll be back soon." He pulled his phone out of his pocket and turned it on so Nate could see. "I have my phone." With that, he fled, down the hall to the stairs, down a flight, and out into a courtyard.

Once there, he dragged in great lungfuls of air as his head pounded in time with his heartbeat. For a long time, he sat on one of the benches in the courtyard, staring unseeing at the ground beneath his feet while the rest of the world passed by him unnoticed. The sky was a little overcast and the air cool enough to soothe the claustrophobic feeling he'd had in the waiting room. He dry swallowed a couple more pills from the outrageously expensive little bottle Nate had bought and waited for the pounding in his temples to ease.

His dad was dying.

But *his* dad, the dad he grew up with, was already dead, a voice in the back of his head reminded him. That man died seven years ago, leaving only a shell behind.

But if he really believed that, then why did it hurt so bad to hear now?

Tim's phone beeped, and he pulled it out of his pocket. He had a text from Nate.

*The nurse says you can visit your dad now. Room 215. I'll be in the waiting room if you need me.*

Tim took a deep breath and then another for courage. His headache had receded to a dull throb, and the panicked feeling had ebbed a bit, so he figured he couldn't put it off any longer. Instead of getting Nate, Tim decided to go alone to his dad's room the first time. When he stepped through the door and saw the body on the bed, Tim had to clench his jaw hard against the tears that welled in his eyes. His dad looked awful, his face pale and swollen to where Tim almost didn't recognize him. He slept fitfully on the bed, moving as much as the machines and tubes connected to him would allow. Even sedated as the doctor said, he looked like he was in pain, and Tim's heart squeezed.

Tim stayed in the room for a little while, but he didn't try to talk to his dad. The man obviously needed what peace he could get, and Tim had no idea what he would say to him even if he could speak. He left the room not long after, part of him wishing he'd never seen his dad like that. The image would stay with him forever now, tainting happier memories. It was probably selfish of him to feel that way, but that didn't change it.

When he stepped into the waiting room, Nate was by his side in a second, his face full of concern. "Are you—" Nate stopped himself and started again. "What can I do?"

"Take me somewhere."

"Where?"

"Anywhere not here."

"Okay." Nate led the way to the elevator, and Tim followed. "Your aunt had to go, but she said to call her if you need her and she'd be back tomorrow."

Tim just nodded, and Nate didn't press.

They walked to a little pizza place, but Tim wasn't really hungry. He ate a piece to make Nate stop fussing, but it was all he could do to swallow each bite. It tasted like cardboard. Nate tried to start a conversation a couple of times, but Tim didn't make it easy, and eventually Nate gave up. Of course he knew he was being selfish. Nate was only trying to help, and Tim was going to screw things up between them if he didn't snap out of it, but he still couldn't seem to stop.

He was silent for the entire cab ride to the hotel Nate found for them during dinner, too caught up in the kaleidoscope of emotions spinning in his chest: fear, grief, disbelief, guilt, denial, anger, hope. Luckily, his heart couldn't decide on any one of them to fixate on, so he had some distance from them all for the time being.

Nate tried to talk to him once they were in their hotel room, but Tim still couldn't do it, not yet.

"I'm sorry," he said wearily. "I'm exhausted. Can we just go to bed? I know we have a lot to talk about, but not tonight, okay?"

"Okay."

Despite the fact that Tim had been a bit shitty to him all day, Nate didn't seem to have any reservations about curling up with him that night. Tim might not have been able to express his gratitude right then, but he felt it all the way to his toes. The warmth of Nate's skin, his quiet breathing and solid presence helped soothe the storm inside Tim and allowed him to let go enough to collapse into unconsciousness. He really didn't know what he would have done if Nate hadn't been there, and that scared him a little.

They both slept late the following morning, probably because of a combination of jet lag and differing time zones. Tim had barely had a chance to get used California time before being pulled back to Houston. He'd barely had time to get used to anything in California, actually. It all seemed like a dream now.

As soon as they were dressed, they got a cab outside the hotel and headed back to the hospital. Tim didn't really want to go, but he knew both Nate and Aunt T would be expecting him to, and he would regret it later if he didn't.

He asked Nate to stay in the waiting room again, and although Nate looked like he wanted to object, he kept quiet and did it anyway. Theresa was already in his dad's room when he got there, reading a book in the chair by the bed. She smiled sadly at him when he came in, put her book down, and stood up.

"Hey there. You disappeared last night. I was worried," she said.

"I just needed to think about some things."

"I understand."

Tim wondered if she really did understand everything that was going through his mind. He hoped not. She was someone he looked up to, and some of his thoughts and feelings weren't anything to be proud of.

"Now that you're here, I'm going to go get something to eat," she said. "He woke up once, early this morning, but he was pretty out of it. I guess that's because of the meds."

"Okay," he replied numbly.

Theresa kissed Tim's forehead as she passed, and then Tim was alone with his dad. Reluctantly, he went to the chair by the bed and sat down. His dad didn't look any better today than yesterday. He watched the man for a while, purposefully trying to keep his mind blank, but it was no good. Eventually the feelings started breaking free. First came the pain, remembered pain and new. The beeping of the machines and clicking of the medication dispenser was all too familiar, as was the smell of antiseptic. Grief long buried welled in him, making his eyes sting and his chest ache.

Soon after came the guilt. He'd broken his promise to his mom. He'd promised to take care of his dad, and he'd failed. He should have done more. He should have tried harder. Maybe if he'd moved in with his dad instead of running in the opposite direction after her death, he could have saved him. And then, as if he hadn't failed her enough, he'd flown off to California to play house with Nate, and now his dad was dying.

Of course, logic insisted that his dad would have ended up there whether he'd gone to California or not. But it was hard to convince his heart of that when it was wallowing in guilt. He stared at his dad's pale, swollen face for a long time until a wave of anger, just as strong and just as unreasoning, replaced his guilt.

*How could you do this to me? How could you be so selfish, fighting me every time I tried to make things better, killing yourself with every bottle, until I have to sit at another bedside and watch another parent suffer and die? How could you do this to your own son?*

Tim wanted to scream at him, wanted to shake him until he opened his eyes and told Tim why. His dad may have lost a wife, but Tim had lost too. He'd lost a mother and a father. Anger he'd buried for years under hopelessness resurfaced, bringing with it memories of all the times he and his dad had fought in the beginning. How he'd begged and wheedled, screamed and threatened until he'd realized none of it did anyone any good. He'd tried sympathy, guilt, tough love... everything he could think of, and it'd changed nothing, so he'd given up, and now look where they were.

"You weren't there for me when I needed you," Tim whispered angrily to the unconscious man on the bed. "You left me to deal with it on my own. I was there for you. I did everything I could think of to make you get help, and you wouldn't. So now I'm supposed to keep on being here for you? I'm supposed to sit here and watch you die because you wouldn't even try to get better?" Tim's fists were clenched in the blankets, and he was panting as if he'd run a marathon, holding back what was raging inside him.

"Timmy?" Theresa's voice was quiet, but it startled him nonetheless. He'd been so wrapped up in his rant he had no idea when she'd come into the room.

"I'm sorry," he said shakily. And he was. Not sorry for what he'd said, he was still too angry for that, but sorry she'd heard it.

"You don't have to apologize to me, sweetie." Her expression held no judgment, only sadness and understanding. "I've shouted the exact same words at your dad a time or two over the years. And sometimes it worked. Sometimes he'd get better for a while, swear off the drink for a couple of weeks. But it never lasted. There wasn't anything either of us could do. I hope you can believe that." She walked over and put her hand on Tim's shoulder. "You're not saying anything he doesn't know already either. He knows he let you and your mom down."

"Then why the hell didn't he do something about it?" Tim leaped to his feet and stormed out of the room. His anger wasn't fading. It was getting worse. He needed to get away from both her and his dad right now. Otherwise he'd say something he couldn't take back.

As he rushed to the stairs for the second day in a row, he passed the waiting room where Nate sat hunched over his laptop. Part of him wanted to call out to Nate, to let Nate comfort him and make everything okay, but he couldn't do it. Nate had done enough already. Tim had disrupted the man's life too much as it was.

By the time Tim reached the courtyard, his anger was already fading. Unfortunately what replaced it wasn't much better. The same sense of hopelessness and helplessness he'd felt just before and nearly every day since his mom passed threatened to drag him under again. He wanted to break free of it. He wanted to run away and live the fantasy with Nate. But he couldn't just leave his dad to die alone.

Theresa would be there to help, but she wasn't his son. No matter how angry and hurt he was, his conscience wouldn't let him walk away. He'd regret it for the rest of his life. But that meant giving up on all his hopes with Nate. Even if Nate were willing, Tim couldn't ask him to wait indefinitely for him. Nate had a life of his own to get back to, a great life, and Tim didn't exactly have much to add, nothing Nate couldn't easily find somewhere else once he bothered to look for it—no matter what Nate said to the contrary. Tim was fully aware, the second Nate chose to put it out there, he'd have men and women lining up for him. Nate would figure that out sooner or later too.

Tim put his face in his hands and groaned, not caring if there was anyone around to hear him. There were things he needed to do. He needed to call Matt and see if he'd sold the car yet. He needed to find someplace to stay. He needed to find out who their caseworker was. But all he could do was agonize over what he was going to tell Nate.

*Hey, thanks for paying to fly me all over the place, making room for me in your home, and taking off work for days and days, but I have to leave now for an undetermined amount of time. Can you pay to ship my stuff back to me? Oh yeah, and wait for me until I can get back? I don't know how long it's going to be, but don't date anyone else while you wait, okay?*

Oh God, what had he been thinking, flying off to California like that? How could he possibly think that kind of fairy tale could be real, that he could just pick up with a guy he knew for less than a week, move in with him, and live happily ever after? He'd quit his jobs, moved his stuff halfway across the country, and now what was he going to do?

Tim wanted to curl up in a ball of misery and pray the whole world would go away and leave him alone for a while.

*All that money—the plane tickets, the hotel, the cabs—how am I supposed to ever be able to pay him back?*

He was just so tired. How much longer could he keep going like this before he gave up just like his dad did? Before he let the world push him down until escape in a bottle was all he had left?

He needed to lie down.

Tim pulled out his phone and texted Nate. He didn't even have the energy to go back inside to get him.

*Can we go back to the hotel, please? I'll meet you out front.*

His phone beeped a moment later.

*OK*

Nate's handsome face was more than a little concerned when he joined Tim outside. "Hey. I didn't even see you leave. I thought you were still in with your dad."

"I needed some air."

"What's wrong?"

For a split second, Tim was so close to biting Nate's head off. It should have been pretty damned obvious what was wrong… *everything.* But he knew Nate was only trying to get him to talk about it, so he choked back all the horrible things that wanted to come raging out of his mouth and shook his head. "Nothing new," he answered shakily.

There were so many things he needed to deal with now, and none of it was Nate's fault *or* his responsibility. Nate had been so wonderful. It was only fair for Tim to give the man the chance to run before he got in any deeper. Tim needed to do it now before he chickened out, quick, like tearing off a bandage.

Maybe if he let Nate go now and didn't drag him into the black hole that was his life, Nate might still be there and willing by the time Tim pulled himself back out of it—whenever that might be. That way, Nate could remember the good parts. His memories of Tim wouldn't be tainted by what was to come, and they could start fresh when the mess was over and done with. It was a small hope but better than no hope at all.

# Chapter Fifteen

NATHAN FOLLOWED Tim back to their hotel room feeling completely useless. Tim wouldn't talk to him, not about anything, and Nathan was at a loss as to what to do about it. He couldn't help unless he knew what was going on. But did he really have a right to intrude if Tim didn't want him to?

God, he wished he'd had more time to get into those relationship books he'd bought. He'd only grabbed one to take with them as an afterthought, but so far, he hadn't been able to find anything pertaining to their current situation in it.

Communication was key. All the books said that. But what happened when the other half wouldn't communicate?

While Nathan had fretted in the waiting room at the hospital, he'd gotten caught up on e-mails, and he and Sean had done a little back and forth about some of the ideas he'd come up with during the previous week when everything had been going so well. Tim had done that for him. Nathan hadn't felt that energized in a very long time—determined maybe, but not inspired like he was all week. Only his inspiration wouldn't talk to him now.

Once the door was closed behind them, Nathan hovered in the middle of the room, waiting for Tim to say something, give him some clue how to proceed. He just needed a direction to go in. He could be the driver if that's what Tim needed. Tim just had to tell him where to go.

But Tim just stood looking out their window at the street below with his arms folded protectively over his chest, rocking on his heels, seeming a million miles away. After about five minutes of this, Nathan couldn't take it anymore. He had to do something. The basic necessities of life were always a good fallback position, so since he wasn't given any other direction, he'd start there.

"You said you were tired. Do you want to lie down?"

"Not yet."

"Are you hungry?"

"Not really."

Nathan sighed and rubbed his forehead as he watched Tim in consternation. "I'm trying to help, but you're not making it easy. Is there anything I can do, or would you rather I leave you alone?"

Nathan thought he'd hidden his frustration pretty well, but Tim flinched anyway. "I'm sorry," Tim whispered.

"You don't have to be sorry. Just tell me what to do."

Tim turned to face him then and let his hands drop to his sides. "Nate, have you thought about what any of this means?"

"I don't understand the question."

Now Tim looked frustrated with him. "What this means. The doctor says he's dying, but they have no idea how long it could take. He's going into a hospice, and I can't leave him there by himself."

"Okay. We won't leave him there by himself." Nathan was missing something here, he was sure of it.

Tim rolled his eyes. "And what if he somehow gets better? Doctors don't know everything. Even if he's in really bad shape, he could hang on for a long time. I have to be here for him. I couldn't live with myself otherwise."

"Okay." It made sense. Of course Tim would want to be there for his dad. It would make their relationship a little harder for a while, but at least Nathan had a direction to go in. His wheels had already started turning when Tim's next words threw up a stop sign.

"Okay?" Tim cried. "Okay? How can you say that? It's not okay. *Nothing* is okay."

*Shit.*

"I didn't mean it that way, Tim. I'm sorry." Nathan rushed to Tim's side, reaching out to touch and soothe, but Tim spun away, putting a few feet between them.

"God, Nate, don't be sorry. You have nothing to be sorry for. You've been great... better than great. I'm the one who should be sorry for all the shit you've had to put up with since you met me."

Now Nathan was even more confused. He wasn't following Tim's line of reasoning at all. "Tim, most of the shit I had to deal with had nothing to do with you. You were the good part, not the bad part. I said I was sorry because I said the wrong thing. What I meant was, I understood that you want to be here for your dad. That's all."

"Nate—" His name came out of Tim on a sob, and this time Nathan didn't try to think. He just went to Tim and wrapped him in his arms.

"It's going to be okay... well, obviously not the part about your dad. But I'll be there to help. We'll figure it out."

"Why?" Tim whispered against Nate's neck.

"Why what?"

"Why would you do all this?"

Nathan was stumped by the question. He was sure they'd already covered this. They were boyfriends now. That's what boyfriends did. Wasn't it?

Tim didn't give Nathan time to come up with an answer. He pulled away and looked at Nathan with anguished eyes. "You still don't get it. I have to come back here. I have no idea how long it's going to take. You said yourself you have tons of work to do and people depending on you. You need to get back to San Diego, and I need to figure out what I'm going to do here."

"But I thought we were boyfriends."

Tim threw up his hands and let out a growl of unmistakable frustration. But Nathan was getting frustrated right back because he truly didn't understand.

Tim stared at him for a few beats before his shoulders slumped and he sighed. "Nate, we've known each other for like two weeks. How could I possibly ask you to deal with all this? How can I even ask you to wait for me when I don't even know how long I'm going to be?"

"But that's what boyfriends do. Isn't it?"

"You could do so much better," Tim said quietly. "You're smart, successful, hot, and just a *really* good person. You could do a hell of a lot better than me, someone who's got his life together already, someone more like you."

"You think I'm hot?"

"Oh my God! Nate!"

Nathan had seen this look on Sean's face a time or two. It was the one that said Nathan was the most infuriating person he'd ever met. He just wasn't sure what he'd said.

"What?"

"Be serious!"

"I am being serious." Nathan closed the distance between them, reached for Tim's hand, and tugged. When Tim resisted, he tugged a little harder until, eventually, Tim relented and allowed himself to be led to the bed. Their room this time wasn't as nice as his usual accommodations, so the only piece of furniture big enough for them to sit next to each other on was the bed.

Nathan took a breath and ordered his thoughts. He'd have to save the "hot" comment for a later date. Right now he needed to concentrate on the rest of what Tim was saying. Apparently Tim needed reassurance that Nathan wasn't going anywhere and had no intentions of finding someone else. That was the baseline. He didn't have to agree with Tim's assessments of his chances out in the dating world. Tim obviously believed it and had insecurities that needed to be soothed. Nathan knew all about insecurities.

"Look," Nathan said as he ran his thumb over the back of the hand he held. "I'm pretty sure what we've got here is the textbook definition of a whirlwind romance. But that doesn't make it any less real for me. You told me you love me, right? Do you still?"

"Of course I still love you. How could I not? I just… this is a lot of shit to dump on anyone, particularly someone who's only known me a couple of weeks. I wanted you to know I wouldn't blame you if it's too much."

"I know all of this was fast. But Tim, I never expected it to be sunshine and roses overnight. I never expected life to stop happening. I'm a problem solver. That's what I do."

"But you barely know me. How can you do all this for me?"

Nathan frowned. "That's not true, you know."

"What's not true?"

"That I barely know you. I don't agree with that, and I hope that's not how you feel about me. I do know you. And you know me."

Tim didn't respond right away, but it looked to Nathan like he wanted to argue that point, so Nathan decided to head him off before he could start.

"I've been thinking a lot about this since I met you. About all the rules there seem to be regarding relationships—this is too fast, they are too different, he's too old, she's too young, we couldn't possibly know each other after only a few nights. I'm just not sure who gets to make those rules. I mean, I think the reason people don't fall in love at first sight is that people don't let others see them as they really are. We all carry these masks around. I know I do it. I had to learn to put one on for work, but that doesn't mean I can't learn to take it off again too. And maybe divorce rates are so high because, even after people are married for years, they still don't learn to drop those masks until it's too late. But with you and me, there was no mask. At least that's the way you described our first night together. You saw me. And then, when we did get together again, you let me see you too—your heart right out there in the open. I know everything I need to know. You're kind, caring, honorable, responsible, proud, honest. All the rest is just surface stuff. It doesn't matter if we don't like the same TV shows or what kind of job you have, as long as I believe, deep down, that you're fundamentally a good person and you're good for me."

Tim's eyes were still anguished, but Nathan thought there might be a little hope there as well.

"But I have no right to ask this much of you. To ask you to wait for me when I have no idea how long I'm going to be," Tim said again.

This time Nathan didn't bother to stop himself. He dismissed that with a wave of his hand. "Okay, so you're not asking. That doesn't mean I can't offer, does it?"

"Well, no. But—"

Nathan growled his frustration. He couldn't help it. "You keep acting like I'm not getting anything out of this, like I'm a saint or something. I'm not. Believe me. I meant what I said about you being good for me. Do you know how many new ideas I've come up with in the week since we've been living together, how productive I've been at work? Do you know how happy I am each and every morning when I wake up and you're right there next to me?

"I may not quite have a handle on how this relationship thing works yet. I may feel a bit lost sometimes, and I will definitely make mistakes. But I know what I want. I know when something makes me happy. I know when something or someone is good for me. You're good for me. And if it takes a little more time than I hoped and a little more investment on my part to get what I want, I'm not afraid of that."

"You make us sound like a work project," Tim said, but he was smiling.

Nathan shrugged. "Well, that's the model I know. This is my pitch. I'll figure out how to make it more 'relationshippy' in time. Just hang in there with me until I get it right. Besides, all the books I've skimmed so far say relationships *are* work, usually in the very first pages, sometimes even in the foreword, so I know of whence I speak."

"Relationshippy?" Tim let out a strangled giggle. The sound wasn't a pleasant one, but it wasn't tears. Nathan wasn't sure he would have been able to handle tears.

Nathan pushed at Tim's shoulders, and Tim finally allowed himself to stretch out on the bed. Nathan settled on his back, and Tim curled against his side with his head resting on Nathan's chest.

They were quiet for a little while until Tim said, "Are you always going to be this amazing? Because I tell ya', it might get a little intimidating down the road."

His tone was joking, and for the first time in what felt like two days, Nathan relaxed. This he could work with. "Of course I'm always this great," he replied. "Didn't I tell you? I think I have a super-boyfriend T-shirt somewhere. Or if I don't, we'll have to order me one."

Tim snuggled closer to him, burying his face against Nathan's neck. "I'm sorry about all the drama. I can't promise it won't happen again," he mumbled sleepily.

"It's okay. That's what boyfriends are for."

Tim was asleep in minutes, and Nathan wasn't far behind. They had plans to make and things to figure out, but they had the basics down, the important parts. He loved Tim and Tim said he loved Nathan. What else was there?

# Epilogue

TIM'S DAD only lasted another three months after his initial
hospitalization, and he never did get to go home again. The caseworker
they were assigned led them through the process step by step—all the
paperwork, moving him to a hospice facility, letting them know all the
resources available to them. But even with all her help and Nathan's
support, those months were incredibly hard.

Tim spent a lot of time alone by his dad's bedside because
Theresa had her own job and life to live, and Nate could only travel
back and forth to Houston so often. Tim's dad was only lucid a tiny
fraction of the time because of the drugs for the pain, and when he was,
mostly he tore Tim's heart out pleading to go home. There were times
Tim had to pry his hand free from his dad's grasp while the man
begged Tim not to leave him there. Those were the worst. Those were
the memories that would haunt him forever and almost made him swear
he wouldn't return to the hospice. But each day he got up again and
dragged himself there anyway.

Nate paid for a room at an extended-stay place not far from the
hospice, and Tim let him without even trying to argue. Tim also let
Nate pay for food and airfare back and forth when he came without any
objections either. He kept a journal of all of it, though, and he would
pay Nate back someday, but his guilt over it wasn't as crushing as he'd
feared it would be. He didn't have any energy left to worry about it.

Nate loved him. Nate wanted to be with him even after everything.
He made Nate happy. And in sappier moments, when they were

cuddled up naked under the blankets on the weekends Nate could make it out, Nate would say that Tim inspired him, and Tim wouldn't feel so much like he was taking without giving anything back.

Luckily, not only did Matt still have Tim's car, but one of Tim's old jobs was okay with letting him come back for the crap shifts. Since daytime was the best time to see his dad and Nate had to be in San Diego most of the time anyway, Tim didn't mind at all. He had no interest in partying on the weekends, and his dad didn't know what day it was most of the time anyway. The money helped him feel like less of a loser, and the job gave him an excuse to get away from the hospice for hours at a stretch. Otherwise he probably would have gone crazy after only a couple of weeks.

Near the end of his dad's life, Tim's grandparents finally came back to Houston for a visit and stayed through the funeral. They invited him to stay at the house with them, but Tim couldn't bring himself to do it. It wasn't only the memories the place held. Tim was angry and resentful toward them even though he tried to let go of it. In his mind he knew they probably wouldn't have made much difference if they had been more involved. They'd given his dad a place to live. They were both in their eighties, and they'd given all they could manage. But his heart couldn't help but feel abandoned by them.

He and Nate flew back to San Diego the day after his dad's funeral. Tim was quiet for most of the trip. He was just so exhausted, now that it was all over, he felt like he could sleep for a week. Nate seemed to sense his mood and didn't press him for conversation. He even slowed to a normal pace going through the airport instead of his usual mad dash to get away from the crowd, and when they got into the cab to head for home, Tim squeezed Nate's hand and gave him a smile to show how grateful he was.

Tim fell asleep in the taxi and was pretty much a zombie when they dragged their bags up to the house. When Nate opened the door and turned on the light in the living room, Tim didn't even remember stumbling in after him. In fact, he didn't remember much of anything until suddenly he was crumpled on the floor with Nate's couch at his back, staring up at a stack of self-help books on death and dying on Nate's coffee table through a haze of tears.

"Tim, are you okay?"

"I—" Whatever else he intended to say was cut off by a sob that caught him completely by surprise. Then it was followed by another and another, and Tim couldn't seem to stop them.

He'd cried at his dad's funeral, a quiet stream of tears, off and on most of the day, but nothing like this. These hurt, wrenched out of his chest against his will, and he was helpless to hold them back. Before he knew it, Nate's arms were around him, and Nate was rocking them on the floor. Tim wanted to say something witty or silly to salvage his pride, but nothing would come out but sobbing. He was crying so hard he was shaking and gasping for breath, afraid it would never stop.

But eventually the gasping sobs faded, the bands around his chest eased enough for him to breathe again, and he was left weak and jittery in Nate's arms.

"I'm sorry," Tim croaked, mortified by what had happened.

"What for?" Nate asked, still rocking them a little.

"Uh, for blubbering all over you like that." Tim grabbed for the box of tissues on Nate's coffee table and blew his nose. "I don't know where that came from."

"Don't be sorry. Obviously you needed it. Besides, how am I supposed to feel comfortable crying all over you in the future if you act all embarrassed about it now?" Nate pulled back and cupped his cheek. "I cry at commercials, you know. That's not a deal breaker, is it?"

Tim laughed. It sounded a little hysterical, but it felt good. After a quiet few minutes, Nate helped him to his feet. "Come on. We're both exhausted. Let's go to bed, and we can do whatever you want tomorrow. Okay?"

"That hardly seems fair," Tim grumbled as they made their way to the stairs. "You've been doing everything for me for weeks now. I think we should do whatever *you* want tomorrow, not the other way around."

"Nope. You can't get out of it that easy. I'll already have what I want, you right there next to me when I wake up. The rest is gravy."

"Oh God. Keep that up and I really am going to have to get you that T-shirt," Tim quipped.

Nathan grinned at Tim over his shoulder. "Too late. Sean already ordered it… in pink, with a rainbow and a unicorn on it, just because he's an asshole like that."

ROWAN MCALLISTER is a woman who doesn't so much create as recreate, taking things ignored and overlooked and hopefully making them into something magical and mortal. She believes it's all in how you look at it. In addition to a continuing love affair with words, she creates art out of fabric, metal, wood, stone, and any other interesting scraps of life she can get her hands on. Everything is simply one perspective change and a little bit of effort away from becoming a work of art that is both beautiful and functional. She lives in the woods, on the very edge of suburbia—where civilization drops off and nature takes over—sharing her home with her patient, loving, and grounded husband, her super sweet hairball of a cat, and a mythological beast masquerading as a dog. Her chosen family is made up of a madcap collection of people from many different walks of life, all of whom act as her muses in so many ways, and she would be lost without them.

E-mail: rowanmcallister10@gmail.com

Facebook: https://www.facebook.com/rowanmcallister10

Twitter: https://twitter.com/RowanMcallister

# HOT MESS

## ROWAN McALLISTER

http://www.dreamspinnerpress.com

http://www.dreamspinnerpress.com

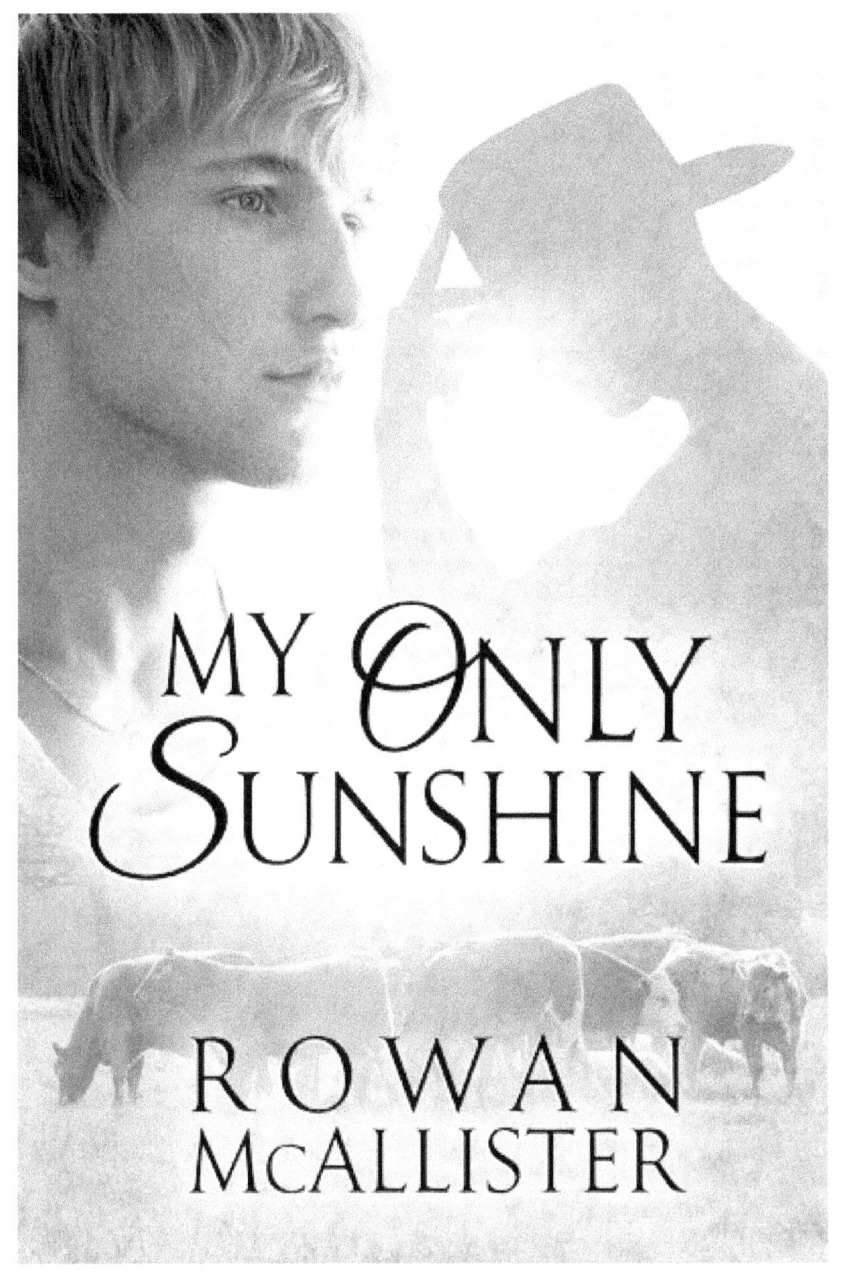

# MY ONLY SUNSHINE

## ROWAN McALLISTER

http://www.dreamspinnerpress.com

http://www.dreamspinnerpress.com

*Cherries on Top*

Rowan McAllister

http://www.dreamspinnerpress.com

http://www.dreamspinnerpress.com

http://www.dreamspinnerpress.com

http://www.dreamspinnerpress.com

# KEEPING SWEETS

## Cate Ashwood

http://www.dreamspinnerpress.com